D1611549

WITHDRAWN

A Garland Series

Foundations of the Novel

Representative Early

Eighteenth-Century Fiction

A collection of 100 rare titles
reprinted in photo-facsimile in 71 volumes

Foundations of the Novel

compiled and edited by

Michael F. Shugrue

Secretary for English for the M.L.A.

with New Introductions for each volume by

Michael Shugrue, *City College of C.U.N.Y.*
Malcolm J. Bosse, *City College of C.U.N.Y.*
William Graves, *N.Y. Institute of Technology*
Josephine Grieder, *Rutgers University, Newark*

Le Diable Boiteux
or the Devil
upon Two Sticks

by

Alain René Le Sage

with a new introduction
for the Garland Edition by
Josephine Grieder

Garland Publishing, Inc., New York & London

Bibliographical note:

This facsimile has been made from a copy in the British Museum (1904.h.8)

Library of Congress Cataloging in Publication Data

Le Sage, Alain René, 1668-1747.
    Le diable boiteux.

    (Foundations of the novel)
    Reprint of the 1708 ed.
    I. Title. II. Title: The devil upon two sticks.
III. Series.
PZ3.L5635Di3 [~~PQ1997~~]   843'.5   73-170518
ISBN 0-8240-0525-2

Introduction

When Alain René Le Sage's novel Le Diable Boiteux
*appeared in France in 1707, it was so popular that, it is
said, two young gentlemen dueled over who should have
the bookseller's last copy. Whether or not the anecdote
is true, the novel did in fact have two French editions in
1707, one in 1708, and another in 1710 and added only
more luster to the reputation of Le Sage, already
distinguished as a comic playwright. It was perhaps not
unexpected that the reputable English publisher, who
already counted in his stable of authors Milton, Waller,
Suckling, and Dryden, should choose to publish a
translation of so celebrated a work.*

*That the title and idea were not original was admitted
by Le Sage in the preface to the (greatly altered) edition
of 1726, where he named* El Diablo cojuelo *(1641) of
Louis Velez de Guevara as his model. He might have
added several other Spanish authors as well — Francisco
Santos, Fr. de Rojas — as sources for anecdotes; and as
for technique, one sees the influence of La Bruyère in
the short, incisive portraits which fill the work. But
unlike his early plays, which closely followed their
Spanish originals,* The Devil upon Two Sticks *is much
more inventive in terms of borrowing and of transposing
a Spanish milieu to early eighteenth-century France.*

There is, properly speaking, only a thin plot. The

5

INTRODUCTION

young scholar Don Cleofas, escaping from the house of his mistress who has hired four bullies to force him to marry her, takes shelter in an apparently empty apartment. He is astonished to hear a bodiless voice who declares himself to be "the most active and indefatigable Devil in Hell" (p. 4) and explains that he has been imprisoned by a necromancer in a glass bottle. Asmodeo — for he soon identifies himself as "the Daemon of Luxury, or to express it genteeler, the God Cupid" (p. 6) — beseeches Cleofas to break the bottle and permit him to escape. Cleofas, after some hesitation, does so; and the grateful devil lifts off the roofs of Madrid's houses to reveal their inhabitants to the scholar and even revenges Cleofas upon his faithless mistress before he is abruptly summoned back to his bottle by the necromancer.

But a carefully plotted novel was not, of course, the goal of Le Sage. Trading on Cleofas' curiosity, Asmodeo promises to show him mankind in all its variety. "In order to furnish you with a perfect Knowledge of Human Life, it is necessary to explain to you what all those People, which you see, are doing. I will disclose to you the Springs of their Actions, and their most secret Thoughts" (p. 17). By lifting off the rooftops, he exposes to Cleofas a tableau of human life; and when the young scholar is naive enough to admire the luxury, art, and industry which he sees spread before him, Asmodeo chidingly reminds him that "there is not one Person in all that Croud who had not better be fast asleep, than employ'd as you see him, if you knew what

6

*he was going about, and what is the Motive of Actions"
(p. 18).
And indeed the panorama which Asmodeo exhibits is
enough to disabuse anyone of his naiveté. Vanity,
selfishness, avarice, self-deception, ingratitude, trickery,
falsity, folly − all are revealed to be the motives of the
people into whose lives Cleofas is permitted to look.
The banker who beats the thieves at their own game by
absconding a day earlier with public funds; the man who
arranges a marriage between two tavern servants, visits
the new innkeeper once too often, and is imprisoned for
his pains; the converted Jew usurer who, untouched by
the priest's sermon on lending, continues his practice
with sang froid − all these are vividly sketched to open
Cleofas' eyes. Professional gentlemen do not go un-
scathed. There is the Clerk of the Court who alters the
register to oblige a guardian. There is the doctor who
assaults passersby in the street so he may have them as
patients. Religion is of little account; the old man who
builds a convent to ease a conscience troubled by his
ill-gotten gains can find no monks who meet his
standards of chastity, sobriety, and humility.
   A favorite milieu of Asmodeo is the theater, for it is
"the truest Picture of Human Life; and the Men who
make the great Figures in the World are no more what
they seem, than that little diminutive Fellow you see
taking off his Buskins and his Feathers in the Tyring-
Room, is the Heroe you saw just now on the Stage" (p.
22). The lawyer Divito takes a mortgage on a theater
only to ogle "the tender Hams of a young Dancer, the*

INTRODUCTION

*heaving Bosom of an Actress to be bred to Tragedy"
(pp. 21-22). A poet composes a magnificent epistle
dedicatory to his magnanimous patron — the name left
blank to be filled in with that of whoever should present
himself. Wits squabble in a coffeehouse over the merits
of a new comedy. A tragic author pompously displays
his latest production to a comic writer, who unblush-
ingly delivers himself of such trenchant criticism that
the former assaults him (the last anecdote contains in
fact a sensible eighteenth-century critique concerning
the virtues of tragedy as opposed to comedy and the
talents necessary to each genre).*

*Because love is Asmodeo's particular province, the
relations between men and women come under close
scrutiny. Asmodeo condemns hypocrisy; "all Persons
who affect Characters unseasonable to their time of
Day" (p. 19) are exhibited without pity. He exposes the
"superannuated Coquet going to Bed, after leaving her
Hair, Eye-brows and Teeth on her Toilet" (p. 23) and
the "amorous Dotard of sixty" who "has already laid
down his Eye, false Whiskers, and Periwig, which hid his
bald Pate, and expects his Man to take off his wooden
Arm and Leg" (pp. 23-24). Women deceive their
husbands; middle-aged virgins hope for the death of
their fathers so they may marry. In fact, women come
out very badly in the novel; scarcely a one is not vain,
demanding, insolent, foolish, or deceiving. After a
catalog of amorous encounters, Asmodeo at last
declares, "It would be endless to show you the Vanities
of the [female] Sex; their Thoughts, Words and*

8

INTRODUCTION

Actions, tend only to Show and Ostentation, for which they sacrifice their Liberty, and all the Pleasures of Life" (pp. 163-164). Can true love ever exist? Not in Madrid, maintains Asmodeo; "To give you a Sight of happy Pairs, I should transport you to Solitudes and Retirements, where Love is a Stranger to Art and Gallantry, and lives amidst its own natural Sweets, Complacency, mutual Esteem, and eternal Constancy; without being diverted by the false Appearances, which under the Colour of advancing its Enjoyments, vitiate the true Relish of 'em" (p. 165).

In spite of these innumerable vignettes of follies and vices, Le Sage still finds some commendable elements in human nature. A short anecdote about a boy who returns to share his new-found wealth with his poor parents indicates that affection and gratitude still exist, and the two long interpolated stories prove it still more. The history of the Count de Belflor and Leonora de Cespides begins with the basest of motives. The very aristocratic Count is much taken by the less noble Leonora and resolves to enjoy her without marriage. He succeeds in corrupting the hitherto strict duenna Donna Marcella with a large sum of money, and, though Marcella is hard put to persuade Leonora out of all the virtuous notions she herself had instilled, she brings the young girl around. Eventually Belflor's conscience gets the better of him, and he is torn by a desire to repair his wrong and his reluctance to marry beneath him. But when her brother Pedro, who has saved his life, refuses to avenge the family honor by dueling him, he is

9

overcome by admiration and gratitude, as well as by Leonora's melancholy letter and tears, and capitulates.
The Count's sudden change of sentiment is, in psychological terms, somewhat insufficiently motivated, but it does at least argue for a heart which, though initially corrupt, may be altered for the better. In "Of the Power of Friendship," the second interpolated story, the sincerity of motive is pure throughout. Don Juan and Don Fadrique, the dearest of friends, both love the virtuous Donna Theodora. The former dissembles his affection for fear of hurting his friend, but Don Fadrique, discovering Don Juan's sentiments and the lady's reciprocal fondness, nobly renounces his pretentions. Donna Theodora is kidnapped by another rival. Don Juan, pursuing her, is captured by pirates and sold into slavery, where he finds Donna Theodora in the harem; he negotiates her escape but is almost killed by Don Fadrique, who mistakes him for the kidnapper. On learning whom he has stabbed, Don Fadrique runs himself through; and his death, though it nearly destroys his friend with grief, facilitates the marriage of the lovers. But even in this story of pure friendship, Le Sage does not let such generous behavior go unscrutinized. Cleofas asks if such extraordinary actions do in fact exist outside of fiction; and in a nicely ambivalent manner, Asmodeo confesses that " 'tis not very common; but 'tis not only to be found in Romances, but in the sublime Nature of Man, and that since the Deluge, in which Compass I have known three instances of it, besides this" (p. 204).

INTRODUCTION

Not only do these two stories tend to restore a balanced view of human nature in a novel where vice and folly are so prominent, but Le Sage's style also contributes to alleviate any depressingly pessimistic view of mankind. Asmodeo neither judges nor moralizes; he exhibits men's baser motives with a sort of bonhommie. Wit and a sharply turned phrase are always at his service. His survey of the cemetery graves shows, for example, "In the second is a Miser, that starv'd himself with Hunger; and in the third his heir, who two Years after dy'd with excessive Eating and Drinking" (p. 166). Or his portrait of "two Servant Wenches, who have lost their Wits; one of them for Grief, for being left out of the Will of an old Batchelor, whom she served; and the other for Joy, at the News of the Death of a rich Treasurer, whose Heiress she was" (p. 143). The juxtaposition of consequences and the irony of fate never fail to provoke the devil to incisive comment in which there is no malice but simply frankness.

It scarcely matters that Le Sage, a Frenchman, chose a Spanish source for The Devil upon Two Sticks. *The story is of neither nationality, but, thanks to the author's astute observation of human foibles, universal in scope. It is perhaps unformed as a novel; but the lucidity and the wit with which Le Sage presents his portraits and the "romantic" elements of the interpolated stories were to find their way into later, better-formed novels of the century.*

Josephine Grieder

LE

Diable Boiteux:

OR, THE

DEVIL

UPON

TWO STICKS.

Tranflated from the Laft Edition at *Paris*,
with feveral Additions.

LONDON:

Printed for *Jacob Tonfon*, within *Grays-
Inn* Gate next *Grays-Inn* Lane. 1708.

UT

CRESCAM   PROSIM

CONSTANTER   ET   PRUDENTER

The Right Hon.ble Sr. Alexr. Campbell
of Cesnok one of the Senators of the
Colledge of Justice and one of the Lords of
Her Maties most Honble Privy Councell & Exchequer
&c: 1707

THE
CONTENTS.

Chap.

CONTENTS.

THE

THE

DEVIL

UPON

TWO STICKS.

CHAP. I.

Necessary to be read in order to the Understanding the rest.

ONE Night in *October*, when thick Darkness had o'er-spread the famous City of *Madrid*, the People, being close at their respective Homes, had left the Streets free to the Lovers inclin'd to sing their Pains or Pleasures under the Balconies of their Mistresses; and accordingly the Guitars had already disturb'd the Repose of the Fathers, and alarm'd the

B   jealous

jealous Husbands; in ſhort, it was almoſt
Midnight, when *Don Cleofas Leandro Perez Zambullo,* a young Scholar of *Alcala,*
very nimbly made his way out of the Garret Window of a Houſe, into which the
indiſcreet Son of the *Cytherean* Goddeſs had
drawn him. He endeavour'd to preſerve
his Life and Honour, by eſcaping from
three or four Bullies, which follow'd cloſe
at his Heels, in order to kill or force him
to marry a Lady, with whom they had juſt
before ſurpriz'd him. Tho' alone, he yet
bravely defended himſelf againſt all of
them, and had not been put to flight, if
they had not wreſted his Sword from him
in the Fight: They follow'd him for ſome
time along the Gutters; but, favour'd by
the Darkneſs, he avoided their Purſuit,
and ſtealing along from one * Houſe-top
to another, made towards a Light which
he perceiv'd a great diſtance off, and which,
feeble as it was, yet ſerv'd him for a Lan-
thorn in this dangerous Conjuncture. After more than once running the Riſque of
breaking his Neck, he reach'd the Garret
whence its Rays proceeded, and enter'd
it by a Window, as much tranſported with
Joy as a Pilot at the Sight of his Veſſel
ſafe at Anchor in the Port, which before
was in danger of Shipwrack.

He

---

* *The Tops of the Houſes in Spain are flat.*

He immediately look'd around him, and was very much furpriz'd to find no Body in this Garret, which feem'd to him to be a very odd Apartment : He obferv'd it with great Attention. He faw a Copper Lamp hung to the Cieling, Books and Papers in Confufion on the Table, Spheres and Compaffes on the one fide, Phials and Quadrants on the other; which made him conclude, that under this Roof liv'd an Aftrologer, which ufually retir'd hither to make his Obfervations.

He reflected on the Dangers he had efcap'd, and was confidering whether he fhould here wait the Approach of Day, tho' very far off, or take another Courfe, when he heard a deep Sigh break forth next to him. He took it for a Nocturnal Illu-fion, or imaginary Fantome, refulting from his prefent difturb'd Mind; wherefore without Interruption he continu'd his Re-flection : But hearing a fecond Sigh, he was put out of doubt of the reality of the former, and tho' he faw no Soul in the Room, could not help crying out, What Devil is it that fighs here? 'Tis me, Siginor Scholar, anfwer'd a Voice which had fome-what very extraordinary in it; I have been a Year enclos'd in one of thefe Glafs-Phials. In this Houfe lives a skilful Aftrologer, which is a Magician, who by the Power

of his Art has kept me fhut up in this clofe
Prifon. You are then a Spirit, faid *Cleofas*, fomewhat confus'd at this uncommon
Adventure. I am a *Dæmon*, reply'd the
Voice, and you are come very opportune-
ly to free me from a Slavery where I languifh in Idlenefs; tho' I am the moft active
and indefatigable Devil in Hell.

Cleofas was fomewhat affrighted at thefe
Words; but being naturally Courageous,
he recollected himfelf, and in a refolute
Tone thus addrefs'd himfelf to the Spirit.
Signior *Dæmon*, pray inform me by what
Character you are diftinguifh'd amongft
your Brethren; Are you a Devil of Quality, or an ordinary one? I am, reply'd
the Voice, a very confiderable Devil,
and am more efteem'd in this and the
other World than any other. Perhaps,
reply'd *Cleofas*, you may be the *Dæmon*
which we call *Lucifer?* No, reply'd the
Spirit, he is the Mountebanks Devil. Are
you then *Uriel?* return'd the Scholar.
Fie! (haftily interrupted the Voice) he
is the Patron of Traders, Tailors, But-
chers, and other third-rate Thieves. It
may be you are *Belzebub*, faid *Don Cleofas*. You deceive your felf, anfwer'd the
Spirit, he is the *Dæmon* of Governantes,
and Gentlemen-Ufhers, or Waiting-men.
This furprizes me, faid the Scholar; I
took

took *Belzebub* for one of the greateſt of
your Number. He *is* one of the leaſt, reply'd the *Dæmon;* you have no true Notion of our Hell. You muſt then, reply'd
Don Cleofas, be either *Leviathan, Belphe-
gor,* or *Aſhtaroth.* Oh! as for thoſe three,
ſaid the Voice, they are Devils of the firſt
Rank; they are the Court Spirits: They
enter into the Councils of Princes, ani-
mate their Miniſters, form Leagues, ſtir
up Inſurrections in States, and light the
Torches of War. Ah! tell me, I entreat
you, ſaid the Scholar, what Poſt has *Flagel?* He is the Soul of the Law, and the
Life of the Bar, reply'd the Devil: It is
he which makes out the Attornies and Bai-
liff's Writs; he inſpires the Pleaders, poſ-
ſeſſeth the Council, and attends the Judges.
But my Buſineſs lyes another Way: I make
ridiculous Matches, and marry old Grey-
beards to raw Girls under Age, Maſters to
their Maids, Virgins of low Fortunes to
Lovers which have none. 'Tis I that have
introduc'd into the World Luxury, De-
bauchery, hazardous Games, and Chymi-
ſtry. I am the Inventer of *Caroufels,* Dancing, Muſick, Plays, and all the new *French*
Faſhions. In a Word, I am the celebrated *Aſmodeo,* ſurnam'd the *Devil upon Two
Sticks.*

B 3   Ah!

Ah! cry'd *Don Cleofas,* you are then the famous *Afmodeo,* fo glorioufly celebrated by *Agrippa,* and the *Claviculd Salomonis?* Really you have not told me all your Amufements; you have forgotten the beft of them. I know that you fometimes divert your felf with affwaging the Pains of unfortunate Lovers, deceiving jealous Hufbands, and tempting of Ladies; and it was by your Affiftance that a young Gentleman, a Friend of mine, crept into the good Graces of a Corregidor's Lady. 'Tis true, faid the Spirit, I referv'd that 'till the laft: I am the *Dæmon* of Luxury, or to exprefs it genteeler, the God *Cupid;* for the Poets have beftow'd that fine Name on me, and indeed painted me in very advantageous Colours; they defcribe me with gilded Wings, a Fillet bound over my Eyes, a Bow in my Hand, a Quiver of Arrows on my Shoulders, and a charming beautiful Face. Which what fort of one it is you fhall immediately fee, if you pleafe to fet me at Liberty.

Signior *Afmodeo,* reply'd *Don Cleofas,* you know that I have long been your fincere Devotee; of the Truth of which the Dangers I juft now run are fufficient Evidences. I fhould be very ambitious of an Opportunity of ferving you; but the Veffel in which you are hidden is undoubted-

ly

ly enchanted, and all my Endeavours to
unftop or break it will be vain; wherefore
I can't very well tell which way to deliver
you out of Prifon: I am not much us'd
to thefe forts of Deliverances; and betwixt
you and I, if fuch a fubtle Devil as you
are cannot make your Way out, how can
fuch a wretched Mortal as I do it? Mankind is endu'd with that Power, anfwer'd
the *Demon*; the Phial in which I am enclos'd is barely a plain Glafs Bottle, which
is very eafie to break; you need only take
and throw it to the Ground, and I fhall
immediately appear in Human Shape. If
fo, faid the Scholar, 'tis eafier than I imagin'd; tell me then in which Phial you are,
for I fee fo many like one another, that I
cannot diftinguifh them. It is the fourth
from the Window, reply'd the Spirit. 'Tis
enough, Signior *Afmodeo*, return'd *Don
Cleofas*; there is now only one fmall Difficulty which deters me: When I have done
you this Service, won't you make me pay
for the broken Pots? No Accident fhall
befall you, anfwer'd the *Demon*; but on
the contrary you will be pleas'd with my
Acquaintance. I will learn you whatever
you are defirous to know, inform you of
all things which happen in the World, and
difcover to you all the Faults of Mankind.
I will be your Tutelar *Demon*, you fhall
B 4   find

find me much more Intelligent than that
of *Socrates*, and I will make you far sur-
pass that Philosopher in Wisdom. In a
Word, I will bestow my self on you, with
my good and ill Qualities; the latter of
which shall not be less advantageous to
you than the former. These are fine Promises, reply'd the Scholar, but you Gentlemen Devils are accus'd of not being very
religious Observers of what you promise
to Men. That is a groundless Charge,
reply'd *Asmodeo:* Most of my Brethren
make no Scruple of breaking their Word,
but I am a Slave to mine; and I swear by
all that renders our Oaths inviolable, that
I won't deceive you. I promise, withal,
that you shall revenge your self of *Donna
Thomasa*, that perfidious Lady, which hid
four Ruffians to surprize and force you to
marry her.

  Don Cleofas charm'd above all with this
last Promise, to hasten its Accomplishment,
immediately took the Phial in which was
the Spirit, and without concerning himself
what might be the Event of it, he threw
it hard against the Ground. It broke into
a thousand Pieces, and overflow'd the
Floor with a blackish Liquor, which by
little and little evaporated, and converted
it self into a thick Smoak, which dissipa-
ting all at once, presented the amaz'd Scho-
                                                    lar

lar with the View of the Figure of a Man
in a Cloak, about two Foot and a half
high, refting on two Crutches. This diminutive lame Monfter had Goats Legs, a
long Vifage, fharp Chin, a yellow and
black Complexion, and a very flat Nofe;
his Eyes, which feem'd very little, re-
fembled two lighted Coals; his Mouth
was extreamly wide, above which were
two wretched red Whiskers, edg'd with
a pair of unparallel'd Lips.

This charming *Cupid's* Head was wrapt
up in a fort of Turban of red Crape,
turn'd up with a Plume of Cocks and Pea-
cocks Feathers. About his Neck he wore
a yellow Linnen Collar, on which were
drawn feveral Models of Necklaces and
Pendants. He was drefs'd in a fhort white
Sattin Coat, and girt about with a Girdle of Virgin Parchment, mark'd with Ta-
lifmanical Charaƈters. On this Coat were
painted feveral Pair of Womens Stays very
advantageoufly fitted for the difcovery of
their Brcafts; Scarves, party-colour'd A-
prons, new-fafhion Head-dreffes of various
Sorts, fome more extravagant than the
reft.

But all thefe were nothing, compar'd with
his Cloak, the bottom of which was alfo
of white Sattin. On it, with *Indian* Ink,
were drawn an infinite Number of Figures,
with

with fo much Freedom, and fuch mafterly
Strokes, that it was natural enough to
think the Devil had a hand in it.   On
one fide appear'd a *Spanifh* Lady cover'd
with her Vail, teazing a Stranger to walk
with her; and on the other a *French* one
practifing new Airs in her Glafs, in order
to try them at a young patch'd and painted
Abbot, which appear'd at her Chamber
Door.   Here a parcel of *Italian* Cavaliers
were finging and playing on the Guitar
under their Miftreffes Balconies; and there
were a Company of *Germans* all in confufion and unbutton'd, more intoxicated
with Wine and begrim'd with Snuff than
the conceited *French* young Abbots, fur-
rounding a Table overflow'd with the fil-
thy Remains of their Debauch.   In one
place was a great *Mahometan* Lord coming out of the Bath, and encompafs'd by
all the Women of his *Seraglio*, officioufly
crouding to tender him their Service.
There the Gamefters were alfo wonder-
fully well reprefented; fome of them, animated by a fprightly Joy, heaping up Pieces
of Gold and Silver in their Hats; and
others, broken and reduc'd to play upon
Honour, cafting up their Sacrilegious Eyes
to Heav'n, and gnawing their Cards with
Defpair.   To conclude, there were as many
curious Things to be feen on it as on the
                                        admirable

admirable Buckler of the Son of *Peleus*, which exhaufted all *Vulcan's* Art; with this difference betwixt the Performance of the two Cripples, that the Figures on the Buckler had no relation to the Exploits of *Achilles*, but on the contrary thofe on the Cloak were fo many lively Images of whatever was done in the World by the Suggeftion of *Afmodeo*.

C H A P. II.

In which the Story of Afmodeo's *Deliverance is continu'd.*

THE *Dæmon* obferving that the Sight of him did not very agreeably prepoffefs the Scholar in his Favour, fmiling faid, Well, Signior *Don Cleofas Leandro Perez Zambullo*, you fee the charming God of Love, the Sovereign Ruler of Hearts. What do you think of my Beauty and Air? Don't you take the Poets for excellent Painters? Why really, anfwer'd *Cleofas*, they do flatter a little. You did not, I fuppofe, appear in this Shape to *Pfyche?* Doubtlefs no, reply'd *Afmodeo*; I borrow'd the Appearance of a beautiful young Swain, to make her doat on me.

me: Vice muft always be cover'd with
a fair Appearance, without which it will
never pleafe. I affume whatever Shape
I will, and could have fhew'd my felf to
you cloath'd with a finer imaginary Body;
but defigning, without any Difguife, to
lay my felf open to you, I was willing
that you fhould fee me in a Shape beft fuit-
ed to the Opinion which the World en-
tertains of me and my Funcions. I am
not furpriz'd, faid the Scholar, that you
are fomewhat Ugly; pardon, if you pleafe,
the harfhnefs of the Term, the Converfation which we have had together requires
freedom. Your Features are very well
proportion'd to the Idea I have of you;
but pray tell me why you are a Cripple.
My Lamenefs, anfwer'd the Devil, is owing to a Quarrel which I formerly had in
France with *Pilliardoe* the Devil of Intereft, who fhould poffefs one *Manceau*, a
Man of Bufinefs, and one of the Farmers
of the Revenues; which being a noble
Booty, we very warmly contefted the Poffeffion of it. We fought in the middle
Region of the Air; *Pilliardoe* was the
ftrongeft, and threw me down to the
Earth, as the Poets tell us *Jupiter* did
Vulcan: Whence from the Refemblance
of our Adventures, my Comrades call'd
me the *Lame Devil*, or *the Devil upon*
                                    Two

Two Sticks; and that Nick-Name, which they gave me in Raillery, has stuck with me ever since: But tho' a Cripple, I can yet go pretty nimbly; you shall be a Witness of my Agility. But, adds he, let us end this Discourse, and make haste out of this Garret. It will not be long before the Magician comes up to labour at the Immortality of a beautiful *Sylphe* which nightly visits him; and if he should surprize us, he would not fail to commit me to the Bottle from whence I came, and confine you to the same. Let's therefore, in the first place, throw away all the Pieces of the broken Phial, that the Enchanter may not discover my Enlargement. If he should find it after our Departure, said *Cleofas*, what would then be the Event? What would be the Event! answer'd the *Demon*; Alas! were I conceal'd at the farthest Part of the Earth, or hidden in the Region where the fiery *Salamanders* dwell; should I descend to the Shades below, or the Bottom of the deepest Sea, I should not be secur'd from his Resentment. His Conjurations are so powerful that all Hell trembles at them. In short, I cannot resist his arbitrary Commands, but shall be forc'd, much against my Will, to appear before him, and submit to whatever Pains he pleases to inflict on me. If so, reply'd
the

the Scholar, I very much fear that our
Converfation will be of no long Dura-
tion; this dreadful Negromancer will foon
perceive our Flight. I don't know that,
reply'd the Spirit, for we can't tell what
may happen. What, faid *Don Cleofas,*
are you not acquainted with Futurity ?
No indeed, reply'd the Devil, we know
nothing of that Matter; but thofe which
depend upon our Affiftance on that Head,
are fine Bubbles; and indeed to this Opinion are to be afcrib'd all the Fooleries
which are impos'd on Women of Quality
by Fortune-tellers of both Sexes, when
they confult them on future Events.   I
don't know therefore whether the Magician will foon difcover my Abfence, but
hope not, for here being feveral Phials very
like that in which I was enclos'd, he may
perhaps not mifs a fingle one.   I am much
in the fame Condition in his Laboratory
as a Law-Book is in the Library of a Man
of Bufinefs, he never thinks of me, and
when he doth, he never doth me the Honour of converfing with me.   He is the
moft infolent Enchanter that I know; for
during the whole Time that I was his Prifoner, he did not once vouchfafe to fpeak
to me.   What fort of a Fellow is this ?
reply'd *Don Cleofas* ;   or what have you
done to draw down his Hatred upon you

I

I cross'd one of his Designs, reply'd *Afmodeo* : There was a Place in the Custom-
House void, he was resolv'd that one of
his Friends should have it, and I was determin'd to make it be given to another.
The Magician prepar'd a *Talisman*, compos'd of the most powerful Characters of
the *Cabala*; but I influenc'd the Mistress
of a Clerk of the same Office to sollicit
it, and she accordingly carry'd it from the
Talisman.

At these Words the *Demon* gather'd
up all the Pieces of the broken Phial, and
after having thrown them out of the Window, Come then, said he to the Scholar,
let us make the best of our way; take hold
of the End of my Cloak, and fear nothing.
However dangerous this Offer appear'd to
Don Cleofas, he yet chose rather to accept
it, than expose himself to the Resentment
of the Magician; wherefore he took as
good hold as he could of the Devil, who
carry'd him out at the Window.

C H A P.

CHAP. III.

Whither the Devil carry'd Don Cleofas,
and what Things he shew'd him.

ASmodeo was not in the wrong when he boasted his Agility; he cleft the Air with as much Rapidity as an Arrow from a Bow, and pearch'd on St. *Saviour's* Steeple. When gotten on his Feet, he said to *Don Cleofas*, Well, Signior *Leandro*, when Men are in a very uneasie, hobling Coach, and cry out, *This is a Coach for the Devil!* do you now think they speak Truth or not? I have just experienc'd the Falsity of that Saying, answer'd *Don Cleofas* very gallantly, and can affirm the Devil's to be not only a very easie Carriage, but also so expeditious that no body can be tir'd on the Road. Very well, reply'd the *Dæmon;* but you don't know why I brought you hither. I intend from this high Place to shew you whatever is at present done in *Madrid.* By my Diabolical Power I will lift off the Roofs of the Houses, and notwithstanding the Darkness of the Night, clearly expose to your View whatever is now under them. At these Words he only extended his right
Arm,

Arm, and all the Roofs of the Houses seem'd remov'd; and the Scholar saw the Insides of 'em as plainly as it was possible at Noon-day.

This View was too surprizing not to employ all his Attention; his Eyes run thro' all Parts of the City, and the Variety which surrounded him, was sufficient to engage his Curiosity for a long time. Signior Student, said the *Demon*, this confusion of Objects, which you survey with so much Pleasure, affords really a very charming Prospect; but in order to furnish you with a perfect Knowledge of Human Life, it is necessary to explain to you what all those People, which you see, are doing. I will disclose to you the Springs of their Actions, and their most secret Thoughts.

Prithee, said the Scholar, since you are so kind a Devil, let me a little look about me from this mighty Precipice, whereon we sit with so much Security. What a very agreeable mixture of Persons and Things do these numberless Candles and Torches, round this great City, present to us? What pretty Arts Men have to extend their Lives, and double their Joys, by this Day of their own making? Tis, methinks, an Argument of the Greatness of Human Life, That the Wit of Man is

C   never

never at reft, but always hurry'd on in
fearch of fomething to give it felf a Satif-
faction, which cannot be drawn from meer
natural Occurrences, but muft be rais'd
from the Embelifhments of Arts, the Entertainment of Inventions, and —— The
Devil had not Patience, but immediately
interrupted the Harangue *Cleofas* was going into, and told him; Sir, if you defire
our Converfation fhall not be merely a
Ramble, like the Labour of filly Travel-
lers, who fill their Heads with Admiration,
and neglect Knowledge, let me befeech
you to wait for my Opinion of what you
fee, before you commend it. The fpacious
Streets taken up with various Bufinefs and
Hurry, the different Ways you fee Equi-
pages, laden Carriages, and Crouds of People moving by Candle-light, make you fall
into Applaufes of the Induftry of Man,
when at the fame time I muft tell you,
there is not one Perfon in all that Croud
who had not better be faft afleep, than
employ'd as you fee him, if you knew
what he was going about, and what is
the Motive of Actions.

Dæmon, reply'd the Scholar, you and
I are fo new Acquaintance, and the Profeffion you are of has fo ill a Reputation
for Sincerity, that I am at a Lofs, both as
to what kind of things you really think
laudable,

laudable, and as to your Veracity in speaking your real Sentiments of what you applaud. Scholar, said the *Demon*, we shall
speak of Things and Persons, as they stand
in the Order of Nature. A Man is to be
commended for what that Man ought to
do; and a Thing is valuable for the Use
it is design'd for; by which plain way
of thinking, Objects keep their Place in
the Opinion, whether the Observer be a
Devil, a Saint, a Philosopher or a Peasant.
Before this Light it is, that grave Politi-
cians of twenty, airy Girls of fifty, lan-
guishing Lovers of sixty, and all Persons
who affect Characters unseasonable to their
time of Day; I say, before this Light it
is, that all Varnish disappears, and Youth
is then only Graceful when it becomes its
Pleasures, and Age when it consults its
Ease.

The Scholar was still entertaining his
Eyes in the gross, with the Variety of
Objects before him, and enjoying the Pleasure of looking into the Houses which his
Companion had until'd, when an Assem-
bly very regularly dispos'd in one of 'em
had fix'd his Attention: He communicated
his Satisfaction to his Familiar; who immediately assum'd a new Air and Mein,
and told him, with an unusual Chearful-
ness, that he was glad he lik'd an Ædifice
C 2   in

in which he had a particular Intereſt. That Structure, ſaid he, is a Theatre, the Maſter of which is ſo near a Relation of mine, that I may call it my own Houſe upon that Foundation, as well as that it is the conſtant Scene of Love-Adventures, of which I am Preſident. I ſee, quoth *Cleoſas*, a pretty ſmug Gentleman ſtand behind the Scenes, with a Cane in his Hand, of a wrinkled Countenance, but an amorous briskiſh Eye; he looks, methinks, as if he had formerly been an old Man, and there is ſomething ſo particularly reſembling your ſelf in the Novelty of his Addreſs, that I preſume he is the Kinſman you boaſt of. Sir, anſwer'd *Aſmodeo*, your Conjecture is juſt; that is Signior *Divito:* You are to underſtand, continu'd he, the Figure you there obſerve is a Twin-Brother of mine, and lay with me in the ſame Cradle, when a certain Emiſſary of the Kingdom of Darkneſs came and ſurvey'd us both; me he obſerv'd to be the more phlegmatick, and conſequently thought I ſhould ſtand in need of continual Inſtigation to Evil, therefore he took me off to make a Devil, and left my Brother to be bred an Attorney, in which Way we are ſure of Mens Services all their Lives, and their Company at the End of 'em. But what has an Attorney to do with the Stage? inter-

terrupted *Cleofas*. Sir, reply'd *Asmodeo*,
an Attorney has hold of any Thing or Person with which he can join his Name in a
Parchment: My Brother had these Premi-
ses for ever fix'd to him by an Instrument
which Men call a Mortgage, with this pe-
culiar Clause, That the Land is for ever
paying, but is never to discharge it self,
which is a Prerogative they of the Facul-
ty have above all other Men; for Lawy-
ers, like Priests, can purchase but not ali-
enate. This my Brother is the newest
Character upon Earth, an hopeful old
Man, and I doubt not before he is seven-
ty he'll make Love with as good an Air as
the best of 'em. He has wholly bid fare-
well to his dusty Parchments, and uses his
Arts as an Attorney but merely as the Pit-
falls and Trap-doors on his Stage, which
serve at once to make his own Escape, and
catch his Pursuers. Well, quoth *Cleofas*,
of all Men living give me the Life of Signior *Divito*: Such Company to visit him!
such a Seraglio to attend him! I may say
it without Vanity, quoth *Asmodeo*, my
Brother has as great an Influence on the
Pains and Joys of Lovers as any Being below my self in the Universe: But such is
the Ingratitude of Mankind, that all his
Cares are neglected. Did you but see him
in his Spectacles examining the tender Hams

of

of a young Dancer, the heaving Bofom of
an Actrefs to be bred to Tragedy; in
fhort, the conftant Correfpondences the
painful Labourer is forc'd to keep with all
the idle Part of Mankind, both Foreign
and Domeftick, you would own him to
be the *Machiavil* for the State of Love.
He can tell you, as foon as any Spirit of
us all, how long fuch a young Virgin will
hold out againft fuch an importunate Lover, how foon that Lover will be weary of
her, and confequently fhe fall under his
Dominions, to Act and Propagate the Paffion which Undid her. I am very glad,
my dear Scholar, you fix'd your Eye there,
for a Theatre is the trueft Picture of Human Life; and the Men who make the
great Figures in the World are no more
what they feem, than that little diminutive
Fellow you fee taking off his Buskins and
his Feathers in the Tyring-Room, is the
Heroe you faw juft now on the Stage. To
make it yet more like the World, do you
look on yonder Couch, and fee how *Lu-
crece* and *Tarquin* agree behind the Scenes.
Such is the Force of Diftance, and well
manag'd Impofture, that the Pitch and Ro-
fin that Fellow is mixing will appear to the
Audience Lightning, and the rolling that
Nine-pin Bowl makes him a Thunderer:
In a Word, the Stage may reprefent to
you

you in the moſt lively Colours the Diſtin-
ctions and Manners among Men. This only muſt be ſaid for the Play-houſe, that it
is much leſs a Cheat than the World: For
the Actor muſt have the Mein, the Ge-
ſture, the Look, the Voice, and the whole
Behaviour of the Heroe whom he perſo-
nates; while the Mock-Worthy, which
Fortune gives you very often, in every
Step he makes is out of his Character, and
ſhows you he either never knew, or has
forgot what is really his Part. To give
you then Inſtances of the Impoſture in each
Place, turn from the Play-houſe, and look
elſewhere.

Obſerve then firſt of all, in the Houſe
on the right Hand, that old Wretch telling his Gold and Silver; he is a covetous
Man: 'Tis ſurprizing to ſee with what
Pleaſure that old Fool contemplates his
Riches! he can never ſatiate himſelf. But
at the ſame time ſee what his Heirs are doing in the next Chamber, they are conſult-
ing a Witch to know when he ſhall die.
In the next Houſe obſerve that ſuperannu-
ated Coquet going to Bed, after leaving
her Hair, Eye-brows and Teeth on her
Toilet. Do you ſee, a little farther, that
amorous Dotard of ſixty juſt come from
making Love? He has already laid down
his Eye, falſe Whiskers, and Periwig which

hid

hid his bald Pate, and expects his Man to
take off his wooden Arm and Leg, in order to go to Bed with the rest.

Cast your Eyes on that magnificent Palace, you will there see a great Lord laid
in a splendid Apartment, with a Casket
full of *Billet-doux*, which he continually
reads to lull him asleep the more pleasant-
ly: They come from the Lady which he
adores, and who puts him to such an Expence, that he will soon be reduc'd to sollicit for a Vice-Royalty to support himself.
In the next House on the left Hand is
Donna Fabula, who has just sent for a
Widwife, and is going to present her Husband *Don Torribio* with an Heir. Are not
you charm'd with that Gentleman's good
Nature? The Cries of his dear Half-self
pierce his Soul, he is wounded with Grief,
and suffers as much as she; with what Care
and Earnestness doth he labour to help
her! Really, said the Scholar, the Man is
in a great Fatigue; but in Reward of all
his Pains, I discern another which sleeps
very soundly in the same House, without
being at all concern'd at the Success of
this Affair. The Business yet relates to
him, said the Cripple, he is the Domestick
that has occasion'd all those Pains his Lady endures. Beyond see that Hypocrite
rubbing himself all over with Coach-wheel
Grease,

Greafe, in order to go to a Meeting of
Sorcerers this Night betwixt St. *Sebaftians*
and *Fontarabia.* I would carry you thither
this Minute, to oblige you with that pleafant Diverfion, if I was not afraid of being known by the Devil which perfonates
the *He-Goat* there. He is a Rafcal that
would betray me, and would not fail to
advife our Magician of my Flight. That
Devil and you, faid the Scholar, are not
then very good Friends. Far from it, reply'd *Afmodeo*; for about two Years fince
we fell out at *Paris,* about a Gentleman's
Son, to the Difpofal of whom we both
pretended: He would have made him a
Factor, and I would have had him a very
fortunate Man; but our Comerades, to
end the Difpute, made a Monk of him. After this we were reconcil'd, and embrac'd,
ever fince which we have been mortal E-
nemies.

Let's leave this fine Affembly, faid *Don
Cleofas,* and purfue our Examination of
what is doing in this City. Content, reply'd the Devil; let's then laugh a little at
that old Mufician finging a paffionate Song
to his young Wife. He would fain have
her admire the Tune which he hath juft
compos'd; but fhe likes the Words better,
becaufe made, and given to her Husband
to fet, by a fine Gentleman that loves
                                    her.

her. Let us divert our felves with that.——
Stay, I befeech you, interrupted *Don Cle-*
ofas, firft pray tell me, what mean thofe
Sparks of Fire which iffue out of that
Cave ? It is, reply'd the Cripple, one of
the moft foolifh amongft all the Works
of Men. He that you fee in that Cave,
at the burning Furnace, is an *Alchimift*,
whofe rich Patrimony the Fire will con-
fume by flow degrees, and he will never
find what he fpends it in fearch of ; for,
betwixt you and I, the *Philofophers Stone*
is no more than a *fine Chimera*, that I
my felf forg'd, to divert my felf with Human Underftanding, which would pafs the
Bounds prefcrib'd to it. And who, reply'd the Scholar, are thofe Women that
I fee at a Table in the next Houfe ? They
are two famous Curtifans, return'd the
Devil, and thofe two Gentlemen who are
committing a Debauch with them, are two
of the greateft Lords of the Court. Ah!
how charming and engaging they feem,
faid *Don Cleofas*. I don't wonder that
Perfons of Quality follow them ; how
they embrace them ? They muft certainly
be deeply in Love with them? Ah! how
young and inexperienc'd you are? reply'd
the Spirit ; you don't know this fort of Ladies, their Hearts are more painted than
their Faces. Whatever Marks of Tendernefs

nefs they exprefs, they have not any
Concern for thofe Lords; they carefs
them to obtain a Protection of one, and
a Settlement of the other. All Coquets
are the fame, and tho' Men very fairly
ruin themfelves for them, they are not the
more lov'd by them; but on the contrary,
whoever pays for Love is treated like a
Husband; this is a Law in amorous Intrigues, which I my felf have eftablifh'd.
But let's leave thofe Noblemen to tafte
the Pleafures which they fo dearly pur-
chafe, whilft their Footmen, who wait
for 'em in the Street, comfort themfelves
with the pleafing Expectation of enjoying
them *gratis.*

Caft your Eye a little farther on that
honeft Apothecary, his Wife and Man,
who are all at work in their Shop at this
late Hour. Do you know what they are
doing? The Mafter is preparing a Proli-
fick Pill for an old Advocate that is to
be marry'd to Morrow; the Man is making ready a laxative Barley Decoction,
and the Woman beating aftringent Drugs
in the Mortar. In the oppofite Houfe,
faid the Scholar, I fee a Man getting out
of his Bed and dreffing in great hafte. It
is, anfwer'd the Spirit, a Phyfician rifing
on a very preffing Occafion. He is fent
for to a Devotee, who cough'd twice or
thrice

thrice within an Hour after he went to
Bed.

Turn your Eyes a little farther on the
Right, continu'd the Devil, and try whe-
ther, by the dull Lamp in that Garret, you
can diftinguifh a Man ftalking in his Shirt.
Yes, yes, I am right, reply'd the Scholar;
I fee a Garret furnifh'd with a wretched
forry Bed, Stool, Table, and the dirty
Walls all over as black as Soot. The
Perfon that is lodg'd fo many Stories
high is a *Poet*, reply'd *Afmodeo*, and what
feems to you to be the Foulnefs of his
Walls, are Tragick Verfes of his own
Compofure, with which he has hung his
Chamber ; for the want of Paper forces
him to write his Poems on the Walls.
By the Hurry and bufie Air of his Gate,
faid *Don Cleofas*, I fhould conclude that
he was compofing fome Piece of very great
Importance. You are not in the wrong to
think fo, faid the Cripple, he yefterday
gave the finifhing Stroke to a Tragedy,
entitul'd, *The Univerfal Deluge*; in which
the Criticks themfelves cannot blame him
for not preferving the Unity of Place, fince
all the Scenes are laid in *Noah's Ark*. I
affure you 'tis an excellent Piece, for all
the Beafts are there introduc'd talking as
learnedly as Doctors themfelves. He defigns to dedicate it, and has already fpent

six

fix Hours in working up the Epiftle Dedicatory, and is at this moment gotten to the laft Line. It may juftly be call'd a Mafter-piece; for not one of the Moral and Political Virtues, nor one of the Topicks of Praife, which may excufably be beftow'd on a Man whofe Anceftors, or his own Merit, hath render'd Illuftrious, are fpar'd; never was Author fo prodigally lavifh of his Flatteries. To whom does he intend to addrefs this Elogy, faid the Scholar? He knows nothing of that yet, anfwer'd the Devil, he has left a Blank for the Name. He is in queft of fome rich Lord, more generous than the Patrons to whom he has dedicated his former Books. But good Cuftomers, which pay well for Dedicatory Epiftles, are very fcarce at prefent; the People of Quality have mended that Fault, and thereby done an acceptable Service to the Publick, which before was continually pefter'd with wretched Performances, by reafon the greateft part of the Books were written to make way for their refpective Dedications.

Let's watch, continu'd *Afmodeo,* thofe Thieves that have broken into a rich Banker's Houfe by his Balcony; obferve them coming out of the Compting-houfe, and returning perfectly empty. What is the Reafon of that? faid the Scholar. The

Banker

Banker has prevented them, return'd the
Demon; he Yefterday made the beft of
his way to *Holland,* with all the Riches
in his Coffers. If I am not miftaken, faid
Don Cleofas, there's another Thief on a
Ladder getting into that Balcony. That
is no Thief, reply'd the Lame Devil, 'tis
a Marquis fcaling the Chamber of a Virgin,
who is very willing to be rid of that Name.
He made her fome fuperficial Promifes of
Marriage, and fhe not in the leaft diftruft-
ing his Oaths, foon yielded; and no wonder, for on Love's Exchange the Marquis's
are Merchants of very great Reputation.

I fee fomething very particular, faid the
Scholar, it is a Man in a Night-cap and
Night-gown that is writing very hard,
whofe Hand is guided by a little black
Figure which ftands at his Elbow. The
Man that writes, anfwer'd the Cripple,
is a Clerk of a Court or Regifter, who,
to oblige a Guardian, is altering a Sentence pronounc'd in favour of his Pupil,
and the little black Figure is Beau *Grifael,*
the Clerks Devil. But, reply'd *Don Cleofas,* this *Grifael,* I fuppofe, fupplies this
Place only as a Deputy, fince *Flagel* being
the Spirit of the Bar, the *Regifters* feem
directly fubjected to his Direction. No,
reply'd *Afmodeo,* the *Regifters* were thought
a Body confiderable enough to have a Devil

vil of their own, and I affure you he has more upon his Hands than he can compaſs.

Oh! oh! exclaim'd the Scholar, there is another Spectacle; every body is up in that great Houſe on the left. Some are making good Chear, others dancing, pray what's the meaning of all this? It is a Wedding, faid the *Dæmon*; but within leſs than three Days, that very Palace which you ſee is at preſent the Scene of ſo much Joy, was the Houſe of utmoſt Mourning. The Story is worth hearing, and I muſt tell it you. At the ſame time he thus began.

CHAP. IV.

The Hiſtory of the Count de Belflor, *and* Leonora de Ceſpides.

THE Count *de Belflor*, one of the moſt conſiderable Grandees of the Court, lov'd young *Leonora de Ceſped* to diſtraction, but never intended to marry her: The Daughter of an ordinary Gentleman did not ſeem a Match conſiderable enough for him, wherefore he only propos'd to make a Miſtreſs of her. 'Twas
with

with this Defign that he purfu'd her where-
ever fhe went, and loft no Opportunity of
difcovering his Love, by the extraordinary
Refpects he paid her: But he could neither fpeak nor write to her, fhe being per-
petually guarded by a fevere and vigilant
Duenna, whofe Name was Madam *Marcella.* This drove him to Defpair, and
feeling his Defires irritated by the Difficulty of attaining 'em, was continually pro-
jecting Ways to deceive the *Argus* which
guarded his *Io.* On the other fide, *Leonora* perceiving the Count's Regard for her,
could not help being touch'd with the fame
Tendernefs for him, which infenfibly
form'd it felf into fuch a Paffion in her
Heart, as at laft grew to be extremely violent. I did not indeed augment it by my
common Temptations, becaufe the Magician which kept me Prifoner deny'd me the
Ufe of all my Functions; but Nature, no
lefs dangerous than my felf, engag'd in it,
and that was enough; and indeed all the
difference that there is betwixt it and me
is, that Nature corrupts Hearts by flow
degrees, whilft I feduce them expediti-
oufly.

Affairs were in this pofture, when *Leonora* and her perpetual Governante, going
one Morning to Church, met an old Woman with one of the largeft String of Beads
that

that ever Hypocrifie yet made: Accofting them with a pleafant fmilling Air, fhe thus addrefs'd her felf to the *Duenna*; The good God preferve you! faid fhe; The Holy Peace be with you! Give me leave to ask whether you are not Madam *Marcella*, the chaft Widow of the late Signior *Martin Rozeta?* The Governante having anfwer'd, Yes: 'Tis very happy that I have met you, faid the old Woman, fince I am to acquaint you, that I have at home an old Relation of mine, who is very defirous to fpeak with you. He is lately arriv'd from *Flanders*, was your Husband's moft intimate Friend, and has fome Particulars of the utmoft Importance to communicate to you. He would have waited on you at home to have imparted them to you, had he not fall'n fick; but the poor Man is at the Point of Death. I live not half a Stone's throw from hence, I befeech you to take the trouble of following me.

The Governante, who wanted not Prudence and good Senfe, being afraid of a falfe Step, knew not what to refolve on; but the old Woman guefling the Reafon of her Uneafinefs, faid to her; Dear Madam *Marcella*, you may fecurely rely upon me, my Name is *la Chicona*; the Licentiate *Marcas de Figuerrea*, and the Batchelor *Mira de Mefqua* will anfwer for

D   me

me as foon as for their Grand-mothers. I
don't defire you to come to my Houfe for
any thing but your own good. My Relation is willing to reftore you a Sum of
Mony, which he borrow'd of your Huf-
band. The very thoughts of Reftitution
engag'd *Marcella* on her fide: Come Girl,
faid fhe to *Leonora*, let's go fee this good
Lady's Relation; to vifit the Sick is an
Act of Charity.

They foon reach'd *la Chicona*'s Houfe;
who led them into a lower Room, where
they found a Man in Bed with a grey Beard,
and if he was not very fick, he at leaft
feign'd himfelf fo. Coufin, faid the old
Woman, prefenting to him the Governante, here is the Lady which you defir'd
to fpeak with, Madam *Marcella*, the Widow of your Friend Signior *Martin Rozeta*. At thefe Words the old Man lifting
up his Head a little, faluted the *Duenna*,
and making Signs for her to come nearer the
Bed-fide, faid in a feeble Tone; I thank
Heav'n, dear Madam *Marcella*, for pro-
longing my Life to this Moment, which
was the only thing I defir'd; I fear'd I
fhould die without having the Satisfaction
of feeing you, and putting into your own
Hands a hundred Ducats which my intimate Friend, your late Husband, lent me,
to help me out of an honourable Quarrel
that

that I was formerly engag'd in at *Bruges.*
Did he never acquaint you with that Adventure? Alas no, anſwer'd Madam *Marcella,* he never mention'd it. God reſt his
Soul! he was generous enough to forget
the Services he did his Friends; and,
very unlike thoſe Boaſters who brag
of what they never did, he never told
when he oblig'd any Perſon. He certainly had a very great Soul, reply'd the old
Man; a Truth which I am more firmly
engag'd to believe than any Man elſe; and
to prove it to you, you muſt give me leave
to relate the Affair out of which I was ſo
happily extricated by his Aſſiſtance; but
having ſomething to diſcloſe of the laſt
Importance with regard to the Memory of
the deceas'd, I ſhould be very glad of an
Opportunity of revealing them to his di-
ſcreet Widow alone.

Very well then, ſaid *la Chicona,* you
need only tell it her in private; in the mean
while this young Lady and I will retire to
my Cloſet. At theſe Words ſhe left the
Duenna with the ſick Man, and conducted
Leonora into another Chamber, where
without any Circumlocution ſhe ſaid, Fair
Leonora, the Moments are too precious to
be miſs-ſpent; you know the Count *de
Belflor* by Sight, he has long'd lov'd you,
and languiſhing dies for an Opportunity to

tell

tell you fo; but the Vigilance and Severity of your *Governante* have always hinder'd him from enjoying that Satisfaction.   In this Defpair he had Recourfe to my Induftry, which I have made ufe for him. The old Man whom you have juft now feen is the Count's young *Valet de Chambre*, and all that hath been done is only a Trick to deceive your *Governante*, and draw you hither.

Thefe Words were no fooner ended, than the Count, who was conceal'd behind the Hangings, appear'd, and running threw himfelf at *Leonora's* Feet: Madam, faid he, pardon the Stratagem of a Lover who could no longer live without fpeaking to you; if this obliging Matron had not procur'd me this Opportunity, I fhould have abandon'd my felf to Defpair. Thefe Words, exprefs'd with a very moving Air by a Perfon not at all difagreeable, difturb'd *Leonora:* She continu'd fome time doubtful what Anfwer fhe ought to make; but at laft recovering her felf, and looking difpleas'd at the Count, faid: Perhaps you believe your felf very much oblig'd to this officious Lady, who has fo well ferv'd your Purpofe; but know that you will reap little Advantage by the Service fhe has done you. At thefe Words fhe made feveral Steps to get out of the
Room,

Room, but the Count ftopp'd her; Stay, faid he, adorable *Leonora*, hear me one Moment; my Paffion is fo pure that it ought not to alarm you; I own you have fome grounds to oppofe the Artifice which I have made ufe of to converfe with you; but have I not hitherto in vain endeavour'd to fpeak to you? I have follow'd you thefe fix Months to the Churches, Walks, Play-houfes, and all publick Places. I have long in vain watch'd an Opportunity of telling you how you have charm'd me; your cruel, your mercilefs Governefs has continually fruftrated my Defigns. Alas then, inftead of turning the Stratagem which I have been forc'd to employ into a Crime, commiferate, fair *Leonora*, my fuffering all the Tortures of fuch a tedious Expectation, and judge, by your Charms, the mortal Pangs they have occafion'd.

Belflor did not forget to reinforce his Words with all the Airs of Perfuafion which gallant Men are us'd to practife with Succefs, accompanying his Words with fome Tears; with which *Leonora* began to be touch'd, and in defpight of her Refolution, fome tender compaffionate Emotions began to arife in her Heart; but far from yielding to them, the more fhe perceiv'd them to grow, the more fhe prefs'd to be gone: Count, faid fhe, all your Talk is in vain, I will not hear you; don't detain me any longer, but let me go out of a House in which my Virtue is alarm'd, or by my Cries I will call in all the Neighbourhood, and expose your Audaciousness to the Publick. This she utter'd in such a resolute Tone, that *la Chicona*, who was oblig'd to stand in Awe of the Magistracy, begg'd of the Count not to push things any farther: Upon which he forbore opposing *Leonora's* Intention, who got out of his Hands, and (what had never before happen'd to any Virgin) quitted the Closet as good a Maid as she enter'd it.

She immediately flew to her *Governante*; Come, good Matron, said she, leave off that foolish Dialogue; we are cheated, let's quit this dangerous House. What's the Matter, Child! with Amazement answer'd Madam *Marcella:* What is the Reason of your so hasty Departure? I'll inform you, reply'd *Leonora;* but let's fly, for every Minute I stay here gives me fresh Uneasiness. However earnest the *Duenna* was to know the Cause of this Haste, she could not then be satisfy'd, but was oblig'd to yield to the Instances of *Leonora.* They both went away in a hurry, leaving *la Chicona*, the Count, and his *Valet de Chambre* in as great Confusion, as a parcel of

Players

Players oblig'd to act a Piece which the Stage-Beaux have already hifs'd.

When *Leonora* was gotten into the Street, with a great deal of inward Difturbance fhe began to tell her *Governante* what pafs'd in *la Chicona*'s Clofet. Madam *Marcella* was very attentive, and when they had reach'd their own Houfe, I proteft, my Daughter, faid fhe, I am extreamly mortify'd at the Thoughts of what you have juft inform'd me; how was it poffible for me to be deluded by that old Woman? At firft, I made a Difficulty of following her: Oh that I had continu'd in the fame Opinion! I ought to have miftrufted her flattering Wheedles. I have committed a Folly not to be forgiven in a Perfon of my Experience. Ah why did not you difcover this Plot whilft I was at *la Chicona*'s Houfe! I would have fcratch'd out their Eyes, call'd the Count *de Belflor* by all the Names I could have thought on, and tore off the Beard of the counterfeit old Man, who told me fo many Lies. But I will this Minute return thither, to carry back the Mony which I honeftly receiv'd, as a real Reftitution of what I fuppos'd my Husband lent, and if I find them together they fhall not lofe by ftaying for me. Thefe Words ended, fhe flew out, and made the beft of her way to *la Chicona*'s Houfe.

The

The Count was yet there, and, by the ill Succefs of his Stratagem, reduc'd almoft to Defpair.   Another would have quitted the Purfuit; but he was not difcourag'd: For, with a thoufand good Qualities, he had one which was very ill; it was the fuffering himfelf to be too much hurry'd on by his amorous Inclinations.   Whenever he lov'd a Lady he was too warm in the Purfuit of her Favours, and tho' naturally an honeft Man, he made no Scruple of violating the moft facred Laws to accomplifh his Defires.   Confidering then that it was impoffible for him to gain his End without the Affiftance of Maoam *Marcella*, he refolv'd to leave no Means unattempted to engage her in his Intereft.   He concluded that this *Duenna*, how fevere foever fhe appear'd, was not Proof againft a confiderable Prefent; and indeed his Opinion was not unjuft, for if there are any fuch things as *Trufty Governantes*, the only Reafon is that the *Gallants* are not rich enough to make fufficient Prefents.

As foon as Madam *Marcella* arriv'd, and found all the three Perfons fhe wifh'd for there, fhe open'd very outrageoufly, loaded the Count and *la Chicona* with a Million of hard Names, and made the Reftitution-Sum fly at the Head of the *Valet de Chambre*.   The Count attempted to appeafe this

this Storm with Patience, threw himself at the *Duenna*'s Knees to render the Scene more moving; he prefs'd her to take the Purfe again, and offer'd her a thoufand Piftoles befides, conjuring her to have Pity on him. As her Compaffion had never been fo powerfully follicited, fo fhe did not prove inexorable. She foon left off her Invectives, and comparing the offer'd Sum with the mean Recompence fhe expected of *Don Lewis*, fhe eafily found that it was more for her Intereff to draw *Leonora* from her Duty, than preferve her in it; which engag'd her, after a few complemental Refufals, to take up the Purfe again, accept the Offer of the thoufand Piftoles, promife to be fubfervient to the Count's Paffion, and immediately prepare to perform her Promife.

Knowing *Leonora* to be a virtuous young Lady, fhe very carefully avoided giving her the leaft Sufpicion of her Correfpondence with the Count, for fear fhe fhould difcover it to *Don Lewis*, her Father; and being refolv'd on more fubtle Meafures to ruin her, fhe thus addrefs'd her felf at her Return: *Leonora*, I have juft now fatisfy'd my enrag'd Mind; I found the three villainous Deceivers confounded at our courageous Retreat. I threaten'd *la Chicona* with your Father's Refentment, and the

the moſt rigorous Severity of the Law; I
call'd the Count *de Belflor* all the ill Names
which Rage could ſuggeſt, and hope that
Lord will no more be guilty of any ſuch
Attempts, and that his Intrigues will no
more exerciſe my Vigilance. I thank
Heav'n that by your Reſolution you have
eſcaped the Net which was ſpread for you.
I weep for Joy, I am raviſh'd to think he
has not been able to gain any Advantage
over you by his Stratagem; for great Lords
make it their Diverſion to ſeduce young
Ladies. Moſt of thoſe who value themſelves on preſerving the ſtricteſt degree of
Probity are not ſcrupulous on this Head,
as tho' the diſhonouring of Families was
no ill Act. I don't abſolutely ſay that the
Count is a Man of this Character, nor
that he aims at deceiving you; we muſt
not always judge ill of our Neighbours,
perhaps his Deſigns are honourable: Tho'
his Quality entitles him to the beſt Match
at Court, your Beauty may yet have made
him reſolve to marry you: I remember alſo, in the Anſwers he made to the hard
Words I gave him, he hinted it to me.
What do you ſay, good *Governante?* interrupted *Leonora;* if he had any ſuch Intention, he would before now have ask'd
me of my Father, who would never have
deny'd a Man of his Quality.

What

What you say is very juft, reply'd the
Duenna, I am of your Mind; the Courfe
which the Count took is fufpicious, or rather his Intentions were ill: I am almoft
in the Mind to return to him, and fcold at
him afrefh.   No, good Madam, reply'd
Leonora, 'tis better to forget what is paft,
and revenge it by Contempt.   'Tis true,
faid *Marcella*, I think that is the beft way;
you are wifer than I.   But on the other
fide, let us not judge amifs of the Count's
Sentiments: How do we know but he
took that Courfe, as the moft refin'd way
of difcovering his Paffion? Before obtaining your Father's Confent, perhaps he
was fond of obtaining your Favour, and
fecuring your Heart by long Services, that
your Union might thereby be render'd
more charming If fo, my Daughter, would
it be a great Crime to hearken to him?
Unbofom your felf, you know my tender
Affection for you; Are you fenfible of any
Alteration in Favour of the Count? or
would you, if it was put to you, refufe to
marry him?

At this malicious Queftion the too fincere *Leonora* caft down her Eyes, and
blufhing own'd that fhe had no Averfion
for him; but Modefty preventing her farther difcovering her felf, the *Duenna* prefs'd
her afrefh to hide nothing from her: She,
over-

over-power'd by the *Governante*'s tender
Professions, went on : Good *Marcella,*
said she, since you will have me talk to
you as my Confident, know that I think
Belflor deserves to be lov'd : I lik'd his
Mein so well, and withal have heard such
an advantageous Character of him, that I
could not help being touch'd with his Addresses. The indefatigable Care which you
always took to oppose them hath frequently given me great Uneasiness, and I own
that I have sometimes deplor'd, and in a
sort by my Tears repair'd the Pains your
Vigilance has forc'd him to bear. I will
farther own to you at this very moment,
that instead of hating him after this rash
Action, my Heart against my Will excuses
him, and throws the Fault on your Severity. Daughter, reply'd the *Governante,*
since you give me Leave to believe his Addresses will be agreeable to you, I will manage this Lover for you. I am very sensible, answer'd *Leonora* in a more moving
Tone, of the Service you are willing to
render me: If the Count was not one of
the Grandees of the first Rank at.Court,
was he only a bare Gentleman, I should
prefer him to all Men; but let us not flatter our selves, *Belflor* is a great Lord, and
doubtless is design'd for one of the richest
Heiresses in the Kingdom. Don't let us
expect

expect that he will ever descend to *Don Lewis*'s Daughter, who has but a mean Fortune to offer him: No, no, adds she, he has no such favourable Thoughts of me; he does not think me worth bearing his Name, and pursues me only to dishonour me.

Ah wherefore, said the *Duenna*, will you think that he does not love you well enough to marry you? Love daily works greater Miracles than that.   You seem to imagine that Heav'n hath set an infinite distance betwixt the Count and you; do your self more Justice, *Leonora*; it would not be below him to join his Fortune to yours; you are of an ancient noble Family, and your Alliance could never put him to the Blush.   Since you have some Inclinations towards him, continu'd she, I must talk with him: I will examine his Intentions, and if I find them such as they ought to be, I will encourage them with some Hopes. Be very careful, reply'd *Leonora*; I am of Opinion you ought not to go in search of him; if he suspects my having any hand in it, he will cease to value me.   Oh I am a Woman of more Address than you imagine, reply'd *Marcella:* I will begin with accusing him of a Design to seduce you, upon which he will not fail to justifie himself; I will hear him,
and

and fhall fee the Event. In fhort, my
Daughter, leave it to me, I'll manage your
Honour as cautioufly as if it were my
own.

The *Duenna* took her Vail, and went out
at the beginning of the Night: She found
Belflor near *Don Lewis*'s Houfe, and gave
him an account of her Difcourfe with her
Miftrefs, not forgetting to value her felf
on her Conduct in the Difcovery of the
Lady's Paffion for him.   Nothing could
oblige the Count more than this News,
wherefore he exprefs'd his Thanks to *Marcella* in the moft fenfible manner ; that is,
he promis'd to give her the thoufand Piftoles on the next Day, affuring himfelf
of the Succefs of his Enterprize; very well
knowing, that a Woman prepoffefs'd is
half feduc'd.   They then parted very well
fatisfy'd with each other, the *Duenna* returning home.

Leonora, who impatiently expected her,
ask'd what News fhe had brought : The
beft that you could ever hear, anfwer'd
the *Governante,* all things fucceed the beft
in the World.   I have feen the Count ; I
can tell you that his Intentions are not
ill, he has no other Defign but that of
marrying you.   This he fwore to me by
all that is facred amongft Men. You may,
perhaps, imagine that I yielded to him
                                        upon

upon this, but I affure you I did not. If you are thus refolv'd, faid I, why don't you make the ufual Applications to *Don Lewis?* Ah, dear *Marcella,* anfwer'd he, without appearing difturb'd at this Queftion, could you think it proper (ignorant as I am whether *Leonora* has any Regard for me) that, hurry'd on by the Tranfports of blind Love, I fhould tyrannically endeavour to obtain her of her Father? No, her Eafe is dearer to me than my own Defires, and I am too honourable to difcover my Paffion, in order to render her unhappy.

All the time that he fpent in expreffing himfelf thus, continu'd the *Duenna,* I obferv'd him with the utmoft Attention, and employ'd all my Experience in difcovering by his Eyes whether his Love was fo fincere as he reprefented it. He feem'd touch'd with a real Paffion, and I with a Joy which without much difficulty I could not conceal. Being then fatisfied of his Sincerity, I thought it not improper to glance at your Sentiments with regard to him, in order to fecure you fuch a confiderable Lover. My Lord, faid I to him, *Leonora* hath no Averfion for you; and, as far as I can judge, your Addreffes are not infupportable to her. Great God, exclaim'd he then all in Rapture, what do I hear!

Is

Is it poffible that the charming *Leonora*
fhould entertain any favourable Thoughts
of me: What is it that I am not indebted
to you, moft obliging *Marcella*, for having
rid me of fuch a tedious Uncertainty? You,
who by a continual Oppofition have loaded
me with fo many Torments. But, dear
Marcella, compleat my Blifs, by obliging
me with an Opportunity of fpeaking with
the Divine *Leonora*; I folemnly promife
and fwear before you, that I will never be
any others but hers. To this, purfu'd the
Governante, he added yet more moving Af-
feverations; in fhort, Daughter, he entreated me in fuch a preffing manner to procure him a private Opportunity of fpeaking to you, that I could not avoid promifing to accomplifh it. Ah, why did you
promife him that? reply'd *Leonora* fomewhat difturb'd. A wife Virgin, you have
a hundred times inculcated to me, is abfolutely oblig'd to fhun thofe Converfations,
which can only be dangerous. I agree to
what you fay, reply'd the *Duenna*, and it
is a very good Maxim; but you may law-
fully difpence with it on this Occafion,
fince you may look on the Count as your
Husband. He is not fo yet, reply'd *Leonora*, and I ought not to fee him before
my Father allows of his Suit.

Madam

Madam *Marcella* now began to repent the good Education which she had bestow'd on the young Lady, since she found it so difficult to subdue her Virtue. But yet resolv'd to compass her End, cost what it would; My dear *Leonora*, said she, I applaud my self, when I see you so reserv'd. Oh happy Fruit of my Cares! You have profited by all the Rules I have given you. I am charm'd with my own Work! But, my Daughter, you exaggerate what I have taught, you strain my Morals too severely, and your Virtue is indeed a little too rude. Tho' I am fond of a strict Severity, yet I cannot approve of a brutish ill-manner'd Caution, indistinguishably and indifferently levell'd against Guilt and Innocence. A Virgin doth not abandon her Virtue, by affording her Ear to a Lover, of the Purity of whose Desires she is satisfy'd; in which case it is not more criminal to answer his Passion, than be sensible of it. Depend upon me, *Leonora*, I have too much Experience, and am too deeply engag'd in your Interests, to draw you into any Measures which can be prejudicial to you.

Alas! where would you have me speak with the Count? said *Leonora.* In your own Apartment, reply'd the *Duenna*, for that is the safest Place; I will introduce

E　　　　　him

him to Morrow Night. Good *Marcella*, reply'd *Leonora*, shall I then admit a Man— Yes, you shall admit him, interrupted the *Duenna*; 'tis no such extraordinary thing as you imagine, 'tis done every Day, and I send up my Wishes to Heav'n that the Maidens which receive such Visits were fortify'd with as good Intentions as yours! Besides, what have you to fear? Shall not I be with you? If my Father should surprize us? reply'd *Leonora*. Never disturb your self in the least about that, return'd *Marcella*; your Father is perfectly satisfy'd with your Conduct, knows my Fidelity, and reposes an entire Confidence in me. Upon this *Leonora*, being so violently push'd on by the *Duenna*, and internally press'd by her Love, was not able to hold out longer, but yielded to *Marcella*'s Proposal.

The Count was immediately inform'd of it, and so joyfully receiv'd the News, that he instantly presented his Female Agent with five hundred Pistoles and a Ring of the like Value: And she accordingly, finding him such a strict Observer of his Word, resolv'd not to fail in the Performance of her Promise. Wherefore next Night, when she concluded all of the Family were asleep, she fasten'd to the Balcony a silken Ladder which the Count had
given

given her, and by that means introduc'd him into his Miſtreſs's Apartment.

In the mean while the young Lady was wholly taken up with a Series of melancholy Reflections, which very much diſturb'd her. Notwithſtanding her Inclination for the Count, and whatever her *Governante* could ſay, ſhe blam'd her eaſie Conſent to a Viſit that would violate her Duty. To receive a Man into her Chamber at Night, whoſe real Sentiments ſhe was ignorant of, and withal without her Father's Knowledge, ſeem'd to her not only criminal, but alſo what might render her contemptible in her Lover's Eyes. 'Twas this laſt Reflection which moſt tormented her, and ſhe was extream full of it when the Count enter'd.

He immediately fell on his Knees to thank her for the Favour ſhe did him. He appear'd throughly touch'd with Love and Acknowledgment, and aſſur'd her of his Intentions to marry her; but not expreſſing himſelf ſo ſatisfactory on that Head as ſhe deſir'd: Count, ſaid ſhe, I am willing to believe that you have no other Deſign than what you have told me; but whatever Aſſurances you can give me, I ſhall always ſuſpect them 'till they are authoriſed and confirm'd by my Father's Conſent. Madam, anſwer'd *Belſlor*, I had

E 2   long

long since ask'd that, if I had not fear'd
the obtaining it at the Expence of your Repose. I don't blame you for having not
yet done it, reply'd *Leonora*, but even approve these more refin'd Punctilio's of your
Love; but nothing at present hinders you,
and you must speak to my Father as soon
as possible, or resolve never to see me
more.

Ah! why never see you more, charming
Leonora! reply'd the Count. How little
sensible are you of the Pleasures of Love!
If you knew what it was to love, as well
as I, you would be pleas'd with my disclo-
sing my Pains in secret, and at least conceal them for some time from your Father's Knowledge. Oh how great are the
Charms of such a private Correspondence
betwixt two Hearts firmly united! They
may prove so to you, said *Leonora*, but
they would be no other than Torments to
me. Such subtle Distinctions of Tenderness very ill become a virtuous Maiden:
Boast therefore no more of the Delights
of a guilty Commerce, which if you valu'd me you would not have offer'd; and
if your Intentions are really such as you
would persuade me they are, you ought
from the Bottom of your Soul to blame
my hearing such Offers so patiently. But
alas, adds she, letting fall some Tears, 'tis
to

to my Weaknefs alone that this Crime ought to be imputed; I have indeed deferv'd it, by doing what I have done for you.

Adorable *Leonora,* cry'd the Count, you wrong me extreamly; your too fcrupulous Virtue takes falfe Alarms. Why fhould you fear, becaufe I have been fo happy as to prevail on you to favour my Love, that I fhould ceafe to value you? How unjuft is this? No, Madam, I am fenfible of the full Value of your Favours; they can never deprive you of my Efteem; I am therefore ready to do what you exact of me, and will fpeak to Signior *Don Lewis* to Morrow. I will ufe my utmoft Endeavour to obtain his Confent to my Happinefs; but I muft not omit telling you, that I fee but fmall Hopes of it. How! reply'd *Leonora,* can my Father poffibly refufe his Confent to a Man of your Quality and Character at Court? 'Tis that very Character and Quality which makes me fear a Denial. You are furpriz'd at what I fay; but will ceafe to be fo, when I acquaint you that fome Days paft the King declar'd he was refolv'd to marry me. He hath not yet nam'd the Lady he defigns me for, but has only given me to underftand that fhe is one of the beft Matches at Court, and that he is firmly bent upon it.

Not

Not knowing at that time what Sentiments you might have with regard to me, (for you very well know that your rigorous Severity never before allow'd me an Opportunity of discovering them) I did not shew any Averseness to obey his Will. After this, judge, Madam, whether *Don Lewis* would run the risque of the King's Displeasure, by accepting me for his Son-in-Law.

No, doubtless, said *Leonora*; I know my Father, how great soever the Advantages of your Alliance might prove, would chuse rather to renounce it, than expose himself to the King's Displeasure. But if my Father should not oppose our Union, we should not yet be the happier; for in short, Count, how can you give me a Hand which the King has engag'd elsewhere? Madam, answer'd *Belflor*, I own sincerely that I at present labour under a very great Difficulty on that side; but yet hope, that by an even and very prudent Conduct with regard to his Majesty, I shall so well manage his Favours and Friendship for me, as to invent a way to avoid that threaten'd Misfortune. You your self, beautiful *Leonora*, may assist me herein, if you think me worth joining to you. Ah! in what manner, said she, can I contribute to the breaking off the Match which the King
has

has propos'd to you? Ah Madam, reply'd
he with a paffionate Air, if you pleafe to
receive my Troth, which I offer to plight
to you, I can preferve my felf for you,
without incurring the King's Difpleafure.
Permit, adorable *Leonora*, adds he kneel-
ing, that I efpoufe you in the Prefence of
Madam *Marcella*, and let her be Witnefs
of the Sanctity of our Engagement; by
this means I fhall eafily efcape thofe miferable Knots with which the World would
bind me: For after that, whenever the
King preffes me to accept the Lady he defigns me, I have nothing to do but pro-
ftrate my felf at the Feet of my Prince,
and inform him that I have long lov'd and
fecretly marry'd you. However defirous
he may be to marry me to another, he
is yet too gracious to fnatch me from
her whom I adore, and too juft to offer
this Affront to your Family. What do
you think, difcreet *Marcella*, adds he turning to the *Governante*, what's your Opinion of this Project with which Love has
this Minute infpir'd me? I am charm'd
with it, faid the *Duenna*; it muft indeed
be own'd that Love is very ingenious! And
you, charming *Leonora*, reply'd the Count,
what do you fay to it? Can your Heart,
tho' arm'd with Diftruft, refufe its Appro-
bation? No, return'd *Leonora*, provided

E 4   you

you will admit my Father into the Secret, who, I doubt not, will fubfcribe to what you will have him.

We ought to be very careful how we intruft this Affair with him, here interrupted the *Duenna:* You don't know *Don Lewis;* he is too nice in Punctilio's of Honour to be affifting to fecret Amours: The very Propofal of a private Marriage will offend him. Befides, his Prudence will not fail to make him afraid of the Confequences of an Union which feems to fhock the King's Defigns. By this indifcreet Step you will fill him with Sufpicions, his Eyes will be continually upon you in all your Actions, and he will deprive you of all Opportunities. Ah! I fhall then die with Grief, cry'd our Courtier. But, Madam *Marcella,* purfu'd he, affecting a melancholy Tone, do you really believe that *Don Lewis* would reject the Offer of a private Marriage? I don't doubt it in the leaft, anfwer'd the *Governante;* but grant that he fhould accept it, he is fo fcrupuloufly religious that he would never yield to the Omiffion of any of the Ceremonies of the Church, and if they are all performed in your Marriage it will foon be publifh'd.

Ah my dear *Leonora,* then faid the Count, tenderly locking his Miftrefs's Hand

betwixt

betwixt his own, must we, to satisfie a vain Notion of Decorum, expose our selves to the terrible Danger of being separated for ever? The Consent of a Father would perhaps spare you some uneasie Thoughts; but since Madam *Marcella* has shew'd us the Impossibility of obtaining it, yield your self to my innocent Desires; receive my Heart and Hand, and when it shall be a proper time to inform *Don Lewis* of our Engagement, we will acquaint him also why we conceal'd it. Well, Count, said *Leonora*, I consent then that you do not so soon speak to my Father; but first found the King's Mind. Before I receive your Hand in private, speak to our Prince, tell him you have privately marry'd me; let's endeavour by this false Confidence——Oh no, Madam, reply'd *Belflor*, I am too great a Hater of a Lie, to dare to maintain this Feint; I cannot thus dissemble. Besides, I know the King, if he should discover that I had deceiv'd him, would not pardon it during his whole Life.

I should never have done, Signior *Cleofas*, continu'd the Devil, if I should repeat *verbatim* all the Expressions which *Belflor* made use of to seduce this young Lady. Wherefore I shall only tell you that he employ'd all the passionate Lauguage which I

suggest

fuggeſt to Men on the like Occaſions: But
he had ſcarce ſworn that he would as ſoon
as poſſible publickly confirm the Promiſe
which he had made in ſecret; he had
ſcarce call'd Heav'n to witneſs his Oaths,
but he found he could not triumph over
Leonora's Virtue, and that the Day being
ready to appear forc'd him againſt his Will
to depart.

The next Day the *Duenna*, believing
her Honour, or rather her Intereſt engag'd
not to abandon her Enterprife, ſaid to
Don Lewis's Daughter; *Leonora*, I don't
know what to ſay further to you; I find
you oppoſe the Count's Paſſion, as tho' it
had no other Aim but that of a bare Gallantry: Have you not obſerv'd ſomething
in his Perſon that diſguſts you? No, good
Marcella, anſwer'd *Leonora*; on the contrary, he never appear'd ſo amiable, and
his Diſcourſe diſcover'd new Charms to
me. If ſo, reply'd the *Governante*, I
don't comprehend you: You are prepoſ-
ſeſs'd with a violent Inclination for him,
and yet refuſe to yield to a thing, the Neceſſity of which has already been repre-
ſented to you. My good Madam, reply'd
Don Lewis's Daughter, you have more
Prudence and Experience than I; but have
you conſider'd throughly the Conſequences which may reſult from a Marriage con-
tracted

tracted without my Father's Knowledge? Yes, yes, answer'd the *Duenna*, I have made all necessary Reflection on that, and am very sorry to see you so obstinately resist the glorious Settlement which his Fortune presents you. Have a Care that your Obduracy does not weary and disgust your Lover, and be afraid lest he should cast his Eyes on the Interest of his Fortune, which the Violence of his Passion has made him neglect. Since he offers to give you his Faith, accept it without farther Deliberation. His Word binds him; than which nothing is more sacred to a Honour. Besides, I am a Witness that he acknowledges you for his Wife. Don't you know that such important Evidence as mine is sufficient to condemn, in a Court of Justice, that Lover which should dare to perjure himself?

It was by such Language as this that the perfidious *Marcella* shock'd *Leonora,* who suffering all Reflections of the Danger that threaten'd her to wear off, in all Simplicity a few Days after abandon'd her self to the Count's wicked Intentions.

The *Duenna* introduc'd him every Night by the Balcony into his Mistress's Apartment, and let him out before Day. One Night having warn'd him to depart somewhat later than ordinary, and *Aurora* beginning

ginning to break through the Darkneſs, he
haſtily endeavour'd to ſlide into the Street,
but by Miſchance ſucceeded ſo ill that he
got a very ſevere Fall. *Don Lewis de
Ceſpedes,* whoſe Bed-chamber was under
that of his Daughter, happening that
Morning to riſe very early for the Diſpatch
of ſome preſſing Affairs, heard the Count's
Fall, and opening his Window to ſee what
was the Occaſion of the Noiſe, perceiv'd
a Man juſt riſen from the Ground with
great Difficulty, and *Marcella* in his Daughter's Balcony; ſhe having drawn up the
ſilken Ladder, which the Count had not
made ſo good uſe of in his deſcending as
in his Aſcent. *Don Lewis* rubb'd his Eyes,
and at firſt took this Spectacle for an Illu-
ſion; but after having conſider'd it, concluded that nothing was more real, and
that the Day-Light, imperfect as it yet
was, did but too much diſcover his Diſ-
grace. Confus'd at the fatal Sight, and
tranſported by a juſt Rage, he haſted in
his Night-Gown to *Leonora's* Apartment,
with a Sword in one Hand, and a Wax-
Candle in the other. He went in queſt of
her and her *Governante,* in order to ſacri-
fice them both to his Reſentment. He
knock'd at their Chamber-door, and commanded them to open it; they knew his
Voice, and trembling obey'd. He enter'd
                                    with

with a furious Air, and difcovering his naked Sword to their amaz'd Eyes; I come,
faid he, to wafh away with her Blood the
infamous Affront that Wretch has thrown
upon her Father, and at the fame time
punifh the villainous *Governante* which has
betray'd the Truft I repos'd in her.

They both fell upon their Knees, and
the *Duenna* began; Signior, faid fhe, before we receive the Chaftifement which
you have prepar'd, vouchfafe to hear us
one Moment. Well, Wretch, reply'd the
old Gentleman, I confent to fufpend my
Vengeance for a Minute: Speak, inform
me of all the Circumftances of my Mif-
fortunes. But what do I talk of all the
Circumftances? I know them all but one,
and that is the Name of that rafh Man
which has difhonour'd my Family. Signi-
or, reply'd Madam *Marcella*, the Count
de Belflor is the Gentleman that hath done
it. The Count *de Belflor!* faid *Don Lewis;* where has he feen my Daughter? by
what Means has he feduc'd her? conceal
nothing from me. Signior, reply'd the
Governante, I will relate the whole Story
to you with all the Sincerity I am capable
of.

She then, with an infinite deal of Art,
recited all the Expreffions which fhe had
made *Leonora* believe the Count had utter'd

ter'd with regard to her: She painted him
in the moſt lively Colours of a tender,
ſcrupulous, and ſincere Lover. But not
being able to elude the Diſcovery of the
whole Truth, ſhe was oblig'd to tell it;
but enlarg'd on the Reaſons that prevail'd
with them to conceal from him the ſecret
Marriage, and gave them ſuch an acceptable Turn, as appeas'd *Don Lewis*'s Rage.
Which ſhe perfectly diſcerning, in order
to compleatly ſoften the old Man, Signi-
or, ſaid ſhe, this is what you deſir'd to
know: Puniſh us this Minute; plunge your
Sword in *Leonora*'s Breaſt. But what do
I ſay? *Leonora* is innocent; ſhe has only
follow'd the Counſels of a Woman which
you intruſted with her Conduct, wherefore
'tis me alone againſt whom your Sword
ſhould point. 'Tis I that have introduc'd
the Count into your Daughter's Apartment, and alone have ty'd the Knot wherewith ſhe is bound. 'Tis I who have wink'd
at all Irregularities in a Contract that was
not back'd by your Authority, in order to
ſecure you a Son-in-Law whoſe Intereſt
you know is the Channel thro' which all
Court Favours at preſent paſs. I had no
other Aim than *Leonora*'s Happineſs, and
the Advantage your Family may reap by
ſuch an important Alliance; and indeed
'tis the Exceſs of Zeal to ſerve your Houſe
which

which alone has drawn me into this be-
traying of my Truft.

While the fubtle *Marcella* was thus ca-
joling the old Gentleman, her Miftrefs
fpar'd no Tears, but difcover'd fuch a fenfible Grief as he could not refift. He grew
tender, his Rage turn'd into Compaffion,
he dropt his Sword, and quitting the Air
of an angry Father; Ah my Daughter!
faid he with Tears in his Eyes, what a fatal Paffion is Love! Alas, you are not fenfible of all the Reafons you have to afflict
your felf. The Shame alone that muft refult from the Prefence of a Father who has
furpriz'd you, muft unavoidably draw
Tears from you; befides which, you don't
yet forefee all the Anxieties your Lover
may perhaps prepare for you. And you,
imprudent *Marcella*, to what a Precipice
has your indifcreet Zeal for my Family
brought you? I acknowledge that fuch a
confiderable Alliance as that of the Count
might dazle your Eyes, and it is that alone
which excufes you to me: But, Wretch
that you are, ought you not to have diftrufted a Lover of his high Quality? The
more Intereft and Favour he can pretend
to, the more you ought to have on your
Guard againft him. If he fhould make no
Scruple of breaking his Faith with *Leono-*
ra, what Courfe fhould I take? Should I
                                    implore

implore the Affiftance of the Laws of the
Land? a Perfon of his Character would
eafily be able to fhelter himfelf from their
Severity: And I wifh that, continuing juft
to his Oaths, he prove willing to keep his
Word with my Daughter; for if the King,
as you fay, defigns to oblige him to marry
another Lady, 'tis very much to be fear'd
that his Majefty will force him to it by the
Vertue of his Prerogative.

Oh Sir, interrupted *Leonora*, that ought
not to alarm you; the Count has very
well affur'd us, that the King will not
commit fuch a great Violence on his Paffion. I am perfuaded, faid *Marcella*, his
Majefty is too fond of his Favourite to
exercife fuch a Tyranny over him, and alfo
that he is too generous to plung into a fatal Grief *Don Lewis de Cefpides*, who has
fpent all his beft Days in the Service of the
Publick. Pray Heav'n it prove fo, reply'd
the old Gentleman weeping, and that my
Fears prove vain! I will go to the Count,
and defire him to explain this Affair. A
Father's Eyes are piercing, and I fhall difcover the deepeft Receffes of his Soul. If
I find him in the Difpofition which I wifh,
I will pardon what is paft; but, adds he
in a more refolute Tone, if by his Difcourfe
I difcover a perfidious Heart, you fhall
both with Tears bewail your Imprudence
in

in a melancholy Retirement the Remainder of your Days. At these Words he took up his Sword, and leaving them to the frightful Thoughts he had rais'd in them, return'd to his Apartment to dress.

Signior *Asmodeo*, said *Don Cleofas* in this Place, before you relate the Sequel of this Story, tell me, I beseech you, what is doing in that Apartment hung with Musk-colour'd Cloth? I see five or six Women crouding and pressing one another to thrust Glass-Bottles into the Hands of a sort of Servant. That is somewhat worth your Observation, answer'd the Devil. In that Apartment an *Inquisitor* lyes sick; he is lodg'd in the Chamber where you see two Women watching with him: They are two of his Penitents; one is employ'd in making Broths for him, and the other at his Boulster is keeping his Head warm. Pray what is his Distemper? said the Scholar. A little Cold in his Head, reply'd the *Demon*; and 'tis to be fear'd the Rheum may fall on his Breast. The other Women which you see in his Anti-Chamber are also devout Ladies, who, on the News of his Indisposition, run thither in all haste with their Medicines. One of them has brought him for his Cough Syrups of *Jujubes*, *Marsh-mallows*, *Coral*, and *Colts-foot*; another, to preserve his

F   Reve-

Reverence's Lungs, is laden with *Syrups* of *Long-life, Veronica, Immortality,* and *Elixir Proprietatis;* another, to fortifie his Brain and Stomach, has brought *Baum, Cinamon,* and *Treacle-Water,* befides the *Divine Water,* and *Effences* of *Nutmegs* and *Amber-grife;* this comes to offer him *Anacardine* and *Bezoartick Confections;* and that, *Tinctures* of *Clove-July-Flowers, Coral, Mille-florum, the Sun,* and *Emeralds.* All thefe Women are boafting the Efficacy of their Remedies to the Inquifitor's Footman; they take him afide one after another, and each of them clapping a Ducat in his Hand, thus whifpers him in the Ear: *Lawrence,* dear *Lawrence,* I entreat you not to fail preferring my Medicines to all the reft. This is what you defir'd, continu'd the Devil, and I will now continue the Thread of my Story.

C H A P.

C H A P. V.

The Continuation and Conclusion of the
History of the Count and Leonora.

DON *Lewis* went early to the Count,
who not suspecting he was discover'd, was surpriz'd with this Visit. He
stept forward to meet him at his Entrance,
and after having tir'd him with Embraces,
How great is my Joy, said he, to see
Don Lewis here! doth he come to offer
me any Opportunity of serving him? My
Lord, answer'd *Don Lewis*, order, if you
please, that we be alone; which *Belflor* accordingly did, and they both sate down,
when the old Man thus began: My Lord,
said he, my Honour and Repose require an
Explanation, which I come to ask of you:
I saw you this Morning go out of *Leonó-*
ra's Apartment; she has confess'd all, she
has told me ——— She has told you that I
love her, interrupted the Count, to avoid
a Discourse which he was not fond of hearing: But she has but feebly express'd all
that I feel for her. I am enchanted; she
is a Lady all over adorable; she has Wit,
Beauty, Virtue; no Perfection is wanting.
I have been told that you have a Son at
the

the Univerſity of *Alcala*; is he like his Siſter? If he hath her Beauty, and reſemble
you in other Excellencies, he muſt be a
compleat Gentleman. I die with Deſire to
ſee him, and offer you all my Intereſt to
ſerve him.

I am indebted to you for that Offer, ſaid
Don Lewis gravely; but to come to ——
He ought to be enter'd in the Service immediately, interrupted the Count again;
I charge my ſelf with the Care of his Fortune; I aſſure you that he ſhall not wade
amongſt the Croud of Officers. Anſwer
me, Count, reply'd the old Gentleman haſtily, and leave off your Interruption. Do
you deſign to keep your Promiſe ——Yes,
without doubt, interrupted *Belflor* the third
time; I will keep my Word which I have
given you to ſtand by your Son with all
my Intereſt; depend upon me, I am a ſincere Man. 'Tis too much, cry'd *Ceſpides*,
riſing up, after having ſeduc'd my Daughter, that you dare inſult me; but know, I
am a Gentleman, and the Injury you have
done me ſhall not remain unpuniſh'd. At
the end of theſe Words he return'd home
with a Heart full of Reſentment, and contriving a hundred Projects to compaſs his
Revenge.

He told *Leonora* and *Marcella* very an-
grily, It was not without ground that I
ſuſpected

fufpected the Count; he is a Traitor, on whom I will be reveng'd: And as for you two, you fhall to Morrow be enter'd in a Convent; you have nothing to do but prepare your felves, and thank Heav'n my Rage contents it felf with that Chaftifement. He then went and lock'd himfelf up in his Clofet, to deliberate what Courfe to take in fuch a nice Conjuncture.

How great was *Leonora*'s Grief when fhe heard *Belflor* was perfidious! She remain'd fome Time without Motion; a mortal Palenefs cover'd her Face, her Spirits fled, and motionlefs fhe fell into the Arms of her *Governante*; who fearing fhe would then die, us'd all her Endeavours to get her out of this Fit: They fucceeded, and *Leonora* reaffuming the Ufe of her Senfes, and feeing her *Governante* very officioufly helping her, How barbarous are you! faid fhe with a deep Sigh; why did you force me out of the happy State in which I was? I was not then fenfible of the Horror of my Fate. Why did you not let me die? You, who well know all the tormenting Griefs which muft difturb the Repofe of my Life, wherefore did you keep me alive?

Marcella endeavour'd to comfort her; but that only encreas'd her Torment. All your Talk is fuperfluous, cry'd *Don Lewis*'s

Daughter,

Daughter; I will hear nothing. Don't lofe
your time in attempting to abate my Defpair, you ought rather to raife it. You,
who have plung'd me into the Abyfs of
Mifery in which I now am? 'Tis you who
vouch'd for the Count's Sincerity; without you I had never yielded my felf to
my Inclinations for him, which I fhould
infenfibly have conquer'd, or however at
leaft he would never have been able to
have gain'd the leaft Advantage over me.
But I will not, continu'd fhe, charge my
Mifery on you, I accufe no body but my
felf. I ought not to have follow'd your
Advice in the Acceptation of a Man's Faith,
without confulting my Father. How daz-
ling foever the Count's Addrefs might appear to me, I ought to have defpis'd rather than complimented it at the expence
of my Honour: In fhort, I ought to have
diftrufted him, you and my felf. Since I
have been fo weak as to yield to his perfidious Oaths, after the Affliction which
I have brought to *Don Lewis,* and the
Difhonour I have done my Family, I hate
my felf; and am fo far from fearing the
Retirement with which I am threaten'd,
that I am fond of hiding my Shame in the
moft difmal Retreat in the World. Thefe
paffionate Words were not only accompany'd with abundance of Tears, but fhe
withal

withal tore her Cloaths in Pieces, and reveng'd the Injustice of her Lover on her
beautiful Hair.

The *Duenna*, to suit her self to her Mistress's Grief, did not spare for Grimaces
and distorted Faces. She dropp'd some of
those Tears she had always at command;
she imprecated a thousand Curses on Mankind in general, and the Count in particular. Is it possible, exclaim'd she, that *Belflor*, who seem'd so full of Justice and Probity, should prove such a Villain as to deceive us both! I cannot extricate my self
out of this Surprize, or rather, I cannot
yet persuade my self that it is so.

When I fansie him at my Knees, said
Leonora, what Maiden would not have
trusted his tender engaging Air, and de-
pended on those Oaths which he so auda-
ciously invok'd Heav'n to witness, and
those Transports which he incessantly repeated? Besides, his Eyes discover'd more
Love than his Mouth expres'd, and the
very Sight of me seem'd to charm him. No,
he did not deceive me; I can't think it.
My Father must not have talk'd with him
so discreetly as he ought; they both grew
warm, and the Count answer'd less like a
Lover than a great Lord. But also perhaps
I flatter my self! I must extricate my self
out of this Uncertainty. I will then write

to *Belflor*, and tell him that I expect him
here this Night: I defire that he fhould fecure my alarm'd Heart, or confirm his Treachery. *Marcella* applauded the Defign,
and was not her felf without hope that
the Count, ambitious as he was, yet touch'd
by *Leonora*'s Tears, might fall from his
Refolution in this Interview, and determine to marry her.

In the mean while, *Belflor* having rid
himfelf of honeft *Don Lewis*, continu'd in
his Apartment, reflecting on the Confequences which might refult from the Re-
ception he had juft given him. He firmly
concluded that the whole Family of the
Cefpides, enrag'd at the Injury done to
their Houfe, would ftudy Revenge ; but
that did not much difturb him: The Intereft of his Love much more employ'd his
Thoughts. He imagin'd that *Leonora*
would be put into a Convent, or at leaft
that fhe would be kept fo ftrictly watch'd,
that in all probability he fhould never fee
her more. This Thought afflicted him,
and his Mind was wholly taken up with
the Search after fome Way to efcape this
Misfortune, when his *Valet de Chambre*
brought him a Letter which *Marcella* had
juft put into his Hands. It was a Billet
from *Leonora*, whofe Contents ran thus:
I am to Morrow to quit the World, and bury
my

*my self in a solitary Retirement, where I
shall have the Horror of seeing my self difhonour'd, odious to my Family and my self;
this is the deplorable Condition to which I
am reduc'd by believing you. I expect you
once more this Night. In my Despair I
hunt after new Torments: Come and own
to me that your Heart had no part in any
of the Oaths which your Mouth swore to
me, or justifie their Sincerity by a Conduct
which alone can soften the Rigour of my
Fate. Perhaps this Meeting may be attended with some Danger, after what has
pass'd betwixt you and my Father; take
care therefore that you be accompany'd by a
Friend. Tho' you have occasion'd all the
Miseries of my Life, I yet feel my self concern'd for yours.*

The Count read this Letter twice or
thrice over, and representing *Leonora* in
the Condition in which she describ'd, he
melted into Compassion. He seriously reflected on what he had done; Justice,
Probity and Honour, all the Laws of which
his Passion had hurried him on to the Vio-
lation of, began to resume their Empire
over him. He suddenly found his Blind-
ness dissipated, and like a Man just got
out of a violent Fever, blush'd at the extravagant Words and Actions which had
escap'd him; he was asham'd of all the base
Artifices

Artifices he had us'd to fatisfie his Defires.
Wretch that I am, cry'd he, what have I
done? What Devil poffefs'd me? I promis'd to marry *Leonora* ; I call'd Heav'n
to witnefs it; I feign'd that the King pro-
pofs'd a Match to me ; I have made ufe
of Lies, Perfidioufnefs and Sacrilege to
corrupt her Innocence; what Madnefs had
feiz'd me? Had I not much better employ'd my utmoft Efforts in the fuppref-
fion of my Love, than by fatisfying it in
fuch criminal ways? But here is a Gentlewoman feduc'd; I abandon her to the Anger of her Relations, who, with her, I have
alfo difhonour'd, and render her miferable
in Reward of her making me happy. Ah,
how barbarous is that Ingratitude! Ought
I not rather to repair the Difgrace and In-
famy I have done her? Yes, I ought; and I
will, by marrying her, difcharge the Promife I made her. Who is there can oppofe fo juft an Intention? Ought her Tendernefs to prejudice me againft her Virtue? No: I know how much her Refiftance coft me to conquer it ; and fhe rather yielded to my fworn Faith, than my
amorous Tranfports.——But on the other
fide, if I confine my felf to this Choice I
fhall be a confiderable Sufferer. I, who may
pretend to the nobleft and richeft Heireffes
in the Kingdom, fhall I content my felf
                                                       with

with a private Gentleman's Daughter of a moderate Fortune? What will the Court think of me? They will say I have marry'd very ridiculously.

Belflor thus divided betwixt Love and Ambition, did not know to which to incline: But tho' he was not yet resolv'd whether he should marry *Leonora* or not, he yet determin'd to go to her that Evening.

Don Lewis, on the other side, pass'd the Day in contriving the Restoration of his Honour. The Conjuncture was very nice; to have recourse to the Laws was to publish his Dishonour; besides, he very much fear'd that Justice might be on one side, and the Judges declare on the other. He durst not throw himself at the King's Feet, for believing that Prince design'd to marry the Count, he was afraid it would be in vain. No Satisfaction was then left besides that of Arms, and it was this he concluded on. In the heat of his Resentment he was tempted to send a Challenge; but beginning to consider that he was too old and feeble to rely on his own Arm, he chose rather to put it into the Hands of his Son, whose Pushes would be more secure than his. He then sent a Footman to *Alcala*, with a Letter for his Son; by which he commanded him to come immediately

mediately to *Madrid*, to revenge an Injury done to the Family of the *Cespides*.

Don Pedro, his Son, was a Gentleman of eighteen Years old, perfectly handsome, and so brave that he pass'd in the City of *Alcala* for the most terrible of all the Scholars of the University; but you know him, adds the Devil, wherefore 'tis needless for me to enlarge farther on his Character. It is true, said *Cleofas*, he has all the Valour and Merit which is possible to centre in such a young Man. He was not then at *Alcala*, as his Father suppos'd, reply'd *Asmodeo*; but the Desire of seeing a Lady which he lov'd had brought him to *Madrid*. The last time he had been there to see his Relations, he made this Conquest. He did not yet know her Name; for she had oblig'd him not to use any means to inform himself; to which cruel Necessity he submitted, tho' with great difficulty. It was a Woman of Quality, who had conceiv'd a Passion for him, and believing she ought to distrust the Discretion and Constancy of a Scholar, she thought fit to try him before she discover'd her self. This unknown Fair One took up more of his Thoughts than *Aristotle*'s Philosophy; and *Alcala* being situate so near this City, he, as you have done, often plaid truant; with this only
dif-

difference, that it was for the fake of an
Object which deferv'd much better than
your *Donna Thomafa.* To conceal the
Knowledge of his amorous Journey from
Don Lewis, his Father, he us'd to lodge
at an Inn in the Out-part of the City,
where he carefully fhelter'd himfelf under
a borrow'd Name. He never went out
but at a certain Hour in the Morning,
when he was oblig'd to go to a Houfe
where the Lady, which occafion'd this
neglect of his Studies, was fo kind as to
come, accompany'd by a Chamber-maid.
He then liv'd lock'd up in his Inn the reft
of the Day ; but in requital, at Night he
walk'd all over the City.

It happen'd one Night as he crofs'd a
By-ftreet, he heard the Sound of feveral
Voices and Inftruments which feem'd
worth his Attention; whereupon he ftopp'd,
and found it to be a Serenade given by a
Gentleman that was drunk, and naturally
very brutifhly rude. He had no fooner
difcern'd our Scholar, than he immediately came to him, and without any other
Compliment; Friend, faid he, in a hafty
Tone, go about your Bufinefs, I don't
love inquifitive People. I might have
withdrawn, anfwer'd *Don Pedro* fhock'd
at thefe Words, if you had defir'd me in
a civiller manner; but I will ftay to learn
                                    you

you how to fpeak. We fhall fee then, faid the Mafter of the Confort, drawing his Sword, which of us two fhall yield the Place to the other. *Don Pedro* alfo pull'd out his Sword, and they began to engage. Tho' the Mafter of the Serenade acquitted himfelf with great dexterity, he could not yet parry a mortal Thruft, upon the Receipt of which he fell dead on the Spot. All the Actors of the Confort, who had by this time quitted their Mufick, and were drawing their Swords to affift him, now came on to revenge his Death. They all at once fell upon *Don Pedro*, who on this occafion fhew'd his utmoft Skill; for befides parrying with a furprizing Dexterity all the Paffes made at him, he himfelf made very vigorous ones, and at once kept all his Enemies employ'd. But they fo obftinately perfifting, and their Number being too great, as able a Fencer as he was, he could not have efcap'd alive, if the Count *de Belflor*, who then pafs'd by, had not taken his part.

The Count wanting neither Courage nor a large fhare of Generofity, could not fee fo many Swords drawn upon one Man, without engaging himfelf on his fide. He drew, and joining with *Don Pedro*, he pufh'd fo briskly at the Serenaders that they all fled, fome wounded, and others for fear
of

of being fo.   After their Retreat the Scholar began to thank the Count for his Affiftance; but *Belflor* interrupting him: No
more of that, faid he, are you not wounded? No, reply'd *Don Pedro*. Let's get
from this Place, reply'd the Count, I fee
you have kill'd a Man; 'tis dangerous to
ftay longer in this Street; you may perhaps be feiz'd.   Upon which they immediately making the beft of their way, got
into another Street; and when they were
advanc'd a good diftance from the Place
where they fought, they ftopp'd.

Don Pedro, very fenfibly influenc'd by
juft and grateful Sentiments, entreated the
Count not to conceal from him the Name
of a Gentleman to whom he was fo much
oblig'd.   *Belflor* made no fcruple of telling
it, and alfo defir'd to know his.   But the
Scholar, unwilling to difcover himfelf, faid
his Name was *Don Juan de Matos*, and
affur'd the Count that he would never
forget what he had done for him.   I would
willingly, faid the Count, prefent you with
an Opportunity of difcharging your Obligation to me this very Night.   I am engag'd to a Meeting not wholly free from
Danger, and was going in fearch of a
Friend to go with me.   I am fenfible of
your Valour, and therefore, *Don Juan*,
I defire your Company.   Your feeming
                                        to

to doubt it renders me somewhat uneasie, reply'd the Scholar; I don't know how to imploy the Life which you have sav'd, better than to expose it for you. Let's make haste; I am ready to follow you. *Belflor* then conducted *Don Pedro* to *Don Lewis's* House, and by the Balcony they both enter'd *Leonora's* Apartment.

Here *Don Cleofas* interrupted the Devil; Signior *Afmodeo*, how was it possible *Don Pedro* should not know his Father's House? That was impossible, reply'd the *Dæmon*, for *Don Lewis* had not remov'd to this House above eight Days; which I design'd to have told you, had not you interrupted me. You are too hasty, and have gotten an ill Custom of breaking the Thread of other Peoples Discourse. Pray correct that Fault in your self.

Don Pedro, continu'd the Devil, did not so much as suspect that he was at his Father's House, nor thought she who introduc'd him was Madam *Marcella*, by reason she receiv'd him in the Dark in an Anti-Chamber, where *Belflor* entreated his Companion to stay as long as he should remain with the Lady: To which the Scholar consented, and sate down with his naked Sword in his Hand for fear of a Surprize. His Thoughts were taken up with the Favours which he concluded Love was
showering

showering on *Belflor*, and wish'd himself as happy as he; for tho' he was not ill-treated by his unknown Miftrefs, she had not yet all the Tendernefs for him which *Leonora* had for the Count. Whilft he was making all the Reflections on this Adventure that could poffibly occur to the Mind of a paffionate Lover, he heard a Perfon foftly endeavouring to open another Door befides that of the Lovers, and difcern'd a glimmering Light thro' the Key-hole. He haftily arofe, made towards the Door that open'd, and prefented the Point of his naked Sword to the Breaft of his Father, who was going to *Leonora*'s Apartment, to fee whether the Count was not there. The good old Gentleman did not believe, after what had pafs'd, that his Daughter and *Marcella* would again venture to admit him, which alone prevented his lodging them in another Apartment. But yet he was apt to think, that before their Entrance into the Convent on the Morrow, they might be willing to take their laft Leave of fpeaking with him. Whoever thou art, faid the Scholar, don't enter this Room, on peril of thy Life. At thefe Words *Don Lewis* look'd at *Don Pedro*, whofe Eyes were fix'd on him with equal Attention; fo that they foon knew each other. Ah my Son, faid the old Gentle-

G   man,

man, with what Impatience have I expected you! why did not you advertise me of
your Arrival? were you afraid of breaking
my Rest? Alas! I am incapable of any
Repose in the miserable Condition in which
I at present am. Oh my Father, said
Don Pedro all in Confusion, is it you that
I see? are not my Eyes deceiv'd by a false
Apparition? Whence proceeds this Surprize? reply'd *Don Lewis:* Are you not
at your Father's House? Did I not acquaint you by my Letter, that eight Days
since I remov'd hither? Just Heav'n, reply'd the Scholar, what do I hear? I am
then at present in my Sister's Apartment.

At these Words, the Count, who had
heard the Noise, and suppos'd that his
Guard was attack'd, came out of *Leonora*'s Chamber with his Sword in his Hand.
The old Gentleman, distracted at this Sight,
and shewing him to his Son, cry'd out,
That is the audacious Villain which has
robb'd me of my Rest, and cast a fatal
Stain upon the Honour of our House; let
us then revenge our selves, let us instantly
punish the Traitor. These Words were
no sooner out of his Mouth than he drew
the Sword he had under his Night-Gown,
and began to attack the Count; but *Don
Pedro* restrain'd him. Stay, Father, said
he, I beg you to moderate the Transports
of

of your Rage. What do you mean, my Son? anfwer'd the old Man: Why do you hold my Arm? You doubtlefs think 'tis too weak to revenge us. Well then, take Satisfaction your felf for the Affront given to our Family, which is the only Reafon why I fent for you to *Madrid.* If you fall, I will fecond you: The Count muft perifh by our Hands, or take away both our Lives, after having robb'd us of our Honour.

Father, reply'd *Don Pedro,* I cannot yield to what your Impatience expects of me. I am fo very far from attempting the Count's Life, that I came hither to defend it; my Word is pafs'd for it, and my Honour demands it. Let's then retire, my Lord, continu'd he, addreffing himfelf to *Belflor.* Hah! bafe Wretch, interrupted *Don Lewis,* looking on *Don Pedro* with a very angry Air, doft thou thy felf oppofe the Execution of a Vengeance wherein all thy Force ought to have been employ'd? My Son, my own Son, correfponds with the perfidious Wretch that has feduc'd my Daughter: But don't think to efcape my Refentment; I will call up all my Domefticks, who fhall revenge me of your Treachery and bafe Cowardice. Sir, reply'd *Don Pedro,* be jufter to your Son, and don't call him Coward, for he

never

never deferv'd that hateful Name. The
Count has fav'd my Life this Night. He
propos'd my going with him, whither I
did not know, but on a certain Appointment: I offer'd to fhare the Dangers he
might encounter, without ever fufpecting
that my Gratitude would imprudently engage my Arm againft the Honour of my
Family. My Word then obliges me to defend his Life here; and in fo doing I fhall
difcharge it: Not that I am lefs fenfibly
touch'd with the Injury he has done our
Family; and to Morrow you fhall fee me
as eager to fhed his Blood, as you now fee
me zealous in the Prefervation of his Life.

The Count, who had hitherto remain'd
filent, being throughly ftruck with the a-
mazing Circumftances of this Adventure,
now fpoke. Perhaps, faid he, addreffing
himfelf to *Don Pedro*, you may meet with
but indifferent Succefs, in revenging this
Injury by Force of Arms: I will offer you
a furer way of re-eftablifhing your Honour. I freely own to you, that to this
Day I never defign'd to marry *Leonora*;
but I this Morning receiv'd a Letter from
her, wherewith I was fenfibly touch'd;
her Tears have juft compleated the Work,
and the Happinefs of being her Husband
is at prefent the utmoft of my Defires. If
the King defigns you another Wife, faid
Don

Don Lewis, how will you difpence with——
The King never propos'd any Match to
me, interrupted *Belflor* blufhing: Pray pardon that Fiction in a Man, whofe Reafon
Love had difturb'd. 'Tis a Crime which
the Violence of my Paffion hurry'd me on
to commit, and which I expiate by confeffing it. My Lord, reply'd the old Gentleman, after an Acknowledgment fo fuita-
ble to a great Mind, I no longer doubt
your Sincerity: I fee you are refolv'd effe-
ctually to repair the Injury we have receiv'd, and my Anger yields to the Affu-
rances you have given me; permit me then
to forget my Refentment in your Arms.
At thefe Words he ran to the Count, who
flew to prevent him: They mutually embrac'd feveral times; and *Belflor* turning
himfelf to *Don Pedro,* And you, you, the
counterfeit *Don Juan,* faid he, you who
have gain'd my Efteem by an unparallel'd
Valour and a noble Mind, allow me to
vow a fincere fraternal Friendfhip to you.
At thefe Words he embrac'd *Don Pedro,*
who receiving his Careffes with a fubmif-
five and refpectful Air, thus anfwer'd him:
My Lord, in promifing me fuch a valuable
Friendfhip, you engage mine; and I entreat that you would always conclude me
one who will continue devoted to you to
the End of my Life.

In the mean while *Leonora*, who was
liſtening all the time at the Chamber-door,
did not loſe one Word of whatever they
ſaid. She was at firſt tempted to throw
her ſelf in the middle of the Swords, without knowing why; but *Marcella* prevented her: And when that dextrous *Duenna*
perceiv'd all things likely to end ſo amia-
bly, ſhe concluded that her Preſence and
that of her Miſtreſs would not prejudice
the Accommodation; whereupon they both
appear'd with their Handkerchiefs in their
Hands, and weeping ran to proſtrate themſelves at *Don Lewis's* Feet. They fear'd,
and not without Reaſon, after their being
ſurpriz'd laſt Night, that the old Gentleman's Anger might return: But raiſing *Leonora*, he ſaid, Daughter, dry up your
Tears, I will not blame you any more;
ſince your Lover is reſolv'd to keep the
Faith which he has ſworn to you, I yield
to forget what is paſt.

Yes, *Don Lewis*, ſaid the Count, I
will marry *Leonora*; and yet better to repair the Injury I have done you, to give
you an entire Satisfaction, and your Son a
Pledge of my Friendſhip for him, I offer
him my Siſter *Eugenia*. Ah, my Lord,
cry'd *Don Lewis* in a Rapture, how ſenſible am I of the Honour you do my Son!
What Father was ever happier? You now
ſhower

fhower as much Joy on me, as before you loaded me with Sorrow.

Tho' the old Man was charm'd with the Count's Offer, yet *Don Pedro* was not: Being wholly taken up with the Thoughts of his unknown Lady, he was fo cifturb'd and confus'd that he could not fay one Word. But *Belflor*, without regarding his Trouble, departed ; telling them he would order all the neceffary Preparations to be made for this double Union, and af-furing them that he was impatient 'till he was fix'd to them by thefe ftrict Bonds.

After his Departure *Don Lewis* left *Leonora* in her Apartment, and went into his own with *Don Pedro;* who with all the Franknefs of a young Scholar faid, Sir, I beg you would difpence with my marrying the Count's Sifter: 'Tis enough that he marry *Leonora;* that will be fufficient to retrieve the Honour of our Family. What, Son! reply'd the old Man; can you refufe to marry the Count's Sifter ? Yes, Father, reply'd *Don Pedro;* that Union, I own, would prove a cruel Torment to me, the Caufe of which I will not conceal. I love, or rather adore a charming Lady; fhe admits me, and fhe alone can render my Life happy. How miferable is the State of a Father! faid *Don Lewis;* he fcarce ever finds his Children difpos'd to do what he

G 4   defires.

defires. But who then is this Lady which
has made fuch violent Impreffions on you?
I don't yet know, anfwer'd *Don Pedro;*
fhe has promis'd to inform me, when fhe
fhall be fully fatisfy'd of my Difcretion and
Conftancy, nor do I doubt but fhe is one
of the moft confiderable Families at Court.
And do you fancy, reply'd the old Man,
changing his Tone, that I will be fo complaifant as to approve your Romantick
Love? That I fhall fuffer you to quit the
moft glorious Eftablifhment that Fortune
can ever offer you, to keep you conftant
to a Perfon of whom you don't know fo
much as her Name? Stifle rather thefe
Sentiments for an Object, which perhaps
may be unworthy of them, and think of
nothing but deferving the Honour which
the Count is doing you. All thefe Di-
fcourfes are in vain, Father, reply'd the
Scholar; I feel it impoffible for me ever
to forget my unknown Fair; nothing can
difengage me from her: Should the *Infan-
ta* be offer'd me——Hold, cry'd the Father haftily; 'tis too infolent to boaft a
Conftancy which raifes my Anger. Be
gone, and never let me fee you again, before you are refolv'd to obey me.

Don Pedro durft not reply to thefe
Words, for fear of drawing on more fevere ones. He retir'd to his Chamber,
where

where he pass'd the rest of the Night in making Reflections equally melancholy and agreeable. He consider'd with Grief that he was going to break with all his Family, by refusing to marry the Count's Sister. But he was perfectly comforted when he represented to himself how his unknown Lady must value him for such a Sacrifice. He flatter'd himself, that after such a shining Proof of his Fidelity, she would not fail to discover her Quality, which he imagin'd little inferior to that of *Eugenia*. With these Hopes, as soon as it was Day, he went to take a Walk on the *Prado*, expecting the appointed Hour to go to the Apartment of *Donna Juana*; for that was the Name of the Lady in whose Lodgings he us'd to meet his Mistress every Morning. He waited the happy Moment with great Impatience, and when it was come, flew to the Place of Rendezvous.

He found his unknown Charmer come thither sooner than ordinary; but touch'd with such a sensible Grief, as express'd it self to *Donna Juana* in showers of Tears. A dismal Spectacle for her Love! All in Confusion he approach'd her, and flinging himself at her Knees: Madam, said he, what must I think of the Condition in which I see you? Doubtless, answer'd she,

you

you don't expect the fatal Blow which I
bring you. Cruel Fortune is feparating us
for ever, and we are never to fee each o-
ther more.

She accompany'd thefe Words with fo
many Sighs, that I don't know whether
Don Pedro was more touch'd with what
fhe faid, or the Grief fhe difcover'd in the
Utterance of it. Juft Heav'n, cry'd he,
with an excefs of Rage which he could not
reftrain, is it poffible for you to fuffer the
breaking of an Union, the Innocence of
which you know! But, Madam, adds he,
perhaps you have taken a falfe Alarm. Is
it certainly true that you will be torn from
the moft faithful Lover that ever was?
Muft I really be the moft miferable of all
Men? Our ill Fate is but too fure, anfwer'd the unknown Fair. My Brother,
on whom I depend, will marry me this
Day, as he has juft this Minute declar'd
to me. Ah! who is that happy Bride-
groom? very haftily reply'd *Don Pedro*;
name him to me, Madam: I will, in my
Defpair—— I don't yet know his Name,
interrupted the Lady; my Brother would
not acquaint me with it. He told me that
he defir'd I fhould firft fee the Gentleman.
But, Madam, faid *Don Pedro*, did you
fubmit to a Brother's Will without Refiftance? Did you fuffer your felf to be
dragg'd

dragg'd to the Altar, without complaining on the Cruelty of the Sacrifice? Did you make no Attempts in my Favour? Alas, I was not afraid of expofing my felf to my Father's Rage, to referve my felf entirely yours! His Threats could not fhock my Fidelity; and with what Rigour foever he may treat me, I will not marry the Lady he propofes, tho' the Match is very advantageous. And who is this Lady? faid the unknown Beauty. 'Tis the Count *de Belflor's* Sifter, reply'd the Scholar. Ah, *Don Pedro*, reply'd fhe, difcovering an extream Surprize, you doubtlefs miftake; you are not fure of what you fay! Is it really *Eugenia de Belflor* which is propos'd to you? Yes, Madam, reply'd *Don Pedro*, the Count himfelf made the Offer. How, cry'd fhe, is it poffible that you fhould be the Cavalier for who my Brother defigns me? What do I hear, cry'd *Don Pedro* in his turn, is my unknown Angel then *Eugenia de Belflor?* Yes, *Don Pedro*, reply'd fhe, but I fcarce believe my felf this Moment to be any longer fo; fo hard is it for me to perfuade my felf of the Reality of the Happinefs of which you affure me.

At thefe Words *Don Pedro* embrac'd her Knees, feiz'd one of her Hands with all the Raptures that a Lover fuddenly remov'd from the Extremities of Pain to an

Excefs

Excefs of Joy could poffibly feel.   Whilft
he thus abandon'd himfelf to the Motions
of his Love, *Eugenia* on her Part gave
him a thoufand Proofs of her Affection,
which fhe accompany'd with tender engaging Expreffions : What racking Pains,
faid fhe, would my Brother have fpar'd
me, had he but nam'd the Husband he
defign'd me? What Averfion had I already
conceiv'd for my Spoufe? Ah, my dear
Don Pedro, how much did I hate you?
Bright *Eugenia*, anfwer'd he, how charming is that Hatred to me? I will deferve it
by adoring you all my Life.

   After thefe two Lovers had given each
other all the moft moving Signs of their
mutual Tenderneffes, *Eugenia* defir'd to
know how the Scholar could gain her
Brother's Friendfhip. *Don Pedro* did not
conceal from her the Amours of the Count
and his Sifter, but related to her all that
pafs'd the laft Night.   She was infinitely
pleas'd to hear that her Brother was to
marry her Lover's Sifter ;   and *Donna
Juana* had too great a fhare in her Friends
Fate, not to be touch'd with this happy
Event.   She teftify'd her Joy as well *Don
Pedro*, who at laft left *Eugenia*, after their
having mutually refolv'd not to feem to
know one another when they appear'd before the Count.

                                            Don

Don Pedro return'd to his Father, who finding him perfectly difpos'd to Obedience, was the better pleas'd, becaufe he afcrib'd it to his refolute manner of deporting himfelf towards his Son the laft Night. They expected News from the Count the very Minute they receiv'd a Letter from him, which advis'd them that he had juft obtain'd the King's Confent to his Marriage, and that of his Sifter, with the Addition of a confiderable Poft for *Don Pedro* ; that on the Morrow both Nuptials might be celebrated, his Orders having been fo diligently executed, that all the Preparations were already far advanc'd. He came in the Afternoon to confirm what he had written, and to prefent *Eugenia* to them.

Don Lewis fhew'd that Lady all imaginable Civilities, and *Leonora* did not neglect tenderly embracing her. As for *Don Pedro*, by whatfoever Motions of Love and Joy agitated, he yet fufficiently reftrain'd himfelf, to avoid the Count's having any Sufpicion of their former Correfpondence. *Belflor* particularly applying himfelf to obferve his Sifter, thought he difcover'd, notwithftanding the Conftraint fhe impos'd on her felf, that fhe did not diflike *Don Pedro*. But the better to affure himfelf of the Truth of his Conjecture,

&ture, he took her afide for a Moment,
and made her own that fhe was extreamly
well pleas'd with her Cavalier. He then
told her his Name and Family, which he
before conceal'd, left the Indifference of
their Quality fhould have prejudic'd her
againft him; all this fhe pretended to hear,
as tho' utterly ignorant of it before.

At laft, after the exchange of a multi-
tude of Civilities on both fides, it was refolv'd that the Weddings fhould be kept
at the Count *de Belflor's* Houfe; and the
Nuptial Feftivities are this Night acting,
but not finifh'd; and that is the Reafon of
the fo great rejoycing in that Houfe, in
which all the Company unanimoufly joins,
except *Marcella,* who has no fhare in it.
She cries whilft the reft laugh; for the
Count *de Belflor,* after his Marriage, confefs'd the whole Story to *Don Lewis,* who
has order'd her to be fent to the * *Mona-
fterio de Arrepentidas,* where the thoufand
Piftoles which fhe receiv'd to betray *Leonora* will ferve her to do Penance the Remainder of her Life.

C H A P.

---

* *A Monaftery in which lewd Women are fhut up.*

CHAP. VI.

Other Particulars which the Scholar saw.

LET's turn to the other side, continu'd the *Dæmon*, and run over some
new Objects. Cast your Eyes on the first
House directly under us, where you will
see something extraordinary; 'tis a Man
considerably in Debt in a profound Sleep.
He must then be some great Lord, said the
Scholar. You have guess'd right, reply'd
the Devil. Observe in the next House an
Author very busie in his Closet; he is surrounded by a thousand Volumes, and is
compiling one, in which there will not be
a Line of his own. He pilfers from all
the Books in his Study, and tho' he only
methodizes and connects his Plagiaries, doth
not want a larger Share of Vanity than a
real Author.

Oh what a diverting Spectacle is that!
said *Don Cleofas:* I see a very fine Woman betwixt a young and an old Man;
and whilst the fond Dotard is embracing
her, she slips her Hand behind him into
that of a young Cavalier, who is doubtless her Spark. Quite contrary, answer'd
Asmodeo, that is her Husband, and the
other

other her Lover. The old Man is a Perfon of Quality, and ruining himfelf for that
Lady, who carefles him for Intereft, and
is by Inclination falfe for her Husband's
Advantage : A very fine Picture really,
faid *Don Cleofas.* That which you fee in
the adjoining Houfe, reply'd the Devil,
does not lefs deferve your Attention. The
Bafhfulnefs of that young Widow deferves
your Admiration ; fhe fcruples receiving
her Shift before her Uncle, but retires into her Clofet to have it put on by her
Gallant, whom fhe has hidden there.

Let me prefent you with fome more
melancholy Images, continu'd *Afmodee*:
Look on the other fide of the Street, into
that feparate Apartment : You fee that
corpulent Man, that unfortunate Canon,
who juft now fell into an Apoplexy ; his
Niece and Domefticks, inftead of affording him any Affiftance, have fuffer'd him
to die for want of it, and are feizing his
beft Effects, and conveying them to a Re-
ceiver of ftoln Goods to hide them ; after
which they will be wholly at leifure to
mourn and lament his Death. Obferve
thofe two Men who are now burying :
They are two Brothers that were both fick
of the fame Difeafe, but took different
Meafures ; one of them rely'd, with an intire Confidence, upon his Phyfician ; the
other

other let Nature take her Course, yet they both dy'd, the former by taking all the Phy-sick the Doctor order'd, and the latter by taking nothing. This is a very perplexing *Dilemma*, said *Don Cleofas*: Alas, what then must a poor sick Man do? That's more than I can tell you, reply'd the De-vil; I very well know that there are such things as good Remedies, but cannot say whether there are any good Physicians.

Do you discern, about two Paces far-ther, a Man in his Shirt stalking in a Sta-ble? Yes, answer'd the Scholar; he seems to have a Curry-Comb in his Hand. So he has, reply'd the Devil; 'tis a Groom, who every Night, as you see him now, walks and curries his Horses in his Sleep; after which he is astonish'd, in the Morn-ing, to find them all dress'd. The People of the House fancy 'tis done by some whimsical Spirit, and the Groom is of their Mind.

Who are those Ladies just going to Bed? They are two coquetting Sisters which lodge together; from seven in the Morn-ing, to this very Minute, they have been talking of nothing but Dresses for them-selves, and Furniture for their Chamber, which they have a Mind to buy; and they have been so infinitely pleas'd with this Conversation, that to avoid all manner of

H   Inter-

Interruption, they have deny'd themfelves
even the Sight of their Lovers. Obferve
their Neighbour, that Lady, juft come
home: She is a great Lover of Scandal; fhe
is juft come from fupping with an old Female Devotee, one of her Friends, with
whofe Converfation fhe has been infinitely
pleas'd. Ah, how perfectly well fhap'd
fhe is, and what a charming Air fhe has!
faid the Scholar. Very well, reply'd *Afmodeo,* but that dapper Beauty can, I affure you, give you an exact Hiftory of the
greateft Part of the laft Century as an Eye-
witnefs. Her Shape, which you admire,
is a very Machine, in the adjufting of
which all the Art of the ableft Mechanicks
was exhaufted; her Breaft and her Hips
are Artificial; and not long fince fhe
dropp'd her Rump at Church, in the midft
of the Sermon.

I hear fuch a difmal Noife, faid the
Scholar, that I cannot help asking you the
Caufe of it. 'Tis a Confort of Kitchen-
Furniture, occafion'd by a Widow of fixty, having this Morning marry'd one of
her Domefticks not yet twenty; upon which
all the merry Fellows in that Quarter are
met together to celebrate the Wedding,
with the ringing of Pots, Frying-pans and
Kettles. You told me, reply'd *Don Cleofas,* that the making ridiculous Matches

was

was your Province; yet you had no Hand in this. No, return'd the Devil; had I been at Liberty, I would not have meddled in't: This Widow had a scrupulous Conscience, and therefore marry'd this young Fellow only in order to enjoy her darling Pleasures without Remorse. I never make such Marriages; I have a much greater Pleasure in troubling Consciences, than setting them at rest.

Notwithstanding the hideous Din of this Serenade, said *Don Cleofas,* I fancy I hear another Noise. Yes, said the Devil, it comes from a Coffee-house, where several Wits have been disputing this five Hours, and the Coffee-man cannot get them out of Doors. The whole Controversie is turn'd on a Comedy which first appear'd on the Stage this Day, the Action of which was interrupted by the Clamours and Hisses of the Audience. Some of them maintain that it is a good Piece, and others as obstinately aver the contrary. They are just going to Fisticuffs, the ordinary End of these Squabbles. If you are desirous to see the Fray I will remove you—— No, no, interrupted the Scholar, rather inform me what that Man is thinking of which sits in his Night-gown in an Elbow-chair. 'Tis an old Officer of the Council of the *Indies,* whose Head is taken up with an

impor-

important-Project. His Eftate is worth about four Millions; but his Confcience fuggefting fome uneafie Reflections on the manner of his acquiring it, he is contriving the Building of a Monaftery; by which he flatters himfelf he fhall footh his troubled Mind. He has already obtain'd Leave to found a Convent; but being firmly refolv'd not to place any Monks in it in whom the Virtues of Chaftity, Sobriety and Humility don't eminently fhine, he is very much puzled in the Choice.

Do you fee a little farther, faid the Devil, that Printer at work in his Printinghoufe? He has fent his Servants to bed, and is privately printing a Book. What is it? faid *Don Cleofas*. 'Tis a Libel, anfwer'd *Afmodeo*; it proves that Religion is preferable to Point of Honour; and that it is better to forgive than revenge an Affront. Ah Rafcal, cry'd the Scholar; he does well to print fuch infamous Books in private; nor would I advife the Author to own it, for I fhould be one of the firft to ftone him: Does Religion forbid the Prefervation of our Honour? Don't let us enter upon that Difpute, interrupted the Devil fmiling. Say what you pleafe, reply'd *Don Cleofas*, for the Author; tell me that his Reafoning is the cleareft in the World, I fhall yet laugh at him: Nothing
in

in the World is fo fweet to me as Revenge; and fince you have promis'd to do me Juftice on my perfidious Miftrefs, I demand that you keep your Word. I yield with Pleafure to the Rage which infpires you, faid the Devil; oh how I love thofe bold Tempers which purfue all their Inclinations without Scruple! Come, I will this Moment fatisfie you, the Time of your Vengeance being now come. *Don Cleofas* then took hold of the End of *Afmodeo*'s Cloak, and that Spirit cleft the Air with him, and fate him down on *Donna Thomafa*'s Houfe.

H ·3   C H A P.

C H A P.   VII.

How Don Cleofas *was reveng'd on his Miſtreſs.*

THAT Lady was at the Table with the four Bullies which had purſu'd the Scholar on the Gutters; he trembled with outrageous Reſentment to ſee them eat a Turky, and empty ſeveral Bottles of Wine, for which he had pay'd and ſent thither. Ah Raſcals, ſaid he, how deliciouſly they feaſt at my Expence, and a fine Mortification to me! I confeſs, ſaid the Devil, 'tis no very pleaſant Sight; but they who will frequent ſuch looſe Ladies, muſt expect Adventures of this kind: They happen every Day in *France* to Abbots, Men of the long Robe, and the rich Farmers of the Revenue. If I had a Sword, reply'd *Don Cleofas*, I would break in amongſt thoſe Villains, and ſpoil their Entertainment. You would be over-match'd, interrupted *Aſmodeo*; leave your Revenge to me, I will compaſs it a better way; I will immediately ſet them together by the Ears, by inſpiring them with a laſcivious Flame.

At

At thefe Words he blew, and out of his
Mouth iſſu'd a Violet-colour'd Vapour,
that deſcended like a ſmall Cloud, and
ſpread it ſelf over *Donna Thomaſa*'s Table.
One of the Gueſts immediately feeling the
Effect of this Blaſt, drew nearer the Dame,
and paſſionately embrac'd her; but the
others, puſh'd on by the Force of the ſame
Vapour, would tear her from him. Each
pretended to the Preference, which they
now began to diſpute, and a jealous Rage
poſſeſs'd all their Minds; they came to
Blows, drew their Swords, and began to
engage very warmly. In the mean while
Donna Thomaſa ſhriek'd in a horrible manner, and the Neighbourhood was immediately in an Uproar; they cry'd out for the
Officers of Juſtice to come, which they
accordingly did, broke open the Curtiſan's
Door, found two of the Ruffians dead on
the Spot, ſeiz'd the reſt and carry'd them
to Priſon with *Donna Thomaſa*, who crying and tearing her Hair, loſt all Patience,
whilſt her Guards were not a jot more
touch'd than *Don Cleofas*, who laugh'd
very heartily with *Aſmodeo*.

H 4 CHAP.

C H A P.   VIII.

Of the Prisoners.

THE Devil and the Scholar in a Moment reach'd the Prison, where they soon saw the two Bullies enter, and clapp'd into a Dungeon. As for *Donna Thomasa*, she was lodg'd on the Straw with three or four loose Women which had been taken up that Day, and who on the Morrow were to be transported to the Place appointed for that kind of Cattle.

Now I am satisfy'd, said *Don Cleofas*; I have had the Pleasure of a full Revenge. Whenever you please we will depart, and continue our Observation of what passes in this City. Stay, answer'd the *Demon*, I must first shew you some Prisoners, and acquaint you why they are confin'd here.

First of all, in that large Chamber on the Right, are three Men asleep on those three wretched Beds which you see. One is a Vintner accus'd of poisoning a Stranger, which t'other Day fell down dead at the Table in his Tavern. 'Tis pretended that the Quality of the Wine kill'd him; but the Vintner alledges that it was the Quantity, and indeed ought in Justice to
be

be believ'd, for the Deceas'd was a *German*. The second is a Citizen, who is in for being Bound for a *Licenciado* that borrow'd two hundred Piftoles to patch up a hafty Marriage with his Maid; and the third is a Dancing-Mafter, that taught one of his Female Scholars a falfe Step.

The two at Cards in the little Chamber next them, are two young Gentlemen of good Families, who were clapp'd up for their Amours. The youngeft of them was difcover'd in Girls Cloaths in a Nunnery, and the other was catch'd, by the Watch, fcaling the Balcony of a Woman of his Acquaintance, whofe Husband was abfent. 'Tis his own Fault that he does not get out, by declaring his Defign was purely Amorous; but he chufes rather to pafs for a Thief, and run the Rifque of his Life, than expofe the Lady's Honour. A very difcreet Lover indeed, faid *Don Cleofas*, it muft be own'd that our Nation out-does others in Gallantry. I dare venture a Wager, that there is not a *Frenchman*, in the World that would fuffer himfelf to be hang'd, like us, by his Difcretion. No, I affure you, faid the Devil, a *Frenchman* would rather clamber up to a Woman's Balcony to publifh her Difgrace.

Caft

Caſt your Eye, continu'd *Aſmodeo*, directly under thoſe two Priſoners, and obſerve that Man in the Dungeon. He was ſeiz'd Yeſterday, and is claim'd by the Inquiſition: I'll relate you his Caſe.

An old Soldier by his Courage, or rather Patience, having mounted to the Poſt of a Serjeant in his Company, came to raiſe Recruits in this City. He enquir'd for a Lodging at an Inn, where he was anſwer'd, That they had empty Rooms, but that they could not recommend any of them to him, becauſe the Houſe was haunted every Night by a Spirit, which treated all Strangers very ill that were raſh enough to lodge there. This did not at all baulk our Serjeant: Put me in what Chamber you pleaſe, ſaid he, do but give me a Candle, Wine, Pipes and Tobacco, and as for the Spirit never trouble your ſelf about it.

He was accordingly ſhewn into a Chamber, where all that he deſir'd was brought to him. He fell to drinking and ſmoaking 'till Midnight, and no Spirit had yet diſturb'd the profound Silence that reign'd in the Houſe; but betwixt one and two the Serjeant, all of a ſudden, heard a terrible Noiſe, like the ratling of old Iron, and immediately ſaw entering his Chamber an Apparition, cloath'd in black, and laden

all

all round with Iron Chains. Not in the least affrighted at this Sight, he drew his Sword, advanc'd towards the Spirit, and with the flat Side of it gave him a very fevere Blow on the Head.

The Apparition, not much us'd to meet with fuch bold Guefts, cry'd out, and perceiving the Soldier going to begin again with him, he moft humbly proftrated himfelf at his Feet, Mr. Serjeant, faid he, for God's fake don't give me any more; but have Mercy on a poor Devil, which cafts himfelf at your Feet. I conjure you by St. *James*, who, as you are, was a great Soldier. If you are willing to fave your Life, anfwer'd the Soldier, you muft tell me who you are, and fpeak without the leaft Prevarication. I am the principal Servant of this Inn, reply'd the Spirit: I am in love with my Mafter's Daughter, and fhe does not diflike me; but the Father and Mother having a better Match in view than me, in order to prevent their making him their Son-in-Law, the Girl and I have concluded that I fhall, every Night, act the Part which I now do. I wrap my felf up in a long black Cloak, and hang the Jack-Chain about my Neck; thus equipt I run up and down the Houfe, from the Cellar to the Garret, and make all the Noife which

you

you have heard. When I am at my Master
and Mistress's Chamber-Door, I stop, and
cry out; Don't hope that; I'll ever let you
rest, 'till you marry *Juanna* to *Guillermo*
your upper Drawer. After having pronounc'd these Words with a hoarse broken
Voice, I continue my Noise, and at a
Window enter the Closet, where *Juanna*
lyes alone, to give her an Account of what
I have done.

Mr. Serjeant, continu'd *Guillermo*, you
see I have told you the whole; I know
that after this Confession you may ruin me
by discovering it to my Master; but if you
please to serve, instead of undoing me, I
swear that my Acknowledgments——Alas,
what Service can I do thee? interrupted the
Soldier. You need do no more, return'd
Guillermo, than to say to Morrow that you
have seen the Spirit, that it so terribly affrighted you——How! terribly affrighted!
interrupted the Soldier; would you have
Serjeant *Antonio Quebrantador* own such
a thing as Fear? You may say what you
please, answer'd the young Man; 'tis no
matter, provided you second my Design.
And when I have marry'd *Juanna* and am
settled, I promise to treat you and all your
Friends nobly for nothing every Day. You
are a very tempting Person, Mr. *Guiller-*
mo,

me, said the Soldier. You propose to me
to support a Trick : 'Tis a serious Affair
which requires mature Deliberation ; but
the Consequences hurry me on. Go, continue your Noise, give your Account to
Juanna, and I'll take care of the rest.'

Accordingly next Morning he said to
his Landlord and Landlady : I have seen
the Spirit, I have talk'd with it. 'Tis a
very honest Fellow, I have concluded a
Treaty of Peace betwixt you and him.
He has promis'd to leave you at quiet, on
Condition that you will marry your Daughter to one *Guillermo* which he talk'd of.
On my part, I took it upon me to oblige
you to consent to this Marriage, and with
your leave it must be so, for I don't love
my Promises should turn to Air. Tho'
the Host was a very simple Fellow, he refus'd to ratifie this Treaty. Have a care,
then, said the Soldier; the Spirit has cry'd
out to you every Night to dispose of your
Daugher to *Guillermo,* and you have feign'd
not to hear it. You don't know what sort
of Gentlemen these Spirits are; after they
have several times declar'd their Intentions,
if they are not follow'd, take notice I warn
you against what they will do.

The Hostess, yet more silly than her
Husband, terrify'd at this Discourse, and
fancy-

fancying that the Spirit was always behind
her, fo earneftly prefs'd her Husband to
confent to the Match, that he yielded to
her Entreaties, and *Guillermo* marry'd *Juanna* the next Day, and fet up in another
part of the Town.

Serjeant *Quebrantador* did not fail to
vifit him often, and he, in Acknowledgment of the Service he had done him,
gave him as much Wine as he car'd for.
This fo pleas'd the Soldier, that he brought
thither not only all his Friends, but lifted
his Men there, and made all his Recruits
drunk. But at laft *Guillermo*, grown weary of fatiating fuch a Crew of greedy
Throats, told the Soldier his Mind; who,
without ever thinking that he had exceed-
ed the Agreement, was fo unjuft as to call
Guillermo little ungrateful Rafcal. The
Hoft anfwer'd, the Serjeant reply'd, and
the Dialogue ended with feveral Strokes
with the flat Side of the Sword, which
Guillermo receiv'd: Several Perfons paffing
by took the Vintner's Part; the Serjeant
wounded three or four, but was fuddenly
fallen on by a Croud of *Alguazils*, who
feiz'd him as a Difturber of the publick
Peace, and carry'd him to Prifon. He
there declar'd all that I have told you, and
upon his Depofition the Officers have alfo
feiz'd

feiz'd *Guillermo*; the Father-in-law requires the annulling of the Marriage, and the holy Office, inform'd of the Affair, have thought fit to take Cognizance of it.

In the next Hole, continu'd the Devil, are four Wretches who will foon end their Days. One of them is a young *Valet de Chambre* which his Mafter's Wife admitted her Lover. One Day the Husband caught them in the Act; the Woman immediately cry'd out for Help, and caught the *Valet de Chambre* at forcing her: The miferable unfortunate Fellow was feiz'd, and will be facrific'd to his Miftrefs's Reputation.

The fecond is a Chirurgeon, convicted of having fent his Wife out of the World the fame way that *Seneca* went. He was this Day tortur'd, and after confeffing the Crime he was charg'd with, own'd, befides, that he had made ufe of a new way to create Practice; he wounded the Paffengers in the Street with a Bayonet, and nimbly efcap'd out of a Back-Door. The wounded Perfon, in the mean while, by his Groans had drawn the Neighbours to his Affiftance. He ran in alfo with the Croud, and finding a wounded Man wallowing in his Blood, he caus'd him to be carry'd into his Shop, where he drefs'd him with the fame

fame Hand which had given the Wound.

The third is by Profeffion an Affaffina-tor, one of thofe which for four or five Piftols, are very ready to oblige all thofe with the ufe of their Arm, who want to be privately rid of an Enemy. The fourth is a young Marquifs's Gentleman, whofe Mafter being robb'd of a thoufand Ducats, he is accus'd of the Crime: He will to Mor-row be put to the Torture, and tho' inno-cent will be tormented 'till he confefs that which was committed by an old Waiting-Woman, who monopolizes the Marchio-nefs's Ear, and no body dare fufpect her.

Signior *Afmodeo,* faid *Don Cleofas,* pray let me entreat you to help this young Gentleman. Keep off, by your Power, the cruel Tortures defign'd him; his Innocence deferves it — You don't confider what you ask, *Don Cleofas,* interrupted the Devil. Can you defire me to oppofe an unjuft Action, and hinder the Deftruction of an innocent Man. You had as good beg of an Attorney not to ruin a Widow or Or-phan. Pray, if you pleafe, be thankful that I don't deal with your felf like an evil Spi-rit: And leave me to the free Exercife of my Hatred and Malice on other Men. Be-fides, if I would deliver that honeft Man out of Prifon, do you think 'tis in my
Power?

Power? How, said the Scholar, have not you Power to fetch a Man out of Prison? No, really, reply'd *Asmodeo*; if you had read *Albertus Magnus's Enchyridion*, you would have known that I cannot, any more than my Brethren, set a Prisoner at Liberty. If even I my self should have the Misfortune to fall into the Clutches of a Justice, I could not extricate my self any other way than by Mony.

I think, said *Don Cleofas*, I see a Woman in that little Room above the Dungeon. Yes, answer'd *Asmodeo*, it is a famous Witch, who has the Character of being able to do Impossibilities. By her Art, 'tis reported, old widow'd Ladies find out Gallants that love them on the Square; Husbands become just to their Wives, and Coquets really enamour'd on those rich Men which keep them. But nothing is more false than this: She is not Mistress of any other Secret, than that of persuading the World she is so, and living handsomely on that Opinion.

Observe in the next Room those two Prisoners, who are talking instead of taking their Rest: They can't sleep, their Circumstances disturb them, and really they are nice enough. The first is a Jeweller, accus'd of having conceal'd stollen Jewels:

I   The

The other is in for Polygamy. He six Months since marry'd an old Widow in the Kingdom of *Valencia* for her Mony, and a little while after espoused a young Woman at *Madrid* to gratifie his Inclination, and gave her all the Riches he had with his *Valencian* Wife. These two Marriages coming out, both his Wives prosecute him. She that he marry'd out of Inclination pursues his Life for Interest, and she that he marry'd for Interest demands it out of Inclination.

Follow my Eyes to that low Hall, where you will see thirty or forty Prisoners lying on Straw; they are Pick-pockets, Shop-lifters, and all the very worst sort of Felons; I'll particularize the Cause of the Commitment of every one of them.——— I beg you not, interrupted *Don Cleofas*; let's leave these Rogues, for I am not fond of hearing the Adventures of the Dregs of Mankind. Pray let's remove from this unpleasant Place; go on, and fix our Observation on more diverting Objects. Very willingly, reply'd the *Demon*, for I have a great many other Things to shew you.

CHAP.

C H A P. IX.

Which contains several short Stories.

Leaving the Prisoners, they flew towards the *Casa * de los Locos;* but before they reach'd it, *Asmodeo* stopping at a great House, said to *Don Cleofas,* Shall I tell you what all those People which you see have this Day done? You will very much oblige me, answer'd the Scholar; but I conjure you to begin with those two Ladies who laugh so loud; they seem to me to be very merry. They are, answer'd the Devil, a Couple of young Ladies that have this Day bury'd their Father, who was a whimsical Humorist, that had such an Aversion for Matrimony that he would never marry them, how advantageous Matches soever were offer'd them. The Character of their deceas'd Father was the perpetual Subject of their Discourse. He is dead at last, said the eldest, our unnatural Father, who took a barbarous Pleasure in preventing our Marriage! He will now no more

I 2   cross

---

* *The Mad-House, or* Bedlam.

cross our Desires. For my part, said the youngest, I am for a rich Husband, and *Don Bourvalas* shall be my Man. Hold, Sister, reply'd the eldest, don't let us be so very hasty in the Choice of Husbands; let's marry those which the Powers above have destin'd for us; for our Marriages are regifter'd in Heaven's Book. So much the worse, dear Sister, return'd the youngest, for I'm afraid my Father will tear out the Leaf. At this the eldest could not hold from an extravagant Fit of Laughter, in which the youngest, equally tickl'd, as heartily joins.

Ah ha, said *Don Cleofas*, in the House over-against that I discern a young Lady looking into a Glafs. 'Tis, answer'd the *Dæmon*, a young Gentlewoman, who lodges in a furnish'd Chamber, and is complimenting her Charms on the important Conquest they have made this Day. She is likewise contriving new Airs, and has already hit on two which will to Morrow give a good Stroke towards the gaining of a new Lover, who is such a very promising Spark that she can't be too sedulous in the Conquest of him: And one of her Creditors coming to dun her, Honest Friend, said she, come within a few Days and you shall be paid, I am just upon
Terms

Terms of Agreement with a confiderable Officer of the Treafury.

Let's turn our Eyes, continu'd the Devil, towards that Captain which is drawing on his Boots; he is going out of *Madrid*, his Horfes wait for him at the Gate, and he is commanded to *Portugal*, in order to join his Regiment. Having no Mony to make the Campaign, he Yefterday apply'd himfelf to an Ufurer: Can't you, faid he, lend me a thoufand Pieces of Eight? Captain, anfwer'd the Ufurer in very obliging Terms, I have not fo much by me, but I will do my beft to find a Man that fhall lend you that Sum; that is, fhall give you four hundred down, provided you give your Note for a thoufand; and out of that four hundred, pleafe to take Notice that I expect fixty for Procuration. Mony is fo very fcarce at this time —— What a hellifh Extortion is this, interrupted the Officer haftily, to ask fix hundred and fixty Patacoons for the Ufe of three hundred and forty! What a horrid Cheat is this! No Paffion, Captain, reply'd the Ufurer with a cool Air; try at another Place. What do you complain of? Do I force you to take the three hundred and forty Patacoons? You are at your Liberty to take or let 'em alone.

I 3   The

The Captain went away, without returning any Answer: But after considering that he must go to his Regiment, his
Time was short, and that he could do nothing without Mony, he returns the next
Morning to the Usurer, whom he met at
his Door in a black Cloak, Collar-Band
and short Hair, with his Beads in his Hand.
Signior *Sanguijela*, says he, 'I am content
to accept your three hundred and forty
Patacoons; my extream want of Mony has
forc'd me to it. I will but go to Mass, answer'd the Usurer very gravely, and at my
Return come again, and you shall have
that Sum. No, no, reply'd the Captain,
go in again; this Affair won't take you up
two Minutes, pray dispatch me immediately, for I am in utmost Haste. I cannot
really, reply'd the Usurer, I every Day hear
Mass before I do any manner of Business;
'tis my constant Rule, which I am resolv'd
to observe most religiously for the Remainder of my Life.

However impatient the Captain was to
receive his Mony, he was forc'd to submit
to pious *Sanguijela's* strict Rules; and as
if he had been afraid he should miss the
Patacoons, he follow'd the Usurer to the
Church, and staid the Mass out with him;
immediately after which he prepar'd to go
                                    out

out of the Church, when *Sanguijela* whi-
fper'd in his Ear, that one of the ableft
Preachers in *Madrid* was juft going to a-
fcend the Pulpit ; and I will not not on a-
ny account, faid he, lofe the Sermon. The
Officer, who thought the Mafs infupport-
ably tedious, was almoft diftracted at this
frefh Delay ; but yet waited the Sermon
out. The Preacher appear'd, and preach'd
againft Ufury; at which the Captain was
infinitely pleas'd, and obferving *Sanguijela's* Looks, he faid to himfelf, If this *Jew*
fhould be touch'd with this Difcourfe!
Should he now give me fix hundred Patacoons, how happy 'twould be! After the
Sermon the Ufurer went out of the Church:
Well, Signior *Sanguijela,* faid the Captain
joining him, what do you think of this
Preacher? was not the Sermon very pathe-
tick? for my part, I own it fenfibly mov'd
me. I am perfectly of your Opinion, with
regard to the Sermon, anfwer'd the Extor-
tioner: He has handled his Subject perfectly well; he is a learned Man, and has
difcharg'd the Duty of his Calling; let us
do the fame in ours.

Caft your Eye, continu'd the Devil, on
that great Houfe beyond the Officer's. Do
you fee that young Lady in the Rofe-co-
lour'd Satin Bed embroider'd with Silver?

I 4   Yes,

Yes, anfwer'd *Don Cleofas*, I difcern a fine
Woman in a profound Sleep, and I think
alfo a Book on her Boulfter.   You are
right, reply'd *Afmodeo*, that Lady is a very
gay, witty, young Marchionefs, which being indifpos'd, and not able to fleep for
three Weeks, fhe this Day refolv'd to fend
for a Phyfician.   He came; fhe confulted
him, and he order'd a Remedy mention'd
in *Hippocrates*.   The Lady began to railly
his Prefcription; but the Phyfician being a
peevifh Animal, was difgufted at her Jeft:
Hippocrates, Madam, faid he, very gravely, is not a proper Man to be ridicul'd.
God forbid, Signior *Carquette*, anfwer'd
the Marchionefs with the moft ferious Air
that it was poffible for her to put on; God
forbid that I fhould laugh at fuch a famous
and learned Author!   I have fuch a high
Value for him, that I am fully perfuaded
the reading of fome of his Tracts only,
would cure my waking Diftemper.   I have
his Works of the laft Edition, which is the
beft Tranflation extant : She accordingly
try'd the Experiment, and at the third Page
fell afleep.

   Pray infrom me, faid the Scholar, what
that tall, meagre Piece of Skin and Bones,
which ftalks about that little Room, is; I
believe his Head is fomewhat difturb'd.
                                            You

You are not miftaken, anfwer'd the Devil, 'tis a Drammatick Poet that underftands French; he has taken the pains to tranflate the *Mifantrope,* one of the beft Comedies of *Moliere,* that famous *French* Author. He has this Day got it acted on the Threatre of *Madrid,* and it has been very ill receiv'd. The *Spaniards* have damn'd it, as dull and tedious : 'Twas about this Play that you heard fuch a noifie Difpute at the Coffee-houfe.

Why, reply'd *Don Cleofas,* had this Comedy fuch an unhappy Fate? Becaufe, return'd the Devil, the *Spaniards* like no Plays that are not full of Intrigue,' and the *French* only thofe which abound with Humour. On this Foot then, faid the Scholar, if our fineft Drammatick Pieces were to be play'd in *France,* they would not fucceed. You are undoubtedly in the right, faid *Afmodeo*; as the *Spaniards* are fteady, and capable of a fix'd Attention, they are fond of being caft into an agreeable Perplexity, and eafily follow the moft complicated Action. The *French,* on the other fide, don't care to be bufied that way, they love to be difingag'd, and are pleas'd to fee their Neighbours ridicul'd, becaufe it tickles their own Satyrical Humour: To conclude, the Tafte of Nations differs.

But

But which fort of Comedy is the beft, anfwer'd *Don Cleofas*, that of Intrigue, or
that of Humour? 'Tis very difputable, reply'd the Devil; but neither *Spaniards* nor
French are to be credited on this Subject,
they are Parties too much prejudiced to
be Judges; and I muft not determine this
Difpute, becaufe, as the *Dæmon* of Luxury, I equally protect all Theatres.

I fee, continu'd he, not far from that
Author, a Banker in whofe Apartment has
lately pafs'd a Scene worth your hearing.
'Tis not two Months fince he return'd from
Peru laden with great Riches, and is now
fet up a Banker in this City : His Father
is a Cobler in a fmall Village about twelve
Leagues from hence, where he lives
throughly contented with his Condition
and his Wife, who is much about the
fame Age with himfelf, that is fixty.

'Tis a long time fince this Banker left
his Parents, to go in queft of a better Fortune than what they could propofe to
leave him; for within the Compafs of
of twenty rolling Years they had not feen
him. They frequently talk'd of him, and
continually pray'd that Heav'n would
pleafe not to forfake him; and the Parfon
being their Friend, they never fail'd to obtain the publick Prayers of the Congrega-
tion

tion for him.   As for the Banker, he had
not forgotten them; but as soon as he was
settled, resolv'd to inform himself of their
Condition.   To this purpose, after having
order'd his Domesticks not to expect him,
he mounted on Horse-back, and went a-
lone to the Village.

'Twas ten at Night before he got thither, and the honest Cobler was a-bed with
his Wife, in a sound Sleep, when he knock'd
at the Door: They then wak'd, and ask'd
who was there? Open the Door, said the
Banker, 'tis your Son *Francillo.* Make
others believe that if you can, cry'd the
old Man, you thieving Rogues go about
your Business, for here is nothing for you;
Francillo, if not dead, is now in the *Indies.*
He is no longer there, he is return'd home
from *Peru,* reply'd the Banker, and it is he
that now speaks to you; open your Door,
and receive him. *Jacobo,* let's rise then,
said the Woman, for I really believe 'tis
Francillo; I think I know his Voice.

They both rose immediately; the Father lighted a Candle, and the Mother,
after getting her Cloaths on with utmost
haste, open'd the Door.   She earnestly
look'd on *Francillo,* and could not longer
doubt his being her Son; she flung her
Arms about his Neck, and clasp'd him
close

clofe to her. *Jacobo*, alfo touch'd by the
fame Sentiments as his Wife, did not fail
to embrace his Son in his turn; and all
three of them, tranfported with the Sight
of one another, after fuch a long Abfence,
could not fatisfie themfelves without expreffing the Marks of the utmoft Tendernefs. After thefe pleafing Tranfports, the
Banker unfadled and unbridled his Horfe,
and put him into the Stable, where he found
an old milch Cow, the Nurfe to the whole
Family ; he then gave the old Folks an
Account of his Voyage, and all the Riches
that he had brought from *Peru.* The Particular was long, and would tire any dif-
interefted Auditors; but a Son that unbofom'd himfelf in the Relation of all his
Adventures, could not fail of the Attention of Father and Mother. They greedi-
ly heard him, and the very leaft Particulars which he related made in them a fenfible Impreffion of Grief or Joy.

As foon as he had ended the Story of
his Fortunes, he told them that he came
to offer them Part of his Eftate, and begg'd
of his Father not to work any longer. No,
my Son, faid Mr. *Jacobo*, I love my Trade,
and will not quit it. Why, reply'd the
Banker, is it not now high time for you to
to give it over, and take your Eafe? I don't
pro-

propose your coming to live with me at
Madrid; I know very well that a City
Life would not please you. I would not
disturb your quiet way of living; but at
least give over your hard Labour, and pass
your Days as easily as you can. The Mother seconded her Son, and Master *Jacobo*
yielded. Very well, *Francillo*, said he, to
please you, I will not work any more for
the Publick; but will only mend my own
Shoes, and those of my good Friend, the
Vicar of the Parish. After this Agreement,
the Banker, fatigu'd with his Day's Journey, went into his Father and Mother's
Bed, and slept betwixt them both, with a
Pleasure which only the most dutiful and
best natur'd Children to their Parents can
imagine.

The next Morning, the Banker, leaving
them a Purse of three hundred Ducats,
return'd to *Madrid*; but Yesterday was
very much surpriz'd to see Mr. *Jocobo* un-
expectedly at his House: My Father, said
he, what brought you hither? *Francillo*,
answer'd the honest Man, I have brought
your Purse, take your Mony again, I desire to live by my Trade, I have been ready to die with Uneasiness ever since I left
off working. Well then, my Father, reply'd the Banker, return to your Village,
work

work at your Trade enough to divert your
felf, but no more. Carry back your Purfe
with you, and don't fpare mine. Alas,
what would you have me to do with fo
much Mony? reply'd Mr. *Jacobo*. Comfort the Poor with it, return'd *Francillo*,
beftow it as your Vicar fhall advife you.
The Cobler, fatisfy'd with this Anfwer, return'd that Morning to his Village.

I need not, faid *Don Cleofas*, ask you
what that Gentleman, which I fee, has been
doing for this whole Day ; he muft of
neceffity have fpent it in writing of Letters.
What a prodigious Quantity do I fee on his
Table! What is moft Comical, anfwer'd
the Devil, is, that all thefe Letters are
Verbatim the fame. This Cavalier has
written to all his abfent Friends the Relation of an Adventure which happen'd to
him this Day after Dinner, and is as fol-
lows: He loves a beautiful, difcreet Widow of thirty ; he makes Addreffes to her,
fhe does not flight him, he propofes to
marry her, and fhe accepts the Offer.
While the nuptial Preparations are making,
he has free leave to vifit her at her own
Houfe, which he accordingly doth daily.
He has been there to Day, and happening
to meet with none of the Family to ask
where fhe was, he enter'd the Lady's Apartment,

ment, where he furpriz'd her afleep on a
Couch in an amorous Undrefs. He approach'd her foftly, and ftole a Kifs; at
which fhe wak'd, and fighing faid: Ah, pray,
Ambrofio, let me fleep! The Cavalier, like
a well-bred Man, very civilly took his
leave at that Inftant, and quitted her A-
partment; he met *Ambrofio* at the Door,
Ambrofio, faid he, your Miftrefs begs that
you would not wake her.

I fhall now ask your frefh Attention,
continu'd the Devil. Three Houfes beyond that of this Cavalier lives *la Chichona,* whom I have already mention'd in the
Story of the Count *de Belflor.* Ah, how
I am ravifh'd to fee her! faid the Scholar.
That good Woman, fo very ferviceable to
young Perfons, is doubtlefs one of thofe
two old Women which I fee in that low
Hall. The one is leaning with her Elbows
on the Table, earneftly looking on the
other, who is telling Mony: Which of
the two is *la Chichona?* She, anfwer'd the
Demon, which leans on her Elbows. The
Name of the other is *la Pebrada*; fhe is a
Lady of the fame Occafion; they are Part-
ners, and at this Moment dividing the
Profits of an Adventure, which they have
this Day brought to bear.

La

La Pebrada has the beft Trade, and deals with feveral rich Widows, to whom fhe carries her Lift to read every Day. What do you mean by her Lift? interrupted *Don Cleofas*. It is, reply'd *Afmodeo*, the Catalogue of all the handfom Strangers which come to *Madrid:* As foon as ever *la Pebrada* hears that any frefh ones are arriv'd in the City, fhe runs to their Inns, and informs her felf exactly of their Country, Birth, Shape, Air and Humour: She then makes her Report to the Widows, who confider of it, and if they are fo inclin'd, *la Pebrada* brings them to the Speech of the Strangers.

This is not only very convenient, faid *Don Cleofas*, but in a fort lawful: For without thefe good Ladies and their Agents, the young Strangers, who have no Acquaintance here, would be oblig'd to the Expence of an infinite deal of time to create fome. But pray tell me whether there are alfo Widows in other Countries? Whether there are? reply'd the Devil: Yes, there are in all Countries, and efpecially in *France*; but an eftablifh'd Reputation is abfolutely neceffary in order to find them. To this purpofe give me leave to tell you, that fome Days paft, a very induftrious Spark, talking on this Head with

one

one of his Acquaintance, faid: My dear, I
muft needs be very unhappy! I have fpent
fifteen whole Days in queft of a yielding Female.   I have gone to *Matins* at all the
Churches; I have furvey'd all the Beauties
of the *Tuilleries*; I have fhew'd my felf on
the *Opera*, appear'd all unbutton'd at the
Play-houfe, where I have fometimes lay a-
long on the Benches, at others ftood upright
behind the Actors, and yet all this avail'd
nothing, I have not fo much as met with
any the leaft Favour from even any one of
fixty; whilft the youngeft and moft beautiful Women of *Paris* are Victims to the
Chevalier *de Tiremailles*, who, without Vanity, I may fay, has neither my Shape
nor Youth.   Oh, don't miftake, interrupted his Friend, the Chevalier *de Tiremailles*, is a known Rover, he has already ruin'd
two Women.   His Actions loudly pro-
claim his Merit, he has the beft Reputation in the World.

What's that I hear? cry'd the Scholar:
What confus'd Noife ftrikes the Air?
Thofe are Mad-men, anfwer'd the Devil,
which are tearing their Throats with fing-
ing and roaring; we are not far from the
Place where they are fhut up.   Ah, faid
Don Cleofas, pray do me the Favour to
K   fhew

ſhew me them, and give me an Account wherefore they ran Mad. I will immediately give you that Diverſion, anſwer'd the Devil; as there are melancholy Mad-men, ſo there are alſo merry ones; you ſhall ſee all ſorts of them. Theſe Words were ſcarce ended, before the Scholar was tranſported to the Top of the *Caſa de los Locos.*

CHAP

CHAP. X.

Of the confin'd mad People.

DON Cleofas caft his Eye into all
the Rooms, and after having ob-
ferv'd all thofe within them, faid the *Demon* to him, Let's examine all thefe one
after another, taking them in a Row as
their Chambers are fituate; and beginning with the Men, I will tell you by
what Misfortune they loft their Senfes,

In the firft Room is a News-Monger,
run diftracted with Melancholy, by read-
ing in the *Gazette,* that a Party of fifty
Portuguefe beat thirty *Spaniards.* His
Neighbour is a *Licenciado,* which has
plaid the Hypocrite at Court for thefe ten
Years only to obtain a Benefice, and fee-
ing himfelf continually forgotten in the
Promotions, Defpair has at laft turn'd his
Head.

The next is an Orphan, whom his Guardian made to pafs for diftracted, that he
might feize his Eftate; and the poor
Youth is really become fo at laft, out of
pure Grief to fee himfelf fhut up here.
Next to him is a School-Mafter, who
                    K 2   loft

loft his Wits in fearch of the *paulo poſt futurum* of a *Greek* Verb.

He which you fee beyond him, is old Captain *Zanubio*, a *Neapolitan* Gentleman, who came to fettle at *Madrid*, and ran mad with Jealoufie. His Story runs thus : He had a young Wife, whofe Name was *Aurora ;* he kept her out of Sight ; his Houfe was inacceffible to all Men. *Aurora* never went out but to Mafs, and then was always accompany'd by her old *Tithon*, who fometimes carry'd her to an Eftate which he had near *Alcantara.* Notwithftanding all his vigilant Care, a certain Gentleman, whofe Name was *Don Garçia Sacheco*, having feen her at Church, had conceiv'd a violent Paffion for her. He was a bold young Spark, and worth the Regard of a handfom Woman ill marry'd. The Difficulty of introducing himfelf to *Zanubio* did not remove his Hopes ; but his Beard not being yet grown, and being a very beautiful Youth, he drefs'd himfelf in Girls Cloaths, took a Purfe of a hundred Piftoles, and went to *Zanubio's* Eftate, whither he had been inform'd, by good Hands, that the Captain and his Wife would very foon come.

He

He addreſs'd himſelf to the Gard'ner's Wife, and in a Romantick Heroick Strain, ſaid to her, I come to throw my ſelf into your Arms, take pity on me; I am of *Toledo,* born of a good Family, and to a good Fortune: My Parents reſolve to marry me to a Man which I hate, and I have this Night eſcap'd their Tyranny, and at preſent want a Shelter from their Rage. They will never come to look for me here; permit me to ſtay here 'till my Relations come to more tender Sentiments for me. Here is my Purſe, adds he, giving it to her, take it; 'tis all I can at preſent offer you. But, I hope, I ſhall one Day be able to acknowledge any Service you ſhall do me.

The Gard'ner's Wife, touch'd with this Diſcourſe, but more eſpecially with the Concluſion: My Daughter, ſaid ſhe, I will ſerve you; I know ſeveral young Women which are ſacrific'd to old Men, and withal know that they are not very well contented with them; alas, I feel part of their Griefs. You could not have addreſs'd your ſelf to a more proper Perſon than my ſelf, I will place you in a little private Chamber, where you ſhall be ſecure. *Don Garcia* paſs'd ſeveral Days here very impatiently, expecting the

Arrival of *Aurora*, who at laſt came, accompany'd by her Husband; who, according to his Cuſtom, ſearch'd all the Apartments, Cloſets, Cellars and Garrets, to ſee if he could not diſcover any Man hidden there. The Gard'ner's Wife, knowing him throughly, prevented his ſearching *Don Garçia's* Chamber, by telling in what manner the pretended Lady had deſir'd a Refuge there.

Zanubio, tho' extream diſtruſtful, had not the leaſt Suſpicion of the Deceit. He was willing to ſee the unknown Lady, who defir'd to be excus'd from the Diſcovery of her Name, pretending ſhe ow'd that Concealment to her Family, whom ſhe diſgrac'd by this ſort of Flight. She then told her Romantick Tale ſo advantageouſly, that the Captain was charm'd with it, and began to find a growing Inclination for the fair Unknown. He offer'd her his Services, and flattering himſelf that this might prove a lucky Adventure, plac'd her with his Wife.

As ſoon as *Aurora* ſaw *Don Garçia* ſhe bluſh'd, and grew diſturb'd; he perceiv'd it, and believ'd that ſhe had obſerv'd him in the Church where he had ſeen her: Wherefore to ſatisfie himſelf, as ſoon as he could ſpeak to her alone, he ſaid, Madam,

dam, I have a Brother which has often
mention'd you to me; he saw you for a
Moment in a Church; ever since that
time he has call'd upon your Name a
thousand times a Day, and is in a Condition which indeed deserves your Pity. At
these Words *Aurora* look'd on *Don Garçia* more intently than she had yet done,
and answer'd, You too much resemble
that Brother for me to be any longer deluded by your Artifice; I see clearly
enough that you are a Cavalier in Petticoats: I remember that one Day, when I
was hearing Mass, my Veil suddenly flew
open, and you saw me. I observ'd you
out of Curiosity, and found your Eyes
always fix'd on me. When I went away
I believe you did not fail to follow me,
to discover in what Street I liv'd, and who
I was. I believe, I say, because I durst
not turn my Head to observe you, because my Husband, who was with me,
would have been alarm'd, and made a
great Crime of it. The next, and the
following Days, I went to the same
Church, where I saw you again, and took
so much notice of your Face, that I know
it again, notwithstanding your Disguise.
Madam, then, reply'd *Don Garçia*, I
must unmask: Yes, I am a Man ensnar'd
by

by your Charms: 'Tis *Don Garçia Pacheco*, whom Love has introduc'd here in this Dress. And you hope, without doubt, said she, that approving your Passion, I should favour this Stratagem, and contribute my Part to keep my Husband in the Error he now lyes under; but there you are deceiv'd. I will immediately discover the whole to him; I am glad of such a handsome Opportunity of convincing him that his Vigilance is less secure than my Virtue, and that as jealous and distrustful as he is, 'tis more difficult to surprize me than him.

She had scarce ended these Words before the Captain appear'd; What are you talking of Ladies? said he. To which *Aurora* immediately answer'd: We were speaking of those young Cavaliers that attempt to get into the Affections of those young Women who have old Husbands; and I was saying, that if any of those Sparks should be so rash as to presume to introduce themselves to you, under any Disguise, I would very severely punish their Impudence. And you, Madam, said *Zanubio*, turning towards *Don Garçia*, how would you treat a young Cavalier on the same Occasion? *Don Garçia* was so disturb'd and confus'd, that he

was

was utterly at a Lofs what Anfwer to return to the Captain, who would have perceiv'd the Perplexity he was in, if a Footman had not come to tell him that a Perfon was come from *Madrid* to fpeak with him. He went to fee what his Bufinefs was; when *Don Garçia* threw himfelf at *Aurora's* Feet: Ah, Madam! faid he, what Pleafure do you take in tormenting me? Will you really be fo barbarous as to deliver me over to the Refentment of an enrag'd Husband. No, *Pacheco,* anfwer'd fhe fmiling; young Women, who have old jealous Husbands, are not fo cruel. Reaffume your Courage; I was willing to divert my felf, by putting you into a little Fright: You fhall be acquitted by it; 'tis not making you pay too dear for my Complaifance in fuffering you to ftay here. At thefe comforting Words *Don Garçia* found all his Fears vanifh, and conceiv'd Hopes that *Aurora* would not deny him.

One Day when they were mutually exchanging fome Marks of their good Underftanding in *Zanubio's* Apartment, the Captain furpriz'd 'em. Had he not been the moft jealous Man in the World, he faw enough to engage him to believe, with good Reafon, that his Fair Unknown was

2

a Cavalier disguis'd: Enrag'd to the highest
degree at this Sight, he runs to his Closet to fetch his Pistols; but in the mean
while the Lovers escap'd; double locking
all the Doors after them, and carrying off
the Keys. They got to an neighbouring
Village, where *Don Garçia* had left his
Valet de Chambre and two Horses. There
he quitted his Petticoats, took *Aurora*
behind him, and conducted her to a Convent, where he desir'd her to enter, and
assur'd her of a Refuge there, the Abbess
being his Aunt. This done, he return'd
to *Madrid* to wait the Issue of this Adventure.

In the Interim, *Zanubio* finding himself
lock'd in, loudly call'd all the Family. A
Footman hearing his Voice, ran towards
him; but the Doors being lock'd, he
could not open them. The Captain endeavour'd to break them open, but not
being able to get out that way quick
enough, yielding to his Rage, he hastily
flung himself out at Window with the
Pistols in his Hand: He fell upon his Back,
hurt his Head, and remain'd senseless on
the Ground. His Domesticks came and
carry'd him into the Hall on a Conch;
they threw Water in his Face, and by
tormenting him, fetch'd him out of his
faint-

fainting Fit; but with his Senses his Rage
return'd: He ask'd for his Wife. The
Servants answer'd him, that they saw her
and the strange Lady go out at the little
Garden Door. He commanded them to
give him his Pistols immediately, and
they were forc'd to obey him. He caus'd
a Horse to be sadled, mounting it without thinking of his Wounds; but happen'd to take a different Road than that
which the Lovers went. He pass'd the
whole Day in a vain Chase, and at Night
stopping at an Inn in a Village to repose
himself, his Fatigue, and the Blood which
he had lost, threw him into a Fever and
Delirium, which almost carry'd him off.

To tell you the rest in two Words, he
lay fifteen Days sick in that Village, after which he return'd to his Estate, where
continually possess'd by his Misfortune,
he by degrees lost his Wits. *Aurora's*
Friends were no sooner inform'd of this,
than they brought him to *Madrid*, and
shut him up in the Mad-house; and his
Wife is yet at the Nunnery, where they
resolve she shall stay some Years, as a
Punishment for her Indiscretion.

The very next to *Zambio*, continu'd
the Devil, is a Merchant who run mad at
the News of the Loss of a Ship. In the
next

next Room is a Soldier, who could not bear the Lofs of his Grand-mother. And the young Man next to the honeft Soldier, faid *Don Cleofas*, what fort of Diftraction is his? Oh! as for him, anfwer'd *Afmodeo*, 'tis a poor Wretch born fimple, he is the Son of a *Dutch* Woman and a fat Officer of the Cuftom-houfe.

Let's remove to that great Man who plays upon the Guitar, and fings to it himfelf. He is a melancholy Mad-man, a Lover whom the Severities of his Miftrefs have reduc'd to this Condition. Ah, how I pity him! cry'd the Scholar, allow me to deplore his Misfortune ; it may be every honeft Gentleman's Cafe. If I fhould be feiz'd by a cruel Beauty, I don't my felf know whether I fhould not lofe my Wits. By this Sentiment you fhew your felf to be a true *Caftilian*; one muft be born in the very middle of *Caftile* to be capable of ever running melancholy Mad for being unable to pleafe. The *French* are not fo tender, and if you will know the Difference betwixt a *Frenchman* and a *Spaniard* on this Head, I need only repeat the Song which that Mad-man fings, and has juft this Minute compos'd.

A

A *Spanish* Song.

Ardo y lloro Sin Sossiego:
Llorando y ardiendo tanto,
Que ni el llanto apaga el fuego;
Ni el fuego consume el llanto.

In Profe thus:

I burn and weep inceffantly, without
my Tears ever quenching my Flames, or
my Flames drying up my Tears.

Thus fings the *Spanish* Cavalier, when
his Miftrefs has us'd him ill; and on the
fame Occafion a *Frenchman*, a few Days
fince, exprefs'd himfelf thus:

A *French* Song.

Th' ungrateful Object of my Love
   Is deaf to all my Pray'rs:
Her cruel Heart no Sighs can move,
   Nor is fhe foften'd by my Tears.
Was ever Mortal curf's'd like me!
   The Light, and ever glorious Sun,
   Henceforth abandon'd will I fhun,
And in the Grave with Payen *lye.*

Payen

Payen is probably a Vintner, said *Don Cleofas.* You've guess'd right, answer'd the Devil. Let's now come to the Women. How comes it, said the Scholar, that I see but five or six! there are less mad Women than I thought. All of 'em are not here, reply'd the *Damon*; but in another Part of the City there is a Place that is quite full of 'em. I'll carry you thither this Minute, if you please. No, no, interrupted *Don Cleofas*, I will content my self with seeing these here; pray inform me of the Causes of their Distraction.

The first, reply'd *Asmodeo*, is an old Marchioness, who lov'd a young Officer that serv'd in *Flanders*. She gave him a large Sum to defray the Charges of his Campaign, and in his Absence consulted a Female Fortune-teller, to know what her Lover did abroad; the Witch shews him to the Marchioness at the Feet of a *Flanders* Lady, in a Glass, at which the old Lady lost her Wits.

The next is a Corregidor's Wife, whose Reason was turn'd by the outrageous Passion she fell into at being call'd a Citizen's Wife by a Court-Lady. The next is a Proctor's Wife, who press'd her Husband very hard to buy her a Cross of Diamonds,

amonds, worth ten thousand Ducats; he absolutely refus'd it, whereupon she ran mad. The next is a Coquet, whose Head is turn'd with Spight for having lost a great Lord, whose Ruin she had contriv'd. In the two little Lodges below those Ladies are two Servant Wenches, who have lost their Wits; one of them for Grief, for being left out of the Will of an old Batchelor, whom she serv'd; and the other for Joy, at the News of the Death of a rich Treasurer, whose Heiress she was.

After having shewn you the mad People which are confin'd, continu'd the Devil, I must shew you those who ought to be treated so.

CHAP.

C H A P. XI.

*Which should be longer than the pre-
ceding.*

LET's turn our Eyes on the Side of
the City, and as I shall discover to
you some Subjects which very well deserve to be plac'd amongst those that are
here, I will give you their respective Characters. I see one already which I will
not suffer to escape. 'Tis a new-marry'd
Man, who eight Days since was told of
the coquetting Tricks of a Jilt that he
lov'd; enrag'd he goes to her, breaks one
Part of her Furniture, throws another
out of the Window, and the next Day
marries her. Such a Man as this, said
Don Cleofas, certainly deserves the first
Vacancy in this House. He has a Neighbour not much wiser than himself, reply'd *Asmodeo;* 'tis a Batchelor of forty
five, who has sufficient to live on, and
yet would enter himself in a Nobleman's
Service.

I see a Lawyer's Widow, a good Woman who is above sixty; her Husband is
just dead, and she has enter'd her self into

to a Nunnery to secure her Reputation,
as she says, from Scandal. I discern a
couple of Virgins of above fifty, each
making Vows to Heav'n to take their Father, who keeps them up as close as tho'
they were under Age. They hope, after
the old Gentleman's Death, they shall
find handsome Men that will marry them
for Love. And why not? said the Scholar: There are Men in the World of as
whimsical a Taste as that. I grant it, reply'd the Devil, 'tis not impossible they
should find Husbands, but they ought
not to flatter themselves with such Hopes;
'tis therein consists their Folly.

There is no Country in the World
where the Women tell their Age truly.
About a Month since, a Maid of forty
eight, and a Wife of sixty nine, went before a Commissary to testifie for a Widow of their Acquaintance whose Virtue
was question'd. The Commissary first
interrogated the marry'd Woman on her
Age, and tho' it was as plainly express'd
in her Forehead as in the Church Register, she yet boldly ventur'd to say she
was but forty. He next interrogated the
Maiden: And you, Madam, said he, how
old are you? Let's pass on to the other
Questions, Sir, answer'd she, for this is

an improper one to be put to us. You
don't confider what you fay, Madam, reply'd the Commiffary; don't you know
that in Juridical Cafes the Truth ought
always to be told? No Law obliges us
to it, anfwer'd the Maiden haftily. But
then I cannot take your Depofition, faid
he, if your Age be not to it, for 'tis a
material Circumftance. If 'tis abfolutely neceffary, reply'd fhe, look upon me
intently, and put my Age down according
to your Confcience, The Commiffary,
without much Examination, put her
down twenty eight. He then ask'd whether fhe had long known the Widow:
Before her Marriage, faid fhe. Then I
have miftaken your Age, reply'd he, in
fetting you down but twenty eight, for it
is twenty nine Years fince the Widow
was marry'd. Well, Sir, return'd the
Maiden, write me down thirty then; I
might at a Year old know the Widow.
That will not be regular, reply'd he, let
us add a dozen. No indeed, interrupted
fhe; all that I can poffibly afford to add
is one Year more, and I would not put a
Month more if it were to fave my Honour. When thefe two Ladies were gone
from the Commiffary's, the marry'd Woman faid to the other, I wonder that im-
                                    pertinent

pertinent Fellow should take us for such
Fools as to tell our Ages truly: 'Tis not
enough indeed that they are regifter'd in
our Parifh Books, but the rude Fellow
would have them upon his Papers, that
all the World may know 'em. Well, I
banter'd him fufficiently; I funk a good
round twenty Years upon him, and you
have done very well in fuppreffing fo many. What do you call fo many? anfwer'd the Maiden very fmartly: You railly me, I am at moft but five and thirty.
Hah! reply'd the other with an angry
Air, who do you tell fo? I faw you born;
'tis a long time fince indeed: I remember
I faw your Father die; he was not young,
and he hath been dead about forty Years.
Oh my Father, my Father, haftily interrupted the Virgin, enrag'd at the other's
Freedom; betwixt you and I, when my
Father marry'd my Mother he was fo old
he was not able to get Children.

I obferve in the fame Houfe, continu'd
Afmodeo, two Men who are not over
wife. One of them is a Pufher of his
Fortune, that goes every Day to the *Le-
vées* of great Lords, and is Fool enough
to believe they remember what he fays to
them a quarter of an Hour afterwards.
The other is a foreign Painter, who draws

Women by the Life: He is a great Artist, he paints well, draws correctly, and hits a Likeness extraordinary well, but does not flatter; and yet is so vain as to think he shall be crouded with Business. *Inter Stultos referatur.* How, said the Scholar, you speak *Latin* to a Miracle! Ought you to wonder at that, said the Devil; I speak all Languages in Perfection, even not excepting that of *Athens*, which I speak a hundred times better than a certain Set of Men who at present value themselves on speaking it well, and yet I am neither the greater Fool, nor the vainer for it.

Cast your Eye into that great House on the left Hand, on a melancholy Lady, surrounded by several Women who watch with her. 'Tis the Widow of an Officer of the Treasury, who is over-run with an Affectation of Nobility: She has this Day made her Will, by which she bequeaths her immense Riches wholly to Persons of the first Quality; not that she so much as knows any one of them, but only for the sake of their great Titles. She was ask'd whether she would not leave something to a certain Person who had done her considerable Services: Alas, no, answer'd she, and I am concern'd at it: I

am

am not so ungrateful as not to own that
I have Obligations to him; but he is but
a Yeoman, and his Name would disgrace
my Will.

Signior *Asmodeo,* interrupted, *Don
Cleofas,* I beg you would inform me whether that old Man which I see reading
so hard in a Closet, may not perhaps
deserve to be plac'd here? He deserves
it beyond dispute, answer'd the *Demon.* He
is an old *Licenciado* in Divinity, he is reading a Proof of a Book which he has under
the Press. The Subject must certainly be moral or divine, said the Scholar: No reply'd
the Devil, 'tis a Miscellany of lewd Poems which he has written; instead of burning them, or at least suffering them to die
with their Author, he prints them in his
Life-time, for fear his Heirs should not
be inclin'd to publish them after his Death;
or out of regard to his Character, should
deprive them of all their Salt and Spirit.

In the Neighbourhood of that *Licenci-
ate,* I see one of the best Authors which
you have. He has an excellent Genius;
his Works abound with the *Attick* Salt;
they are sprinkled all over with noble
and shining Thoughts: He does not
want New Turns; his Expressions are
bold, and always happy. Let's pass on to

L 3   his

his Neighbour. 'Tis a Man———Oh, not so fast, precipitately interrupted *Don Cleofas*; you have said nothing but what is excellent of this Author, and yet have shewn him to me amongst the Fools. That is indeed true, reply'd the Devil; I forgot his Fault. When he reads his Performances, he stops at all those Places which seem to him to deserve Applause, to leave his Auditors time to give it him, and withal have the Pleasure himself of tasting all their Excellencies.

Observe in that House on the right, three Persons drinking Chocolate: One of them is a Count which sets up for a Lover of Polite Learning: The other is his Brother, a *Licenciado*; and the third is a Wit, which hangs on 'em. They are always inseparable, and never visit asunder. The Count's sole Business is to praise himself; that of the *Licenciado*, or young Divine, to praise his elder Brother and himself: But the Wit's Business is of a larger Extent, he praises both of 'em, intermixing his own Commendations with theirs.

I was going to pass by a simple Woman, which I discover in a little House. She is so much possess'd with her very little Merit, that she is drawing up a List of

her

her Lovers, in which she inserts all Men in general who ever spoke to her. About two Paces farther I discern a rich Batchelor, tainted with a very particular Folly. He lives frugally, tho' 'tis neither for Mortification, nor Sobriety: But to amass Riches. For what? To distribute in Alms? No. He buys Pictures, rich Furniture, Jewels, China and Bawbles, not to enjoy the use of 'em during his Life, but only to make a Figure in his Inventory. What you tell me is unnatural and forc'd, interrupted *Don Cleofas*. Is there really a Man in the World of this Character? Yes, I tell you, reply'd the Devil, he is one of that sort of Madmen. Does he, for Instance, buy a very fine *Scrutore*; he causes it to be pack'd up neatly, and lock'd up in his Garret, that it may appear perfectly new to the Brokers who shall buy it after his Death. In short, he pleases himself with the Thoughts that the Inventory of his Goods will be admir'd,

With this Batchelor lives an Author, which succeeds very well in a grave way of Writing; and is only fit for what he now does: Yet he believes himself capable of every thing, and will not write Plays, Because, says he, my

L 4   Comedy

Comedy would be too fublime to pleafe
the Pit. If he faid too cool, I fhould take
a fpecial Care how I rank'd fuch a fenfible Man amongft the Fools and Mad-
men.

Should I, *Don Cleofas*, attempt to fhew
you all thofe which deferve to be fhut up,
I fhould never have done. Wherefore, to
vary the Pleafures I intend you, I will
carry you to another Place, and divert
you with different Objects. But before
we quit where we are, I muft hint to
you a certain Author, which I have juft
now found. He is a perfect Mafter of
the *Greek* and *Roman* Authors, from
whom he borrows all the Thoughts which
he puts in his Works; and yet he believes
himfelf to be an Original, and allows none
to be Plagiaries, but thofe who fteal
from *Lope de Vega Carpio*, or *Pedro Cal-
deron*.

CHAP. XII.

The L O V E R S,

I Muſt confeſs, ſays *Cleofas,* the Obſervations you have made are very Inſtructive, but tend to things for which a Man of my Age and Complexion has but little Reliſh. You are to remember 'twas a Love-Adventure brought me into the Honour of your Converſation; and, dear *Cupid,* ſince you preſide over that Paſſion, confine your Diſcourſe to what you are Maſter of. Shew me then the Joys and Anxieties, the Politicks and Follies of Lovers, if you would improve me in a real uſeful Knowledge. I ſhould be ſhy, ſaid the *Demon,* of giving you that Information, for fear of loſing a Votary, did not I know it is an inſeparable Quality in Lovers to ſee and yet indulge their Miſery and Weakneſs, for which Reaſon I am under no Apprehenſion of your growing Wiſer from the Folly of others. But prethee, quoth the Scholar, before you go any further, let me know what that Gentleman is, who is ſtriking Fire at his Tinderbox; do you obſerve

yonder,

yonder, how he appears and vanishes as the Sparks fly about him. That vigilant Person, reply'd *Asmodeo*, is a Lover, who has been this Evening in his Mistress's Company. She, in her Discourse on indifferent Things, began two or three Censures with a customary Phrase of hers, *There are some People in the World.* This he took no notice of at the Time she spoke it; but upon second Thoughts in his own Lodgings, very wisely discover'd that she meant him by that ambiguous Expression. After taking several Turns in his Chamber, he call'd for Pen, Ink and Paper, kick'd his Footman down Stairs, and resolv'd to tell his Mistress plainly he knew whom she aim'd at in her late Reflections. He had not gone thro' the first Line of his Letter, before he was interrupted by a sudden Thought which set all things right again, convinc'd him that his Suspicions were groundless, and that he was still in her good Graces. He immediately grew the most satisfy'd Man in the World, went to Bed in the Height of good Humour, gave his Man a Crown, and bid him good Night. What Disaster, says *Cleofas*, can have befall'n him since? He seems to blow his Tinder in an unusual hurry; how his Cheeks swell, and his

Eyes

Eyes glare! 'Tis the moſt dreadful Night-piece I ever ſaw. You muſt know, ſays the *Dæmon*, he had compos'd himſelf with great Tranquillity for half an Hour, and was juſt falling aſleep, when he ſtartled on a ſudden, and bethought himſelf *if ſhe did not mean him, whom could ſhe mean.* This threw him into ſo great a Ferment, that he jump'd out of his Bed, with a Reſolution to do ſomething which yet neither he nor I know any thing of. I heartily pity the poor Fellow, ſaid *Cleofas*, for I find he loves in earneſt. Had he not, reply'd the *Dæmon*, ſhe had been his own before now; but 'tis the Frailty of that weak Sex to prefer an acted Paſſion to a real one. That is a Frailty, ſays the Scholar, into which they may naturally fall. A perſonated Lover can aſſume all the Graces, and avoid all the Imperfections of the Paſſion. Diſquietudes, Jealouſies and Expoſtulations always accompany, but very ill recommend a Heart throughly enamour'd. But look, the Man has lighted his Candle, and blown it out again. Ay, ſays the *Dæmon*, he was quieted the very Moment he had litt it, by calling to mind that he had one Day heard his Miſtreſs ſay, Nothing was ſo graceful in a Man as an high Forehead,

head, which you may obferve he has, to the apparent Detriment of his Chin, Cheeks and Eyes. On how flight a Foundation is rais'd the good and evil of Lovers! cry'd *Cleofas*. Perhaps fhe who creates all this Diforder is in perfect Tranquillity. That you fhall fee immediately, faid *Afmodeo:* Caft your Eyes on the great Houfe in the Corner of the fame Street; does not a Watch-light difcover to you a Lady lying half out of her Bed, and talking to a Servant, who fits by her fide? You are to underftand, by the way, that the Woman of a Lady in Love never goes to Bed 'till four in the Morning. As foon as fhe has undrefs'd her, and laid her on her Pillow, her Bufinefs of putting her to Reft is but begun; for fhe is then to fit down by her, hear her Sentiments of the humble Servant, and confute all her Sufpions of his Infidelity or want of Love; and by that time the good Lady is ten times throughly convinc'd, and her Maid as often perjur'd, in hopes to be difmifs'd, the Story is to begin again. The prefent Anguifh of our wakeful Veftal is occafion'd by a merry Tale that the Gentleman in his Shirt told her in their laft Converfation; which diverted her fo much that fhe is afraid he has not Grief at Heart, who could talk with fo much

Hu-

Humour: This gives her a thousand Fears,
that he has broke his Fetters; but she
now receives Comfort, the Wench having almost perfuaded her that the Perfon
for whom her Ladyfhip has fo much Tendernefs went away in very great Diforder,
and in all probability is at this Moment
upon the Rack.

I know, by Experience, fays the Scholar, there is nothing fo difagreeable to one
in her Ladyfhip's Condition as a State of
Indifference; your true Lover muft be
always giving either Pleasure or Pain.
But who is that pretty Creature fighing
before her Glafs at this time of Night?
Why does she bite her Lips, glance her
Eyes, and examine her Face in fo many
different Views? You know, faid *Afmodeo*, the Cuftom among you young Fellows, of publifhing a Lift every Winter
of the Beauties who are to be the Ty-
rants of the Year, and have their Healths
drank by Crouds of fecond-hand Lovers,
that never faw 'em, but are to be enamour'd by Hearfay, and die for 'em becaufe 'tis the Fafhion. The Lady before
us, after a Reign of three Years, was left
out in Yefterday's Nomination, which is
the Subject of her prefent Contemplati-
on; wherein she appeals to her Glafs,
from

from the Injuftice of the Electors. To be reveng'd on the Town, fometimes fhe is refolv'd to marry a faithful Lover fhe has long laugh'd at, and fpend the Remainder of her Life in Devotion; but upon furveying her felf more narrowly, fhe finds things are not come to that Extremity, and now intends to drefs, and try the Fortune of her Features in all publick Places for one Year more, in order to revive her Pretenfions againft the next Election. But we muft not dwell fo long on Particulars, if you would have an Idea of the Extent of my Command; you fee my Followers in every Quarter of the City.

Yonder's a young Lady getting out of a Window, to run away with her Father's Footman; and at that Corner is a Lord attending with a Coach and Six, to fteal a Manteau-maker's Journey-woman. The Gentleman you fee in the Porch has made an Affignation to meet his Miftrefs in that Place to Morrow Morning at feven, and in order to it took his Station there at ten laft Night. Excufe Interruption, faid the Scholar; pray tell me the Circumftances of the Perfon yonder that lyes on his Back with his Hands lifted up, and his Head erected, like a Figure on a
Tomb;

Tomb; he seems falling asleep in an Act of Devotion. 'Tis the only Person I have seen well-employ'd; he is taken up much better than in these Vanities. Nothing less, answer'd the *Demon*; he lyes motionless, as you see, that a Plate of Black-Lead on his Forehead may have its due Effect in preserving it smooth. His Hands are ty'd up, that they may be white in the Morning, and his Waste brac'd in with an Iron-Bodice, to preserve his Shape. In this extraordinary Posture he is calling upon cruel *Belinda,* and amidst a thousand cutting Reflections on the ill Success of his Passion, it is no small Mortification to him, that by the Itching of the left Side of his Nose, he finds he shall have a Pimple there before Morning.

But pray tell me, says *Cleofas,* the History of that studious Gentleman that stands in his Night-gown looking upon his Candle. He rubs his Head, as if it teem'd with some extraordinary Project. Hah! my old Friend *Leandro,* says the *Demon,* are you there? This Gentleman, says he, turning to *Cleofas,* about fifteen Years ago, fell in Love with a young Widow, who did not discourage his Addresses. He's a good-natur'd sensible Fellow, and fond to Death of his fair Idol, but

but at the same time so over-run with
Modesty that he can't find Courage enough
to reveal his Passion, and ask her Consent. She has given him a thousand Opportunities of breaking it to her, and he
has made as many Resolutions of doing
it the next time he sees her, but they are
no sooner left together, but he falls into
Confusions and Palpations, looks like an
Ass, and wishes somebody would come
into the Room to disembarrass him, and
spoil an Opportunity that perhaps he has
long'd for several Months before. She
took him Yesterday into the Fields. The
Lover, who would have given half his
Estate for so favourable an Occasion, fell
a praising the Prospect, and after a great
many Efforts to enter on the Grand Affair, resolv'd to put it off to another
time. His Passion began in the Year 1692,
and in 1695 was in a fair way, had he
press'd it; ever since that time he has
been endeavouring to communicate his
Heart, but it fails him, and 'tis very probable he may be pass'd the Functions of
Love before he has Courage enough to
make it. This would have been a rare
Fellow to have made Love before the
Deluge, says *Cleofas*; a Man might then
have languish'd an hundred Years for a
Girl,

Girl, and afterwards, upon her Difdain, have had two or three Centuries of Youth to rake in; but at prefent, Courtfhip, Marriage, and Confummation are drawn into a Span. We muft huddle up our Amours as foon as poffible, if we intend to tafte the Sweets of 'em. But, faid *Afmodeo*, commend me to that bufie Gentleman whom you fee writing in a penfive Pofture. He is a paffionate Lover, that is, an angry one: An honeft Soul, that fhews his Sincerity to his Miftrefs, by never difguifing his Refentments. This Morning he took the innocent Freedom of fhaking her by the Shoulder, and calling her a dirty Baggage; upon which, after having deliberated whether he ought to hang himfelf, or beg her Pardon, he has juft now finifh'd a penitential Letter to her, wherein he fubfcribes himfelf the Vileft of Men, and moft miferable of Lovers.

Unhappy Wretch! let him go fleep, if he can, faid the Scholar; but I grow fick with looking upon Fools fo like my felf. You'd oblige me more if you'd fhow me the Weaknefs of the Enemy, and let me fee, that with all thefe Difadvantages, we are equal to the Sex we have to deal with. There is hardly one of them, faid the Devil, who do's not deftroy, by her Infolence, the Paffion fhe raifes by her Beauty.

Yonder's a Wife on her Bed faft afleep, that has given Orders to her Maid not to

M   let

let in her Husband, 'till fhe has call'd her up
to rattle him for making her fit up fo late:
In that Tavern you may fee the good Man
calling for another Bottle, becaufe he's afraid
of going home at fo ill an Hour. There's a
Merchant's Heirefs who languifh'd for the
Honour of being Noble, and is tranfported with the Pleafure of taking Place of
her old Acquaintance all Day, tho' every
Night fhe is kick'd out of Bed by her Lord
for being born a Citt, and paying his
Debts. A little farther you may fee a private Gentleman that's marry'd to a Dutchefs,
but divorc'd for a Fortnight for offering to
lay Hands on her Grace's Linnen, without
mentioning her Title.

There's a Gaming Lady juft come home
from lofing 500 *l.* at *Ombre*; fhe can't go
to Bed 'till her Maid has brought her a
Pack of Cards, and wakes her Husband to
fhew him how fhe loft the laft Game; then
falls into a Paffion, goes raving to Bed,
and rails at the good Man all Night for
not getting a Place at Court.

If you had as good Ears as I, you
would hear that Lady, who frisks to and
fro in her Apartment with fo much Uneafinefs, cry Coxcomb, Fop, Clown, No-
vice, at every little Stop fhe makes in her
Walk. Her Mifery is, that according to
Form, fhe told a plain Fellow with a good
Eftate, who propos'd himfelf to her, fhe
wonder'd

wonder'd he could make her fuch an Offer, and folemnly protefted fhe could never like him: The Swain believ'd her, and is gone to his Country Seat; upon which fhe is now cafting about, by what means to explain to the Ruftick the Nature of Gallantry, and make him underftand, that a Man's Profeffion of Love, and a Woman's Refufal, in this refin'd Age, are equally meer Words.

But I obferve a Lady, who of all I have feen, faid *Cleofas,* touches me with the greateft Compaffion; her ftreaming Eyes, and difhevel'd Hair, fpeak a perfect *Magdalen*: What can be her Diftrefs? who could be fo barbarous to a Creature made up of fo much Softnefs? That difconfolate Dame, quoth *Afmodeo,* was three Hours ago one of the greateft Coquets in *Madrid,* and is breaking her Heart too late for want of knowing it time enough. She had long lov'd a Gentleman of Merit, but play'd with his Paffion and her own by fo many repeated Slights, that he grew tir'd of the Chafe, and Yefterday difpos'd of himfelf to another. 'Tis for this Reafon that fhe abandons her felf this Night to Prayer and Harts-Horn, and intends to Morrow to fhut her felf up in a Nunnery for ever. It would be endlefs to fhow you the Vanities of the Sex; their Thoughts, Words and Actions, tend only to Show and Oftentation, for which they facrifice their Liberty, and all the Pleafures

M 2 of

of Life. Look at the fumptuous Apartment in that Palace, and the wrought Bed
which reaches up to the Roof of it: Don't
you fee in it an old Man juft fallen afleep,
and by his Side a beautiful young Lady
looking at a Picture in Miniature. The
Avarice of her Mother tore her from
the young Gallant, whofe Figure fhe is
contemplating, to bury her in the Embrace
of one fhe loaths. And now all the Hopes
fhe has left is, to lay her old Man in his
Winding-Sheet, and one Day or other come
into the Arms of her firft Love. At the
next Houfe is a more diverting Sight: The
Brute who ftaggers into that Chamber is
reeling to the Bed of that delicate Creature, whom her prudent Parent proftitu-
ted to his Embraces. The beaftly Sot was
Rival to one of a very agreeable Character; their Fortunes were equal, but I
dare fay you'll laugh at the Merit which
preferr'd this Worthy to the Choice of the
provident Mother. You muft know he
had a Pidgeon-Houfe upon his Eftate,
which the other wanted. This turn'd the
Ballance in his Favour, and determin'd
the Fate of that unfortunate Lady. If you
can fhow us only unhappy Effects of this
Paffion, faid *Cleofas*, I muft defire you'd
entertain me with another Set of Objects.
Don't be difcourag'd, anfwer'd the *Demon*, at the Profpects I have laid before
you.

you. There are in Nature pleasing A-
mours and happy Marriages, but these are
not to be look'd for in *Madrid*.   To give
you a Sight of happy Pairs, I should transport you to Solitudes and Retirements,
where Love is a Stranger to Art and Gallantry, and lives amidst its own natural
Sweets, Complacency, mutual Esteem,
and eternal Constancy; without being diverted by the false Appearances, which
under the Colour of advancing its Enjoyments, vitiate the true Relish of 'em. 'Tis
when we Spirits behold Mortals in this
Condition, that we suffer our greatest Pangs
of Envy, and wish for Flesh and Blood, to
taste the Gratifications bestow'd upon 'em.

Of the Tombs.

ASmodeo, resolv'd to shew *Don Cleofas*
some new things, carry'd him to a-
nother Part of the City, and they fix'd
on a lofty Church fill'd with magnificent
Tombs.   Let's here continue the Thred
of our Observation, said the Devil; and
before we pursue our Reflections on the
Living, let's for a few Moments disturb
the Repose of the Dead bury'd in this
Church.   Let's run thro' these Sepulchers,
detect what they conceal, and see wherefore they were erected.

The first of those eight Tombs, which
you

you fee on the right Hand, contains the
Corps of a young Lover, who dy'd with
Grief for not being able to carry the Prize at
the Ring. In the fecond is a Mifer, that
ftarv'd himfelf with Hunger; and in the
third his Heir, who two Years after dy'd
with exceffive Eating and Drinking. In
the fourth lyes a Father, which could not
furvive the Rape of his only Daughter. In
the next is a young Man, who threw himfelf into a Pleurifie by taking cooling Phy-
fick. In that beyond him, are contain'd
the fad Remains of an Officer, which after
having faithfully ferv'd his Country, like
another *Agamemnon*, at his Return from
the Army found an *Ægifthus* in his Houfe.
The feventh covers an old Maiden Lady
of Quality, ugly and poor, whom Grief and
Envy confum'd; and in the laft refts the
Wife of an Officer of the Treafury, who
dy'd with Difguft for being oblig'd, in a
narrow Street, to turn her Coach to make
way for that of a Dutchefs.

Who are they, faid the Scholar, in thofe
five Tombs on the left Hand? I'll tell you,
anfwer'd the Devil: One of them contains
the ridiculous Conjunction of an old Huf-
band, and a young Wife. The Husband,
when he marry'd her, had Children by a
former Venture, and was juft ready to have
fign'd their Ruin, when an Apoplexy carry'd him off; and their Mother-in-Law,
four

four and twenty Hours after, dy'd with Vexation, that he did not die two Days later. In the next lyes an old Canon, too foon hurry'd out of the World by making his Will when in perfect Health, and reading it to his Domefticks, to whom, like a good-natur'd Mafter, he had bequeath'd feveral Legacies: His Cook, too impatient to ftay for his, foon difpatch'd him. Beyond this imprudent Canon lyes a beautiful Lady, facrific'd to the Sufpicions of her jealous Husband. In the fourth is a Bigot, who loft his Life by walking in his Garden half an Hour without an Umbrella; and in the laft is a devout Lady, that dy'd of the exceffive Ufe of Phlebotomy, by way of Precaution.

In the midft of all thefe ftately Tombs, faid the Devil, there are feveral Perfons very plainly interr'd, and amongft the reft a *German*, who dy'd by drinking three Healths with Tobacco in his Glafs, in a Debauch; a *Frenchman* which loft his Life for prefenting (according to the Civility of his Nation) a Lady with Holy Water at her Entrance into the Church, as he was going out of it. There lyes a Player, that by flow Degrees confum'd himfelf in envying thofe of his Comerades, who kept their Coaches, whilft he was oblig'd to go a-foot. There is an Actrefs, which over-heating her felf, in playing the Part of a Veftal-Virgin,

mif-

mifcarry'd, and dy'd of it behind the Scenes; and next to her is interr'd a Dramatick Author, who fuddenly dy'd of Envy, at the Pits clapping one of his Friend's Plays the firft Day.

Signior *Afmodeo*, faid the Scholar here, pardon me if I interrupt you to ask the Reafon of thofe piercing Cries which deaffen my Ears. They proceed, anfwer'd the Devil, from that fine Houfe on the left Hand; where this very Moment is acting one of the moft melancholy Scenes that ever was reprefented on the Theatre of the World: Fix your Eyes on that deplorable Spectacle. Ah, why, reply'd *Don Cleofas*, does that Lady which tears her Hair, and ftruggles in the Woman's Arms, appear fo afflicted? Look in the oppofite Apartment, return'd *Afmodeo*, and you will fee the Caufe. Obferve that Man laid out on that ftately Bed; 'tis her Husband, he is juft dead, and fhe is inconfolable. Their Story is very moving, and deferves to be written; I have a great Mind to tell it you: You will oblige me, faid the Scholar; I am not lefs fenfible of Objects of Compaffion, than diverted by thofe of Ridicule. 'Tis fomewhat long, reply'd the Devil, but too moving to be tirefome. He then began the Relation in thefe Terms.

C H A P.

CHAP. XIII.

Of the Power of Friendſhip.

A STORY.

A Young Gentleman of *Toledo,* accompany'd by his *Valet de Chambre,* travell'd ſeveral long Days Journies from his native Country, to avoid the Conſequences of a tragical Adventure. He was two little Leagues from *Valencia,* when at the Entry of a Wood he met a Lady deſcending haſtily out of her Coach. No Vail cover'd her Face, in which Beauty ſhone in Perfeċtion. This charming Lady ſeem'd ſo diſturb'd and diſtraċted, that the Cavalier, concluding ſhe wanted Aſſiſtance, did not fail to tender her that of his Courage. Generous Unknown, ſaid the Lady, I won't refuſe your Offer; Heav'n ſeems to have ſent you hither to my Aſſiſtance, and to avert the Misfortune which I dread. Two Gentlemen are met upon an Appointment in this Wood; I this Minute ſaw them enter; I can tell you no more; but, if you pleaſe, follow me, and you ſhall know the whole. At the end of theſe Words ſhe flew into the Wood, and the *Toledan,* after leaving the Care of his Horſe

N   to

to his Man, made after her as faſt as he
could.

They had ſcarce advanc'd an hundred
Paces before they heard the claſhing of
Swords, and ſoon diſcover'd two Men fu-
riouſly engag'd. The *Toledan* ran to part
them, which having done, partly by Force
and partly by Entreaty, he ask'd them the
Cauſe of their Quarrel. Brave Unknown,
ſaid one of the two Cavaliers, my Name
is *Don Fadrique de Mendoça,* and my Ad-
verſary is *Don Alvaro Ponce:* We both
love *Donna Theodora,* the Lady which you
accompany: She has always ſlighted our
Addreſſes, and notwithſtanding all the
Tenderneſſes that Love could ſuggeſt to
pleaſe her, the obdurate Fair would never
treat us better. As for me, I deſign'd to
continue her Slave in ſpight of her Indifference; but my Rival, inſtead of taking the
ſame Reſolution, ſent me a Challenge.
'Tis true, interrupted *Don Alvaro;* I concluded that if I had no Rival, *Donna Theodora* might look on me; wherefore I endeavour'd to take away the Life of *Don
Fadrique,* to rid my ſelf of a Man that oppos'd my Felicity. Gentlemen, then ſaid
the *Toledan,* I don't approve your Duelling; 'tis an Affront to *Donna Theodora:*
'Twill ſoon be publiſh'd in *Valencia* that
you have fought for her; and your Miſtreſs's

ftrefs's Honour ought to be dearer to you
than your own Repofe and Lives. Befides, what Advantage could the Vanqui-
fher reap by his Victory? After having ex-
pos'd his Miftrefs's Reputation, could he
expect fhe would look on him with a favourable Eye? Ridiculous Stupidity! Take
my Advice, make a more noble Effort on
your felves, more worthy the Names that
you bear : Conquer thefe furious Tranfports, and by an inviolable Oath engage
your felves to fubfcribe the Articles of Accommodation which I fhall propofe to you.
Your Quarrel fhall end without Bloodfhed.
Hah! how? faid *Don Alvaro.* This Lady muft declare, reply'd the *Toledan,*
whether fhe will chufe *Don Fadrique* or
you, and the unhappy Lover, far from
arming againft his Rival, muft leave him
the Field. I confent, faid *Don Alvaro,*
and fwear by all that is moft facred to ac-
quiefce in her Choice, whether fhe determine in Favour of me or my Rival; for
even that Preference will be more fupporta-
ble than the miferable Uncertainty under
which I now labour. And as for me, faid
Don Fadrique in his Turn, I call Heav'n
to Witnefs, that if the Divine Object
which I adore does not pronounce in my
Favour, I will remove my felf far diftant

from

from her Charms, and if I cannot forget
her, at leaſt will never ſee her more.

The *Toledan* then turning towards *Theodora*, Madam, ſaid he, 'tis your part to
ſpeak; 'tis in your Power with one Word
to diſarm theſe two Rivals; you need only declare him whoſe Conſtancy you pleaſe
to reward. Sir, anſwer'd the Lady, ſearch
for another Expedient to reconcile them:
Why ſhould I be the Sacrifice of their A-
greement? I really value *Don Fadrique* and
Don Alvaro, but I don't love either of
them; and it is unjuſt that to prevent the
Stain which their Duelling might caſt upon my Honour, I ſhould be oblig'd to give
thoſe Hopes which my Heart will never
own. 'Tis too late to diſſemble, Madam,
reply'd the *Toledan*; you muſt declare your
ſelf. Both theſe Cavaliers are equally
handſom, and I am certain you have more
Inclination for one than the other. I re-
fer my ſelf to the mortal Agony in which
I ſaw you. You miſ-interpret that Fright,
reply'd *Donna Theodora*; the Loſs of either of theſe Gentlemen would very ſenſibly touch me, and I ſhould never give o-
ver blaming my ſelf on that account, tho'
I am only the innocent Cauſe; but if you
ſaw me alarm'd, 'twas only to the Danger
which threaten'd my Reputation that any
Fear was owing.

D

Don Alvaro Ponce, who was naturally very fierce, at these Words lost all Patience: 'Tis enough, said he very warmly; since the Lady refuses to end this Dispute amicably, the Sword shall immediately decide it; upon which he aim'd a Pass at *Don Fadrique,* who was prepar'd to receiv'd it. The Lady, rather affrighted by this Action, than determin'd by her Inclination, amaz'd cry'd out: Hold, Gentlemen, I will satisfie you; if there be no other way to end an Engagement in which my Honour is concern'd, I declare that I give the Preference to *Don Fadrique de Mendoça.*

She had no sooner ended these Words, than the discarded *Ponce,* without uttering one Syllable, immediately loosen'd his Horse which was fasten'd to a Tree, and retir'd, casting very angry Looks at his Rival and Mistress. The happy *Mendoça,* on the contrary, was o'erwhelm'd with Joy; sometimes he fell on his Knees before *Donna Theodora,* at others he embrac'd the *Toledan,* and was utterly at a Loss for Expressions strong enough to represent the Sentiments of Gratitude with which he was throughly touch'd. In the mean time the Lady returning to her natural Temper, after the Departure of *Alvaro,* began to reflect how anxious it would prove to her

to

to suffer the Addresses of a Lover, whose
Merit tho' she really valu'd, yet withal for
whom her Heart had never been prepossess'd with any the least Tenderness. *Don
Fadrique*, said she, I hope you won't abuse
the Preference which I have given you;
you owe it to the Necessity to which I was
reduc'd, to declare betwixt you and *Don
Alvaro*. My Sentence is not owing to my
valuing you much more than him, tho' I
know very well he has not all the good
Qualities which you have, and I shall but
do you Justice by saying that you are the
most compleat Gentleman in *Valencia*. I
will farther own to you, that the Addresses of such a Man as you might very well
flatter a Woman's Vanity; but how honourable soever it may be to me, I must
tell you, I look upon them with so little
Relish, that you are really to be pity'd for
loving me so tenderly as you appear to do.
I will not yet deprive you of all Hopes of
touching my Heart: My Indifference, perhaps, may be only the Effect of the yet re-
maining Grief which seiz'd me a Year
since for the Loss of *Don Andrea de Cifuentes*, my Husband. Tho' we did not live
long together, and he was of an advanc'd
Age, when my Parents, dazled with his
Riches, oblig'd me to marry him, yet was
I very much afflicted at his Death. I shall
                                    bemoan

bemoan it all my Life; and indeed did he
not deserve my Sorrow? He was not like
those four and jealous old Men, which never being able to persuade themselves that
a Woman may be discreet enough, to excuse their Weakness, continually watch all
her Motions, or entrust that Charge to a
Duenna devoted to their Tyranny. Alas,
he had such an entire Confidence in my
Virtue, as even a young Husband, tho'
ador'd, is scarce capable of. Besides, his
Complaisance was endless; I dare venture
to say, that his sole Care was to prevent
me in all things which I seem'd to desire:
Such was *Don Andrea de Cifuentes*; you
may then, *Mendoça*, easily judge, that 'tis
not easie to forget a Man of such an agreeable Character. He is always present in
my Thoughts, which does not a little contribute, doubtless, to turn them from fixing
on whatever is done to please me.

Don Fadrique could not help interrupting *Donna Theodora* here. Ah! Madam, cry'd he, how happy am I to learn
from your own Mouth, that your former
despising my Addresses did not result
from any Aversion to my Person. I hope
that you will one Day yield to my Constancy. 'Twill not be my Fault if your
Passion does not succeed, reply'd the Lady,
since I allow you to visit me, and some-
N 4 times

times mention your Love. Endeavour to
make me relifh your Endearments; ufe all
your Arts to make me love you. I will
never conceal from you any favourable
Sentiments which I may have for you; but
if, after all your Efforts, you can't compafs your End, remember, *Mendoça*, that
you will have no reafon to blame me.
Don Fadrique would have reply'd, but had
not time, by reafon the Lady took the
Toledan by the Hand, and nimbly turn'd
towards her Equipage. He loofen'd his
Horfe, which was ty'd to a Tree, and lead-
ing him by the Bridle, follow'd *Donna
Theodora*, who mounted her Chariot with
as much Precipitation as fhe had before
defcended from it, tho' the Reafon was
utterly different. The *Toledan* and he accompany'd her on Horfe-back to the Gates
of *Valencia*, where they parted. She went
to her own Houfe, and *Don Fadrique* carry'd the *Toledan* to his.

He made him fit down, and after having very well entertain'd him, he ask'd
him what particularly brought him to *Valencia*, and whether he thought of making
a long Stay there. I fhall continue here as
little while as poffible, anfwer'd the *Toledan*; I came this way only to go towards
the Sea-fide, to embark in the very firft
Veffel which fails from the Coaft of *Spain*,
for

for I care not much in what Part of the World I finish the Course of an unfortunate Life, provided it be far distant from these fatal Climates. What do you tell me, reply'd *Don Fadrique* surpriz'd, what can have turn'd you against your Country, and made you hate what all Men naturally love? After what has happen'd, return'd the *Toledan*, my Country is odious to me, and I aim at nothing in the World but to quit it for ever. Ah, Sir, said *Mendoça*, touch'd with compassionate Concern, how impatient I am to know your Misfortunes? If I can't relieve your Pains I will share them with you. The Air of your Face has prepossess'd me in your Favour; your Deportment charms me, and I find my self strenuously interested in your Fortune.

'Tis the greatest Consolation which I am capable of receiving, *Don Fadrique*, answer'd the *Toledan*; and in some measure to acknowledge the Affection which you have discover'd for me, I must also tell you, that when I saw you with *Don Alvaro Ponce*, my Inclinations declar'd on your side. An internal Motion, which I was never before sensible of at the first sight of any Person, made me fear lest *Donna Theodora* should prefer your Rival, and I was touch'd with Joy when she determin'd
in

in your Favour. You have fince fo much ftrengthen'd that firft Impreffion, that inftead of hiding my Uneafineffes I earneftly defire to lay them before, and find a fecret Pleafure in the unbofoming my felf to you. Hearken then to the Relation of my Misfortunes.

Toledo is my native Place, and *Don Juan de Zarate* my Name; almoft from my Infancy I have loft thofe which gave Life, fo that I began betimes to enjoy an Annual Eftate of four thoufand Ducats, which they left me. My Heart being at my own Difpofal, and believing my felf rich enough not to confult any thing but my own Inclination in the Choice of a Wife, I married a Virgin perfectly beautiful, without delaying on account of the Meannefs of her Fortune, or the Inequality of our Conditions. I was charm'd with my Felicity; and to give the greater Relifh to the Pleafure of poffeffing the Perfon which I lov'd, a few Days after my Marriage, I carry'd her to an Eftate which I have fome Leagues from *Toledo*.

We liv'd there in a charming Union, when the Duke of *Naxera*, whofe Seat is near my Eftate, came one Day, when he was hunting, to refrefh himfelf at my Houfe. He faw my Wife and fell in Love with her: I fufpected it at leaft; but what fully convinc'd

vinc'd me of it, was, that he immediately
made the moſt preſſing Inſtances in the
World to obtain my Friendſhip, which he
never before ſet any Value on. He introduc'd me to his hunting Acquaintance,
forc'd me to accept of ſeveral Preſents,
and made me ſeveral Offers of his Service.
Being immediately alarm'd by his Paſſion,
I intended to return to *Toledo* with my
Wife ; and doubtleſs that Thought was
inſpir'd by Heav'n: For had I wholly depriv'd the Duke of all Opportunities of
ſeeing her, I ſhould have avoided thoſe
Misfortunes which have fall'n on me ; but
my confident Reliance on her Virtue ſe-
cur'd me. I thought it impoſſible for a
Woman which I marry'd without a Fortune, and rais'd from a low Condition,
to be ſo ungrateful as to forget my Favours. Alas, what a wrong Judgment did
I make! Ambition and Vanity, thoſe two
Vices natural to the Sex, were her greateſt
Faults.

As ſoon as the Duke got an Opportunity to diſcover his Sentiments, ſhe was
ſecretly pleas'd at ſuch an important Con-
queſt. The Paſſion of a Man adorn'd with
the Title of his Excellence, tickled her
Pride, and fill'd her Mind with extravagant Chimera's: Whence ſhe began to value him more and me leſs ; and all that I
had

had done for her, inftead of exciting her Gratitude, ferv'd only to render me contemptible in her Eyes. She look'd on me as a Husband unworthy of her Beauty, and fancy'd that if this Grandee, who was now conquer'd by her Charms, had feen her before her being a Wife, he had certainly marry'd her. Intoxicated by thefe foolifh Imaginations, and feduc'd by feveral engaging Prefents, fhe yielded to the Duke's private and prefling Importunities.

They frequently wrote to each other, without my ever fufpecting their Correfpondence; but at laft I was unhappy enough to be cur'd of that Blindnefs. One Day returning from hunting fooner than ufual, I went into my Wife's Apartment, who did not expect me fo foon. She had juft receiv'd a Billet from the Duke, which fhe was preparing to anfwer. She could not hide her Uneafinefs from me. I trembled, and finding Pen, Ink and Paper ready on a Table, I concluded fhe had betray'd me. I prefs'd her to fhew me what fhe was writing; which fhe fo abfolutely deny'd, that I was oblig'd to ufe fome Violence to fatisfie my jealous Curiofity; and notwithftanding all her Refiftance, I tore from her Bofom a Letter containing thefe Words: *Shall I for ever languifh in expectation of a*
fecond

second Interview ? How cruel are you, to give me the most charming Hopes, and thus long delay the fulfilling them ! Don Juan *goes every Day a hunting, or to* Toledo ; *should we not make use of these Opportunities ? Have more regard to the violent Flames which consume me. Pity me, Madam; consider that if it be a Pleasure to obtain our Desires, 'tis a Torment to wait long for the Enjoyment of 'em.*

I could not read out this Letter without t'ᵉ utmost Transports of Rage. I clapp'd my Hand on my Dagger, and at first was tempted to take the Life of that faithless Wife who had depriv'd me of my Honour; but considering that would be only to revenge my self by halves, and that my Resentment requir'd yet another Victim, I conquer'd my Rage, dissembled, and said to my Wife, with the least disturbance possible; Madam, you were to blame to hearken to the Duke; the Lustre of his high Quality ought not to have dazled your Eyes ; but young Women are fond of pompous Titles; I am willing to believe that this is all you've yet proceeded to, and that you have not yet done me the last Injury ; wherefore I excuse your Indiscretion, provided you will return to your Duty, and becoming throughly sensible of my Tenderness, you will think of nothing
more

more than to deferve it. After thefe
Words I retir'd to my Apartment, as
well to leave her to recover her felf, as becaufe I wanted fome Retirement to cool
my Rage, which had fufficiently enflam'd
me. If I could not recover my Temper,
I at leaft put on a very eafie Air for two
Days; and on the third pretending Bufinefs of the laft Confequence to *Toledo*, I
told my Wife, that I was oblig'd to leave
her for fome time, and entreated her
to take care of her Honour during my Abfence.

I left her, but inftead of going to *Toledo*, I privately return'd home at the beginning of the Night, and conceal'd my felf
in the Chamber of a faithful Domeftick,
where I could fee whoever enter'd my
Houfe. I did not doubt the Duke's being
inform'd of my Departure, and concluded
he would not mifs the Opportunity. I hop'd
to furprize them together, and promis'd
my felf an entire Vengeance ; but I was
deceiv'd in my Expectation: For inftead
of finding my Houfe preparing for the Re-
ception of a Lover, I faw on the contrary
the Doors very clofe fhut at their time;
and three Days paffing without the Appearance of the Duke, or even any of his
Servants, I perfuaded my felf that my
Spoufe repented her Fault, and broke off all
                                    manner

manner of Communication with the Duke.

Prepossess'd with this Opinion, I lost all desire of Revenge, and yielding to the Motions of a Love, which angry Resentment had suspended, I flew to my Wife's Apartment, embrac'd her with transporting Raptures, and said, Madam, I restore you all my Esteem and Tenderness. I have not been at *Toledo:* I pretended that Journey only to try you. You ought to pardon a Snare laid by a Husband, whose Jealousie was not groundless. I fear'd that your Mind, seduc'd by splendid Illusions, was not capable of undeceiving it self: But, thanks to Heav'n, you are sensible of your Error, and, I hope, nothing for the future will ever disturb our good Agreement.

My Wife seem'd touch'd at these Words; and letting fall some Tears, How unhappy am I, said she, to have given you Reason to suspect my Virtue! Tho' I have to the last Degree abhorr'd that Fault which so justly irritated you against me, my Eyes have in vain kept from closing these two Days to make way for my Tears; yet for all my Grief, and all my Remorse, I shall never regain your intire Confidence in me. I restore it you, Madam, said I, perfectly softned by the Sorrow which she express'd;

I

I will no more remember what is paſt, ſince you ſo ſincerely repent. According-ly from that very Moment I had the ſame Regard for her as before, and began again to taſte thoſe Pleaſures which had been ſo cruelly interrupted. The Reliſh of them was heighten'd; for my Wife, as tho' ſhe reſolv'd to efface out of my Mind all the Marks of the Injury ſhe had done me, was much more ſollicitous to pleaſe me than ever. I found her Careſſes more tender, and al-moſt rejoyc'd at the Diſcontent which had occaſion'd this happy Change.

I then fell ill, and tho' my Diſeaſe was not dangerous, 'tis not to be imagin'd what Fears my Wife diſcover'd. She ſtaid all Day with me, and in the Night, I being in a ſeparate Apartment, ſhe conſtantly came two or three Times to ſatisfie her ſelf how I was. She ſeem'd extreamly ſol-licitous to prevent all the Aſſiſtance I wan-ted, and her Life ſeem'd to be inſeparable from mine. On my ſide, I was ſo ſenſible of all the Marks of Tenderneſs which ſhe gave me, that I could not help teſtifying my Acknowledgement of them to her; and yet, *Mendoça,* they were not ſo ſincere as I imagin'd.

One Night, when I began to recover, my *Valet de Chambre* wak'd me: My Lord, ſaid he, very much confus'd, I am ſorry I am oblig'd to difturb your Repofe; but am too faithful to conceal what is now acting in your Houfe. The Duke of *Naxera* is with my Lady. I was fo ftupify'd at this News, that for fome time I look'd on the Fellow, without being able to fpeak. The more I thought of what he told me, the lefs I believ'd it. No, *Fabio*, cry'd I, 'tis impoffible that my Wife fhould be guilty of fuch a horrid perfidious Crime! You are not fure of what you fay. My Lord, reply'd *Fabio*, would to God 'twas poffible for me to doubt of it ; but I am not deceiv'd by falfe Appearances. Ever fince your Indifpofition, I have fufpected the Duke's being every Night introduc'd into my Lady's Apartment. I hid my felf to remove my Sufpicions, and am but too well convinc'd that they are juft.

At thefe Words, I rofe diftracted with Rage; took my Night-Gown and Sword, and made directly to my Wife's Apartment, accompany'd by *Fabio*, who lighted me.

At the Noife of our Entrance, the Duke which was fate on the Bed, rofe, and catching a Piftol from his Girdle fir'd at me ; but with fuch great Confufion and Precipitation, that he mifs'd me. I then violently rufh'd upon him, and run him into the Heart; after which I addrefs'd my felf to my Wife, who was rather dead than a-

O   live :

live: And thou, said I, infamous Wretch
receive the Reward of all thy Falshoods.
At these Words I plung'd my Sword, yet
reaking with her Lover's Blood, into her
Breast. I condemn my Passion, *Don Fadrique*, and own I might have sufficiently
punish'd a perfidious Wife, without taking
away her Life; but what Man could keep
his Reason intire in such a Conjuncture?
Paint to your self all the Demonstrations
of tender Love which this false Woman
made; represent all the Circumstances,
the Enormity of the Treason, and judge
whether a Husband, fir'd by a just Rage,
ought not to be pardon'd her Death.

To conclude so tragical a Story in two
Words; after having fully satiated my Vengeance, I dress'd my self with utmost haste,
concluding that I had no time to lose, that
the Duke's Relations would hunt for me all
over *Spain*, and that the Interest of my
Family not being sufficient to balance that
of theirs, I should never be safe 'till gotten
into a Foreign Country: Wherefore I se-
lected two of my best Horses, and with all the
Mony and Jewels I had, left my House before Day, follow'd by the Servant which
has so well approv'd his Fidelity. I chose
the Road to *Valencia*, designing to put my
self on Board the first Vessel which should
Sail to *Italy*; and this Day passing near
the

the Wood where you were, I met *Donna Theodora*, who entreated me to follow her, and endeavour to part you.

After the *Toledan* had done, *Don Fradrique* said: *Don Juan*, your Revenge on the Duke of *Naxera* was juft, don't therefore difturb your felf at the Purfuit his Relations may make: You fhall, if you pleafe, ftay with me, 'till an occafion offers to Embark for *Italy*. My Uncle is Governor of *Valencia*, and you will be fafer here than any where elfe, and will befides be with a Man who defires for the future to be engag'd to you by the ftricteft Ties of Friendfhip. *Don Juan* anfwer'd *Mendoça* in Terms full of Acknowledgement, and accepted the offer'd Refuge.

The Power of Sympathy is very furprizing, *Don Cleofas*, purfu'd *Afmodeo*; thefe two young Cavaliers were touch'd with fuch a mutual Affection for one another, that in a few Days it created a Friendfhip betwixt them, as intire as that of *Oreftes* and *Pleiades*. Befides the Equality of their Merit, there was fuch a Harmony in their Humours, that whatever pleas'd *Don Fadrique*, the other could not diflike. They both made up but one Character, and they were made to love one another. *Don Fadrique*, who above all was enchanted with the Deportment of his Friend, could not

for-

forbear boafting of it every Moment to
Theodora.

They both frequently vifited that Lady, who continually look'd on *Mendoça's*
Addreffes with Indifference; at which he
was extreamly mortify'd, and complain'd of
it to his Friend: Who told him, to comfort
him That the moft infenfible Women fuffer
themfelves to be touch'd at laft: That nothing was wanting to Lovers, but Patience
enough to wait that favourable time: That
he fhould not be difcourag'd: That his
Lady, foon or late, would regard his Services. This Advice, tho' founded on Experience, did not encourage the faint-heart-
ed *Mendoça,* who very much fear'd he
fhould never be able to pleafe the Widow
Cifuentes; and this Fear threw him into
fuch a languifhing Condition, as excited
Pity in *Don Juan,* who was foon after in
a more deplorable State himfelf.

What Reafon foever the *Toledan* had to
be difgufted againft the Sex, after the horrible Falfity of his Wife, yet he could not
help loving *Donna Theodora;* tho' he was
fo far from abandoning himfelf to a Paffion
which injur'd his Friend, that he only
thought of ftruggling againft it; and fully
perfuaded that he could not better conquer
it, than by keeping at a Diftance from
thofe Eyes which occafion'd it, he refolv'd
never

never to fee the Widow *Cifuentes* again. Accordingly, whenfoever *Mendoça* would have carry'd him with him, he always found fome Pretext to excufe it. But *Don Fradique* never made one Vifit to the Lady, that fhe did not ask why *Don Juan* had left off coming thither. One Day when fhe put that Queftion, he anfwer'd fmiling, that his Friend had his Reafons. Hah! what Reafons can he have to avoid me? faid *Don Theodora.* Madam, return'd *Mendoça,* when I defir'd him to come along with me this Day, and exprefs'd fome Surprize at his Refufal, he told me in Confidence, what I am oblig'd to reveal to you to excufe him; 'twas, that he had engag'd a Miftrefs, and that not having long to ftay in this City, his Moments were precious.

I can't be fatisfy'd with this Excufe, bluſhing reply'd the Widow *Cifuentes*; Lovers are not allow'd to abandon their Friends. *Don Fradrique* obferving *Donna Theodora's* changing Colour, thought it only owing to her Vanity, and believ'd that Spight to fee her felf neglected, was the Caufe of her Bluſhing: But his Conjecture was wrong. A more violent Impulfe than that of Vanity, occafion'd the Motions which fhe betray'd; but for fear of his difcovering her Sentiments, fhe

turn'd

turn'd the Difcourfe, and affected a Gaye-
ty during the reft of their Converfation,
which would have thrown the Blame on
his Difcernment, if he had not foon perceiv'd the Alteration.

As foon as the Widow *Cifuentes* was
alone, fhe turn'd extreamly thoughtful.
She then felt the utmoft Force of her Paffion for *Don Juan*, and imagining her felf
worfe recompenc'd than fhe really was: How
cruel and unjuft, faid fhe fighing, is that
Power which delights in inflaming difa-
greeing Hearts ; I don't love *Don Fadrique*,
and he adores me, and I burn for *Don Juan*, whofe Thoughts are taken up by another! Ah, *Mendoça*, no more reproach my
Indifference; thy Friend has fufficiently
reveng'd it. At thefe Words, ftruck with
a quick Senfe of Grief and Jealoufie, fhe
dropp'd feveral Tears; but Hope, which
affwages Lovers Pains, foon reprefented
various flattering Images to her Mind. It
fuggefted to her, that perhaps her Rival
might not be dangerous: That *Don Juan*
might be lefs feized by her Charms, than
amus'd by her Favours, and that 'twas
no hard Matter to get rid of fuch feeble
Ties. But to enable her to judge her
felf what fhe ought to believe of the *Toledan*, fhe was refolv'd to fpeak with him
in private. She fent for him, he came,
and

and when they were alone, *Donna Theodora* thus began.

I never thought that Love could make a
well-bred Man forget the Complaisance
due to the Ladies; yet, *Don Juan*, since
you have been in Love, you came no more
near me; I think I have reason to complain of you: But I am yet willing to believe that 'tis not of your own accord that
you fly me; perhaps your Lady may have
forbid you seeing me. Confess it to me,
Don Juan, and I will excuse it. I know
Lovers Actions are not free; they dare
not disobey their Mistresses. Madam,
answer'd the *Toledan*, I grant that my Conduct ought to surprize you; but let me
beg of you not to put me to justifie it.
Satisfie you self with knowing that I have
Reason to avoid you. What can that
Reason be? reply'd *Donna Theodora*, not
a little mov'd, I desire you would tell it
me. Well, Madam, reply'd *Don Juan*,
you must be obey'd; but I shall not pity
you, if you hear more than you desire to
know.

Don Fradique, adds he, has related to
you the Adventure which oblig'd me to
quit *Castile*. In my travelling to *Toledo*,
with a Heart full of Resentment against
Women, I defy'd the whole Sex ever to
surprize me. With this fierce Disposition

I

I approach'd *Valencia*, I met you, and
what perhaps no other Man has been able
to do, I fuftain'd the firft Sight of you
without being mov'd. I even look'd on you
again afterwards with Impunity; but alas,
how dear I pay'd for a few refolute Days!
You at laft conquer'd my Refiftance; your
Beauty, Wit and Charms have exercis'd
themfelves on a Rebel; in a Word, I have
all the Love for you, which you are capable of infpiring. This, Madam, is what
keeps me from you. The Lady which you
were told monopoliz'd my Thoughts, is
but an imaginary one, and I only feign'd
the making *Mendoça* my Confident, to prevent any Sufpicions I might raife in him,
by my Refufal to vifit you along with
him.

This unexpected Difcourfe fill'd *Donna
Theodora* with fuch an extraordinary Joy,
that fhe could not help difcovering it. 'Tis
indeed true fhe did not concern her felf at
all to hide it; but inftead of arming her
Eyes with fome fort of Severity, looking
on the *Toledan* with a very tender Air, fhe
faid, You have told me your Secret, *Don
Juan*, and I will alfo difcover mine. Infenfible of the Sighs of *Don Alvaro Ponce*,
little mov'd at *Mendoça's* Flames, I led an
eafie undifturb'd Life, when Chance brought
you near the Wood where we met. Not-
with-

withstanding the Confusion I was in, I yet obſerv'd you offer'd me your Aſſiſtance with a very good Grace, and the way in which you parted the two furious Rivals rais'd in me an advantageous Opinion of your Valour and Addreſs. But the Means you propos'd to reconcile them diſpleas'd me. I could not without difficulty reſolve on the Choice of either of them. But not to conceal any thing from you, I believe you had then a ſmall Share in my Repugnance; for at the very Moment that my Mouth, forc'd by Neceſſity, nam'd *Don Fadrique,* I felt my Heart declare for the *unknown Cavalier.* From that Day, (which I may call happy, ſince you have own'd your Paſſion) your Merit augmented my Value for you.

From you, continu'd ſhe, I conceal no part of my Thoughts, but impart them to you with the ſame Frankneſs that I told *Mendoça* I did not love him. A Woman who has the Misfortune to conceive a Paſſion for a Perſon that can never love her, is in the right to reſtrain her ſelf, and at leaſt revenge her Weakneſs by an eternal Silence; but I take it for granted, that I may without Scruple diſcover an innocent Tenderneſs to a Man whoſe Intentions are lawful: Yes, I am in Raptures to find you love me, and for that Bleſſing render

Thanks

Thanks to Heav'n, which doubtlefs deftin'd us for each other.

After thefe Words the Lady remain'd
filent, to give *Don Juan* leave to fpeak,
and room to difcover thofe fhining Tranfports of Joy and Gratitude with which
fhe believ'd fhe had infpir'd him; but inftead of appearing enchanted with what he
had heard, he was profoundly thoughtful
and melancholy. What do I fee, *Don
Juan?* continu'd fhe. When to make you
a Fortune, which another would think
worth enjoying, I forget the ftrict Modefty of my Sex, and fhew you a Soul char-
med with you, can you refift the Joy fuch
an engaging Declaration ought to raife in
you? You remain in a frozen Silence, nay
I fee even Grief in your Eyes: Ah, *Don
Juan,* what ftrange Effects have my Favours produc'd!

Alas! what other Effects, Madam, interrupting her with a melancholy Air, faid
the *Toledan*, could they produce on a Heart
like mine? The greater degrees of Paffion
you difcover for me, fo much the more
miferable I am. You are not ignorant
what *Mendoça* has done for me, and know
the facred Friendfhip in which we are mutually engag'd. Can I then found my Happinefs on the Ruins of his moft charming
Hopes? You are too nice, faid *Donna Theodora,*

odora, I never promis'd *Don Fadrique* any thing which can obstruct my offering you my Faith without incurring his Censure, and your receiving it without Injustice. I own that the Thoughts of an unhappy Friend ought to give you some Uneasiness; but, *Don Juan,* can that counterbalance the happy Fate which attends you? Yes, Madam, reply'd he warmly; such a Friend as *Mendoça* has more Power over me than you imagine. If you could conceive all the Tenderness and Force of our Friendship, what a miserable Object of Pity would you find me! Should I thus treat *Don Fadrique,* who has hidden nothing from me? My Interests are become his, and the least Concerns of mine never escape his vigilant Care; to say all in a Word, I share his Soul with you. Alas! if you would have had me accepted your Favours, you should have shewn them before I had enter'd into such strict Bonds of Friendship: Then, charm'd with the Happiness of pleasing you, I should have look'd on *Mendoça* with no other Eyes than those of a Rival; my Heart, guarded against the Affection he express'd for me, would not have return'd it, and I should not have had those Obligations I have at present to him. But, Madam, 'tis now too late; I have receiv'd all the Services he could render

der me; I have follow'd the Inclination I
had for him; Gratitude and Affection have
ty'd me up so close, and at last reduc'd me
to the cruel Necessity of renouncing the
glorious Fortune which you offer me.

Here *Donna Theodora*, whose Eyes
were cover'd with Tears, dry'd them up
with her Handkerchief. This disturb'd the
Toledan; he felt his Resolution shaken and
decaying; wherefore he said, with a Voice
continually interrupted with Sighs, Adieu,
Madam, adieu; I must fly, to preserve
my Virtue; I cannot bear your Tears, they
render you too formidable: I separate my
self from you for ever, and deplore the
Loss of so many Charms which my inexorable Friendship forces me to sacrifice.
These Words ended, he retir'd with the
poor Remains of Constancy, which were
not a little difficult to retain.

After his Departure the Widow *Cifuentes* was agitated by a thousand confus'd E-
motions. She was asham'd of having declar'd her self to a Man whom she could
not keep. Yet not being able to doubt but
that he was violently seiz'd by the tender
Passion, and that the Interest of his Friend
alone was what made him refuse the Hand
she offer'd, she was so just as to admire so
very rare an Instance of Friendship, instead
of being offended at it.   Notwithstanding
which

which she could not avoid being afflicted
at missing her desir'd Success, wherefore
she resolv'd for the Country on the next
Day to divert her Melancholy, or rather
to augment it; for Solitude naturally tends
rather to strengthen than weaken Love.

Don Juan, on the other side, not finding *Mendoça* in his Apartment, lock'd himself up in his own, abandoning himself
wholly to his Grief; for after what he had
done for his Friend, he thought he might
be allow'd at least to sigh. But *Don Fadrique* soon came to interrupt his Thought-
fulness; and concluding by his Face that
he was indispos'd, he discover'd no small
Concern; so that *Don Juan,* to remove it,
was forc'd to assure him he wanted nothing
but Rest. *Mendoça* instantly left him to
his Repose, but with such an afflicted Air,
as more sensibly touch'd the *Toledan* with
his Misfortune. O Heav'n, said he to
himself, why must the most tender Friendship in the World occasion all the Misery
of my Life!

The following Day *Don Fadrique* was
not yet risen, when Word was brought
him that *Donna Theodora* and her whole
Family were gone to her Seat of *Villa Real,* from whence it was not probable they
would soon return. This News less disturb'd him on the Pains he knew he should
suffer

suffer by the Distance of his belov'd Object, than that her Departure was made a Secret to him. Without knowing what to think, he took it for an ill Presage. He rose to visit his Friend, as well to talk with him concerning it, as to enquire after his Health. But having just got dress'd, *Don Juan* enter'd his Chamber, saying; I come my self to remove the Uneasiness I gave you; I am very well to Day. That good News, answer'd *Mendoça*, a little consoles me after the Ill I have receiv'd. The *Toledan* ask'd what that was, and *Don Fadrique*, after sending away his Servants, said, *Donna Theodora* is this Morning gone into the Country, where 'tis believ'd she intends a long Stay. I am very much surpriz'd at it; why should she hide it from me? What think you of it, *Don Juan?* Have not I reason to be alarm'd at it?

The *Toledan* carefully avoided telling him his real Sentiments, and endeavour'd to perfuade him that *Donna Theodora* might go out of Town, without giving any reason for his Fears. But *Mendoça*, very little satisfy'd with the Reasons which his Friend gave to hearten him, interrupted him: All this Difcourse, said he, cannot remove the Jealoufie I have conceiv'd. Perhaps I may imprudently have done fomething which may have difpleas'd *Donna Theodora*, and

to

to punifh it, fhe leaves me without condefcending fo far as to let me know my Crime. However 'tis, I can't live in this uncertain Condition; *Don Juan,* let's go after her: I will go and get Horfes ready. I advife you, faid the *Toledan,* not to take any body with you: This Explanation of her Conduct ought to be without Witneffes. *Don Juan* will not be accounted more than proper, reply'd *Don Fadrique; Donna Theodora* is not ignorant that you know all that paffes in my Heart. She values you; and far from being an Obftacle, you'll be affifting in the appeafing her in my Favour. No, *Don Fadrique,* reply'd he, my Prefence cannot be ferviceable to you; I therefore conjure you to go alone. No, dear *Don Juan,* return'd *Mendoça,* we will go together, I expect this Complaifance from your Friendfhip. How tyrannical is that! cry'd the *Toledan* with an Air of Grief; why do you exact from my Friendfhip what it ought not to grant you?

These Words which *Don Fadrique* did not comprehend, and the warmth with which they were utter'd, ftrangely furpriz'd him. He look'd very intently on his Friend. *Don Juan,* faid he, what is the Meaning of thofe Words I have juft heard? What horrid Sufpicion rifes in my Mind! Ah, you too much afflict me by

your

your too great Conftraint! Speak; what is the Caufe of the Unwillingnefs to go along with me, which you exprefs'd? I would willingly hide it from you, anfwer'd the *Toledan*; but fince you your felf force me to difcover it, I muft no longer conceal it, Let's us never more, *Don Fadrique*, applaud the Agreement betwixt our Affections; it is but too perfect. The Beauty which has wounded you, has not fpar'd your Friend *Donna Theodora*—— You will then be my Rival! interrupted *Mendoça* turning pale. Ever fince I difcern'd my Love, return'd *Don Juan*, I have ftruggled againft it. I have continually avoided the fight of the Widow *Cifuentes*, you know it, and your felf have blam'd me for it: I triumph'd at leaft over my Paffion, tho' I could not deftroy it; but Yefterday that Lady fent to acquaint me, that fhe defir'd to fpeak with me at her Houfe. I went; fhe ask'd why I feem'd to avoid her. At laft I was forc'd to difcover the true Caufe; believing that after that Declaration fhe would approve my Intention of always flying the Sight of her; but by a fantaftical Turn of my ill Stars: Shall I tell you? Yes, *Mendoça*, I muft tell you, I found *Donna Theodora* paffionately prepoffefs'd with a Paffion for me.

Tho'

Tho' *Don Fadrique* was the best natur'd and most reasonable Man in the World, he was seiz'd with a Fit of Rage at these Words; and here interrupting his Friend: Hold, *Don Juan*, said he, rather pierce my Breast, than pursue this fatal Recital. You are not contented with owning your self my Rival, but also inform me that she loves you: Just Heav'n, what is it that you venture to impart to me! You put our Friendship to too severe a Trial. But why do I say our Friendship? you have long since violated it by encouraging the perfidious Sentiments you have now declar'd to me. How much was I mistaken? I thought you Generous and Magnanimous, but find you a faithless Friend, since you can entertain a Passion which wounds me; I am sinking under this unexpected Blow, which I feel the heavier for being given by a Hand—— In the Name of God, *Mendoça*, interrupted the *Toledan* in his turn, allow your self a Moment's Patience; I am not a false Friend: Hear me, and you will repent calling me by that odious Name.

He then related what had pass'd between the Widow *Cifuentes* and him; the tender owning of her Passion, and the Persuasions she us'd to engage him to yield without scruple to his Love. He repeated

P   his

his Answer; and as he advanc'd in the
Relation of what a firm Resolution he discover'd, by the same Degrees *Don Fadrique* perceiv'd his Anger to wear off. At
last, adds *Don Juan*, Friendship over-
came Love, and I refus'd to give my Faith
to *Donna Theodora*. She wept in angry
Despite; but, great God, how insupport-
able was the Grief which her Tears occasion'd! I can never remember them without trembling afresh at the Danger I ran.
I began to believe my self barbarous; and
for some Moments, *Mendoça*, my Heart
became unfaithful to you. I did not yet
yield to my Weakness, but escap'd those
dangerous Tears by a hasty Flight. But
'tis not enough to have avoided this Danger, it ought to be fear'd for the future; I
must hasten my Departure: I will no more
expose my self to *Theodora*'s Eyes. After
all this, will *Don Fadrique* any more
accuse me of Ingratitude and Perfidious-
ness?

No, reply'd *Mendoça*, embracing him,
I return you all your Innocence; my Eyes
are open, pardon the unjust Reproaches
of a Lover who had lost all his Hopes.
Alas, ought I to think that *Donna Theodora* could see you long without loving
you, and yielding to those Charms whose
Power I have my self try'd? You are a
true

true Friend; I will no more charge my
Mifery on any thing but Fortune; and
far from hating you, I feel my Tendernefs
for you increafe each Minute. Ah! you
renounce the Poffeffion of *Donna Theodora!* You offer up to Friendfhip fuch a
great Sacrifice, and fhould I not be touch'd
with it! You can conquer your Love, and
fhall not I make an Effort to reftrain mine!
I ought to equal you in Generofity: *Don
Juan,* follow the Inclination which draws
you; marry the Widow *Cifuentes*; let my
Heart, if it will, figh. You prefs me in
vain, reply'd the *Toledan*; I confefs I have
a violent Paffion for her; but your Repofe
is dearer to me than my own Happinefs.
Ought then, anfwer'd *Don Fadrique*,
Donna Theodora's Repofe to be indifferent? Let's not flatter our felves; the Inclination fhe has for you decides my Fate.
Tho' you fhould remove your felf, tho' to
yield her to me you fhould fpend a deplorable Life in far diftant Countries, I fhould
be never the better for it; fince, as fhe never yet was pleas'd with me, fhe never will:
Heav'n has referv'd that Glory for you
alone; fhe lov'd you from the firft Moment fhe faw you; fhe has a natural Inclination for you: In a Word, fhe cannot
be happy without you. Accept then the
Hand which fhe offers, accomplifh her De-

fires,

fires, and your own: Leave me to my ill
Fortune, and don't make all three miserable, when one may exhaust all the Rigour
of Destiny.

Asmodeo was here oblig'd to interrupt
his Discourse to hearken to the Scholar,
who said, What you tell me is surprizing;
are there really any People in the World
of this extraordinary Character? I see no
Friends in the World who don't quarrel,
I don't say for such Mistresses as *Theodora*,
but even for Coquetting Jilts.   Can a Lover renounce the Object which he adores,
and which loves him, to avoid rendring
a Friend unhappy? I don't believe it
possible in Nature, 'twill pass no where
but in a Romance. I agree with you,
answer'd the Devil, that 'tis not very
common; but 'tis not only to be found in
Romances, but in the sublime Nature of
Man, and that since the Deluge, in which
Compass I have known three Instances of
it, besides this.   But to return to our
Story.

The two Friends continu'd to sacrifice
their Passion, and the one resolving not
to yield in Point of Generosity, their amorous Sentiments remain'd suspended for
some Days. They ceas'd to speak of *Donna Theodora*, they durst not mention her
Name.   But whilst Friendship thus triumph'd

umph'd over Love in the City of *Valencia;* Love, as tho' he would revenge himself, reign'd at another Place with a tyrannick Sway, and forc'd an abfolute Obedience without the leaft Refiftance.

Donna Theodora abandon'd her felf to that tender Paffion at her Seat of *Villa Real,* fituate near the Sea; fhe inceffantly thought of *Don Juan,* and could not but hope fhe fhould marry him, tho' fhe had no reafon to expeft it, after the rigid Sentiments of Friendfhip for *Don Fadrique* which he difcover'd.

One Day, after Sun-fet, as fhe was diverting her felf by walking on the Sea-fide with one of her Women, fhe perceiv'd a fmall Shalop juft got to Shore. At firft fight there feem'd to be on board feven or eight very ill-look'd Fellows; but after having look'd on them nearer, and obferv'd them with more Attention, fhe concluded that they had miftaken Masks for Faces; accordingly they were really mask'd, and arm'd with Swords and Bayonets. She trembled at their frightful Afpeets, and from thence fearing that the Defcent which they were going to make boaded no good, fhe return'd haftily to her Houfe. She look'd back from time to time to obferve them, and perceiving that they were landed, and began to purfue her, fhe ran as faft

as

as she could; but not being so nimble foot-
ed as *Athalanta*, and the mask'd Men being strong and swift, they overtook her at
her own Door, and there seiz'd her.

The Lady and her Woman shriek'd out
so loud that they drew some Domesticks
thither, who alarm'd the whole House,
and all *Donna Theodora*'s Footmen ran
thither arm'd with Forks and Clubs.
Whilst two of the lustiest of the mask'd
Gang, after having seiz'd in their Arms
the Mistress and the Maid, carry'd them
to the Shalop, mauger all their Resistance, the Remainder made head against
the Family, who began to press very hard
upon them. The Fight was long; but at
last the Maskers succeeded in their Enterprize, and regain'd their Shalop, fighting as
they retreated. 'Twas now time they should
retire, for they were not embark'd before
they saw coming from the *Valencia* Road
four or five Cavaliers, who rode full Speed
that way, and seem'd to come to the Re-
lief of *Donna Theodora*. At this sight they
made so much haste to get out to Sea, that
all the Cavaliers Endeavours were in vain.

These Cavaliers were *Don Fradrique*
and *Don Juan*. The first of them had receiv'd a Letter, by which he was advis'd,
that 'twas reported by good Hands that
Don Alvaro Ponce was at the Isle of *Ma-*
jorca;

jorca; that he had equipp'd a fort of Tar-
rane, and affifted by twenty Men of de-
fperate Fortunes, he defign'd to feize and
carry off the Widow *Cifuentes*, the firft
time fhe fhould be at her Country Seat.
On this News the *Toledan* and he, with
their *Valets de Chambre*, inftantly fet out,
to acquaint *Donna Theodora* with this
News. At a good diftance they obferv'd
a very great Number of People on the Sea-
fhore, who feem'd engag'd againft one
another; and not doubting but that it was
as they fear'd, they fpurr'd on their Horfes
full fpeed to oppofe *Don Alvaro's* Project. But whatever Hafte they could make,
they arriv'd only foon enough to be Witneffes of the Rape which they defign'd to
have prevented.

In the mean time *Alvaro Ponce*, trufting
to the Succefs of his audacious Attempt,
made off from the Coaft with his Prey;
and his Shalop reach'd a fmall arm'd Veffel, which expected him out at Sea. 'Tis
not poffible to be fenfible of a greater Sorrow than that which *Mendoça* and *Don
Juan* felt. They pour'd out a thoufand
Imprecations againft the Ravifher, and
fill'd the Air with Complaints as lamentable as vain. All the Domefticks of *Donna
Theodora*, animated by fuch excellent Ex-
amples, did not fpare their Tears. The

Shore

Shore refounded with mourning Cries;
Rage, Defpair and Defolation reign'd on
the melancholy Strand ; nor did the Rape
of *Helen* occafion a greater Confternation
in the *Spartan* Court.

C H A P. XIV.

Of the Broil betwixt a Tragick and Comick Author.

HERE the Scholar could not help
interrupting the Devil: Signior *Afmodeo,* faid he, tho' the Story you are tel-
ling is extreamly moving, yet I am not able
to refift my earneft Defire to know the
Meaning of what I there fee. I difcern
two Men in their Shirts in a Chamber,
pulling and tearing each other by the
Hair, and feveral Men in their Night-
Gowns endeavouring to part them. Thofe
Perfons whom you fee fighting in their
Shirts, anfwer'd the Devil, are two *French*
Authors; and thofe who are parting them
are two *Germans,* a *Dutchman,* and an
Italian, all which are lodg'd in the fame
Inn, which is frequented by none but Fo-
reigners.

One

One of thefe Authors writes Tragedies, and the other Comedies. The firft, attracted by his Curiofity to fee *Spain,* crouded himfelf into the *French* Ambaffador's Retinue; and the other, difcontented with his Circumftances at *Paris,* came to *Madrid* in queft of a better Fortune; and if thefe Authors Quarrel is really Comical, the Caufe of it is much more fo. The Tragick Poet is really a diverting Original, who has fpoil'd his Genius by reading the Antients, which fometimes makes great Fools, as well as great Men. To keep his Mufe in breath, he writes every Day. Not being able to fleep this Night, he began a Play, whofe Plot is taken from *Homer's Iliad.* He has finifh'd but one Scene; and his leaft Fault being that of the reft of the Poets, an impertinent Inclination to pefter other People with their Performances, he rifes, fnatches up his Candle, and in his Shirt knocks very hard at the Chamber-Door of the Comick Author, then afleep; but foon waking at the Noife, open'd the Door to the other, who faid, entring the Room like a Man poffefs'd, Fall down, my Friend, fall at my Feet, and adore a Genius which *Melpomene* has honour'd. I have juft brought forth fome Verfes——But why do I fay I have juft done it? 'Tis *Apollo* himfelf which dictated them to me.

If

If I were at *Paris*, I would this Day read them from House to House, and I wait only for Day-light to charm Monfieur, the Ambaffador, and all the *French* at *Madrid* with them. But before I fhew them to any body, I will repeat them to you.

I thank you for the Preference, anfwer'd the Comick Author, with a powerful Yawn; but the worft on't is, that you have chofen an unfeafonable Time, when I am fo very fleepy, that I will not promife to hear all the Verfes you have to repeat without Nodding. Oh, I'll anfwer for that, reply'd the Tragick Author; tho' you were dead, the Scene which I have juft now written would reftore you to Life again. My Verfification is not a Rhapfody of ftale common Thoughts and trivial Expreffions, fupported barely by Rime: 'Tis a noble Mafculine Poem, which moves the Heart, and ftrikes the Intellect. I am none of thofe Poetafters, thofe petty Authors who publifh the wretched Trifles which refult from their own barren Genius; but I have drawn mine from the grand Springs, and will venture a Wager that I have not put one Thought into my Tragedies, which is not in fome *Greek* Author. I would not be underftood to mean that I fteal from the Antients; no; but by vertue of reading the *Sophocles's* and the *Euripides's*, the *Ho-*
mers

mers and the *Pindars*, I have render'd thofe
great Men fo familiar to me, or rather my
favourable Stars fo perfectly infpir'd me
with their Genius at the Moment of my
Birth, that if by an uncommon Misfortune we fhould lofe the Remains of their
Works which we now have, they would
be found again in my Writings. You fhall
judge your felf. But hear my Tragedy.
The Death of *Patroclus.* Scene the firft.
Brifeis and other of *Achilles's* Captives appear tearing their Hair, and beating their
Breafts, to exprefs their Grief for the Death
of *Patroclus.* Wholly unable to fupport
themfelves, being utterly difpirited by
Defpair, they fall down on the Stage. This
will be new and extreamly moving; *Phe-*
nix, Achilles's Governor, is with them,
and opens the *Drama* with thefe Verfes.

Priam *fhall lofe his* Hector *and his* Troy;
Achilles *to revenge his Friend prepares:*
See glitt'ring thro' the Air on every fide,
Pikes, Lances, Helmets, Cuiraffes and Darts.
The ratling Hail in lefs abundance pours.
The Greeks *all fwear t' appeafe* Patroclus
      Ghoft.
Fierce Agamemnon, *and divine* Camelus,
Old honour'd Neftor, *equal to the Gods,*
Leontes, *dextrous at the manag'd Spear,*
Strong Diomede, *and Silver-tongu'd* Ulyffes.
                              And

And see! Achilles *comes—Godlike he drives*
His Steeds immortal towards Troy's *proud*
    Walls,
And leaves the distanc'd Winds far off be-
    hind;
Then thus he shouting cries——O vigorous
    Race,
Podargus, Xanthus, Balius! *quick advance!*
And when with Spoil and Carnage we are
    tir'd,
Haste to regain our Camp,—but not without
    your Master.
Fleet Xanthus *bows his Neck, and thus re-*
    plies,
For Juno *gave him Speech—*Achilles, *know,*
Your faithful Horses shall your Will obey;
But your dark Hour of Fate is drawing near.
He spoke—and now the winged Chariot flies,
Th'exulting Greeks *behold, and shouting loud,*
With Sounds of Joy shake all th' adjacent
    Coast.
Drest in Vulcanian *Arms the Conqu'ring*
    Prince
Appears more glitt'ring than the Morning
    Star,
Or than the Sun commencing his Career,
When he moves on to bless the World with
    Day;
He flames like Fires which on some Moun-
    tain Top
Are made at Night by the rejoicing Swains.
                                            I

I ftop here, continu'd the Tragick Author, to give you a Moment's breathing-time; for if I fhould repeat the whole Scene at once, the too great Multiplicity of fhining Paffages and fublime Thoughts would overcome you. Obferve the Beauty and Juftice of that Comparifon; As bright as Fires made on the Top of a Mountain at Night. Every Body won't difcern it; but you, who have Wit and juft Senfe, you, I fay, ought to be ravifh'd with it. I am, doubtlefs, anfwer'd the Comick Poet with a malicious Smile; nothing is fo fine; and I hope you will not forget, in your Tragedy, the Care which *Thetis* took to drive away the Flies from *Patroclus's* Body. I affure you, replies the Tragick Author, 'tis the moft proper Incident in the whole Play to furnifh pompous Lines.

All my Works, added he, as you fee, are ftamp'd with the Image of venerable Antiquity; and when I read them, obferve how they are applauded! I ftop at every Verfe to receive their due Praifes. I remember I one Day read a Tragedy in a Houfe at *Paris* where the Countefs of *Vieillebrune* was, who has an admirable delicate and nice Tafte, and fcalding Tears trickled down her Cheeks at the firft Scene

As

At thefe Words the Comick Author was
ready to burft with laughing: Ay, faid he,
I very well remember that Countefs is of
that Humour; fhe is a Woman who can't
bear Comedy; fhe has fuch an utter Averfion for it, that fhe runs out of the Box
as foon as the Mufick has done, to vent
all her Grief. Tragedy is her favourite
Paffion; let the Play be good or bad, provided there be unhappy Lovers in it, you
are fure of that Lady's Company; and to
be free with you, if I wrote ferious Poems, I fhould be glad of other Applauders
than her Ladyfhip. Oh, I have others alfo, faid the Tragick Poet, I have the Ap-
probation of the Learned. I had rather
have that of the Pit, return'd the Comick
Author. Fie, fie, reply'd the other, I don't
write for the Pit; I labour only for the
Learned and the Court: I wifh the Pit
would do Juftice; that Part of the Audience has no manner of Right to judge of
my Poems, which are above their Jurif-
diction: I wifh it would content it felf
with the Exercife of its Tyranny in judg-
ing Comedies, which is its Province. Comedies being but Trifles, wretched, feeble
Productions of Wit——Not fo faft, good
Sir, interrupted the other Author, ftop a
little, if you pleafe: You don't think how
you rave. You fpeak contemptibly of Comedy!

medy! Do you believe a Comick Piece
less difficult to write than a Tragedy? or
that 'tis easier to make well-bred People
laugh than cry? Undeceive your self, and
be assur'd that an ingenious Subject, which
turns on the Manners of Men, does not
cost less Pains than the finest Heroick
Piece.

Igad, said the Tragick Poet with an Air
of Railery, I am surpriz'd to hear you express your self thus: But, Monsieur *Calidas*, to avoid all Dispute, I will for the
future like your Works, tho' I have hitherto despis'd them. I don't value your Contempt, Monsier *Lorgicles*, hastily return'd
the Comick Author; and to answer your
insolent Airs, which you have also drawn
from the grand Springs, I will now tell
you, in my turn, what I think of your
Works. The Verses you have just recited
are ridiculous, and the Thoughts, tho' taken out of *Homer*, are neverthelefs flat.
Achilles talks to his Horfes, and his Horfes answer him; that's a mean, low I-
mage, as well as the Comparison of the
Fire the Peasants make on a Mountain.
To pillage the Antients in this manner, is
not to do them any Honour; in your
Works you confound the Beauties which
Time formerly respected, with those it has
since destroy'd; and paint the Manners of
former

former Ages; without accommodating your felf to the Delicacy of our own. Your *Greek* Authors indeed abound with admirable Beauties, but more Senfe and a better Tafte than you have is requifite to make a happy Choice of what ought to be borrow'd from them. That is the Difference betwixt the great *Racine*, and thofe who, like you, render themfelves ridiculous by keeping too fcrupuloufly clofe to the *Greek* Words.

Since your Genius is not fufficiently elevated to difcern the Beauties of my Poem, and to punifh your Rafhnefs in prefuming to criticize on my Scene, you fhall not hear a Line more of it. I have been too feverely punifh'd, return'd *Calidas*, in hearing the Beginning. It becomes you indeed very well to defpife my Comedies! Know then, that the very worft I could ever write, will always appear far fuperior to your beft Pieces. Affure your felf, 'tis much eafier to take a Flight, and foar on lofty Subjects, than to hit upon a delicate nice Raillery; and to prove that I am convinc'd of what I fay, when I return to *France*, if I do not fucceed in Comedy, I will defcend to the writing of Tragedy.

For a Farce Scribler, interrupted the Grave Author, you have indeed a great deal of Vanity. For a moft wretched Verfifier,

fifier, faid the Cómick Author, you have really an extravagant Opinion of your felf. You are an infolent Fellow, reply'd *Longicles*; I tell you, diminutive Monfieur *Calidas*, if I was not in your Chamber, the Çataftophre of this Adventure fhould teach you how to refpeft the Buskin. Oh, let not that Confideration with-hold you, great Monfieur *Longicles*, anfwer'd *Calidas*; if you have a mind to fight, I will engage you here as readily as any where elfe. At thefe Words they tore one another by the Throat and Hair, and both box'd very warmly, without fparing each other. An *Italian*, who lay in the next Room, heard the whole Dialogue, and by the Noife of the Blows concluded they were fighting. He then rofe, and tho' an *Italian*, out of Compaffion for them call'd up the Houfe. A *Dutchman* and two *Germans*, whom you fee in Morning-Gowns, came along with the *Italian*, to part the Combatants.

This is a very pleafant Fray, faid *Don Cleofas*; but by what I fee, it is plain that the Tragick Authors in *France* think themfelves much more confiderable Men than thofe who write Comedy. Undoubtedly, anfwer'd *Afmodeo*, the former fuppofe themfelves as much above the latter, as the Heroes of their Tragedies are above the Foot-

Q   men

men in the Comick Plays. Upon what Pretence can they found their Arrogance? reply'd the Scholar; is it that 'tis more difficult to write a Tragedy than a Comedy? No, really, return'd the Devil; my Decision of the Queſtion is, that to form an excellent Plot for a Comedy does not require a leſs Effort of Genius, than to lay the fineſt Plan in the World for a Tragedy. But with regard to the working up the Play in the latter, the majeſtick Grandeur of the Subjeſt ſupports it, and inſpires ſuch noble Thoughts, that the ſole Aſſiſtance of good Senſe is requiſite to finiſh ſuch Tragedies as are at preſent written in *France*: But to write Comedies with Succeſs at this time of Day, ſomething beſides good Senſe is requiſite. In a Word, lofty Subjeſts furniſh the Writer with almoſt all that is neceſſary, whilſt in mean Charaſters he is expeſted to provide all. According to this Deciſion, ſaid the Scholar, I conclude that Tragedy, by vertue of its Name, is above Comedy; but in requital, that Comick Authors are to be preferr'd before the Tragick. Let's end this Digreſſion, reply'd the Devil, and I will re-aſſume the Thread of my Story, which you interrupted.

C H A P.

CHAP. XV.

The Continuation and Conclusion of the Story of the Power of Friendship.

THO' *Donna Theodora*'s Servants could not hinder her being forc'd away, they yet courageously oppos'd it, and their Resistance was fatal to some of *Alvaro*'s Men; amongst others they wounded one so dangerously, that unable to follow his Comerades, he remain'd almost dead on the Sand.

This unfortunate Wretch was known to be one of *Alvaro*'s Footmen, and *Donna Theodora*'s Servants perceiving that he yet breath'd carry'd him to her House, where they spar'd nothing that could contribute to the Recovery of his Spirits; and they gain'd their End, tho' the great Quantity of Blood which he had lost render'd him extream feeble. To engage him to speak, they promis'd to secure his Life, and not deliver him up to the Severity of Justice, provided he would tell where his Master design'd to carry *Donna Theodora*. Flatter'd by this Promise, tho' in his Condition there appear'd but small Hopes of his ever taking the Benefit of it, he recollected

Q 2   his

his little Remainder of Strength, and in a
very feeble Tone confirm'd the Advice
which *Don Fadrique* had before receiv'd;
and added, that *Don Alvaro*'s Defign was
to carry the Widow *Cifuentes* to *Saffari*
in the Ifland of *Sardinia*, where he had
a Relation whofe Intereft and Authority
was very great, and who he knew would
certainly protect him.

This Confeffion fomewhat abated the
Defpair of *Mendoça* and the *Toledan*. They
left the wounded Man in the Houfe, where
he dy'd fome Hours after, and returning to
Valencia confulted what Meafures to take.
They refolv'd to purfue their common
Enemy to the Place of his Retreat. Accordingly they both embark'd very foon
after at *Denia* for Port *Mahone*, not doubting their meeting with an Opportunity
there of going to the Ifle of *Sardinia*.
Their Hopes prov'd true, for they were
no fooner arriv'd at *Mahone*, than they
were inform'd that a Veffel freighted for
Cagliari was juft ready to Sail, and they
took the Opportunity.

The Ship put off with the moft favourable Wind they could defire; but five or
fix Hours after they were perfectly be-
calm'd, and at Night the Wind turning
directly contrary, they were oblig'd to
fteer from one fide to the other, without
hope

hope of its changing. They fteer'd thus for three Days, and on the fourth, at two after Noon, they difcover'd a Veffel making all poffible Sail to them. They at firft took it for a Merchant-man, but obferving that it came within Cannon-fhot of them without fhewing any Colours, they did not doubt but that it was a Pirate.

They were not deceiv'd, it was a *Tunis* Ship which fuppos'd that the Chriftians would yield without fighting ; but when they perceiv'd that they clear'd their Ship and prepar'd their Guns, they concluded them in earneft for fighting; wherefore they ftopp'd, did the fame, and prepar'd to engage. They began to fire, and the Chriftians feem'd to have fome Advantage ; but an *Algerine*, larger and provided with more Guns than both the other, coming in the midft of the Action, and taking the Part of the *Tunis* Ship, made full fail to the *Spaniard*, and oblig'd him to fuftain the Fire of both Ships.

At this Sight the Chriftians defpairing, and refolving not to continue an Engagement now become too unequal, gave over firing, when there appear'd on the Poop of the *Algerine* a Slave, who cry'd out to them in *Spanifh*, that if they expected Quarter they muft furrender to the *Algerine*. Thefe Words ended, a *Turk* difplay'd

Q 3

play'd the *Algerine* green Taffata Flag with
Silver Half-Moons. The Chriftians, confidering that all Refiftance would be vain,
no longer thought of defending themfelves, but yielded with all the Grief which
the horrid Idea of Slavery could caufe in
Freemen; and the Mafter of the Veffel,
fearing a longer Delay might irritate the
barbarous Conquerors, took the Colours
from the Poop, threw himfelf into the
Pinnace with fome of the Sailors, and went
on Board the *Algerine*; and that Pirate fent
a parcel of Soldiers to plunder the *Spanifh*
Ship, as he of *Tunis* likewife gave the
fame Order to fome of his Crew, fo that
all the Paffengers were in an inftant dif-
arm'd and fearch'd, and fent on Board the
Algerine, where the two Pirates divided
their Prey by Lot.

It had been at leaft a Confolation for
Mendoça and his Friend, to have both
fall'n into the Hands of the fame Pirate.
Their Chains would have been lighter, if
they could have join'd in the bearing them;
but Fortune, refolv'd they fhould experience all her Severity, fubjected *Don Fadrique* to the *Tunis* Robber, and *Don Juan*
to the *Algerine*. Imagine the Defpair that
feiz'd thefe Friends when they faw they
were going to part. They threw themfelves at the Pirate's Feet, and conjur'd
him

him not to separate them. But these Savage Villains, whose Barbarity is Proof against any Sight, could not be mov'd; but on the contrary, concluding these two Captives to be considerable Men, who could pay a large Ransom, they resolv'd to keep them, as they were, divided.

Mendoça and the *Toledan,* seeing they could not soften these merciless Wretches, cast their Eyes on each other, and by their Looks express'd the Excess of their Affliction. But when the whole Booty was divided, and the *Tunis* Pirate was going to return on Board his own Ship with his Slaves, the two Friends were ready to expire with Grief. *Mendoça* ran to the *Toledan,* and clasping him in his Arms, We must then, said he, separate; Oh terrible Necessity! Is it not enough that the audacious Villainy of a Ravisher remain unpunish'd, but we must be incapacitated to unite our Complaints and Sorrows? Ah! *Don Juan,* what have we done to Heav'n, that we must in such a cruel manner experience its heavy Displeasure? Ah, look no where else for the Cause of our Misfortunes, answer'd *Don Juan,* they ought only to be imputed to me; the Death of the two Persons which I sacrific'd, tho' excusable in Mens Eyes, must undoubtedly have irritated Heav'n, which punishes

you

you for having engag'd in Friendſhip
with a miſerable Wretch whom Juſtice
purſues.

At theſe Words they both ſhower'd
down Tears in great abundance, and ſigh'd
with ſuch violence, that the other Slaves
were not leſs touch'd with their Grief than
their own Misfortune. But the *Tunis* Soldiers, yet more barbarous than their Maſter, obſerving that *Mendoça* did not haſte
to the Veſſel, brutally ſnatch'd him out of
the *Toledan's* Arms, and forc'd him along
with them, loading him with Blows.
Adieu, dear Friend, cry'd he, I ſhall never
ſee you more! *Donna Theodora* is not yet
reveng'd ; the Ills which I expect from
theſe cruel Men will be the leaſt of the
Sufferings of my Slavery. *Don Juan* could
not anſwer theſe Words; the Treatment
which he ſaw his Friend receive threw him
into a Fit that render'd him ſpeechleſs.
The Order of the Story requiring us to follow the *Toledan*, we will leave *Don Fadrique* on board the *Tunis* Ship.

The *Algerine* return'd to his Country,
where being arriv'd, he carry'd the new
Slaves to the *Baſha*, and thence to the publick Slave-Market. An Officer belonging
to the Dey *Mezzomorto* bought *Don
Juan* for his Maſter, and ſet him to work
in the Gardens belonging to *Mezzomorto's*
                      * *Haram.*

* *Haram.* Tho' this Employ muft needs
prove very painful to a Gentleman, yet the
Solitude, which it requir'd, render'd it a-
greeable; for in his prefent Circumftances
nothing could more divert him than the
Reflection on his Misfortunes; on which
he inceffantly employ'd his Thoughts, and
was fo far from endeavouring to diflodge
thefe moft afflicting Images, that he feem'd
to take Pleafure in the Remembrance of
them.

One Day, not perceiving the Dey, who
was walking in the Garden, he fung a melancholy Song as he was working; *Mezzomorto* ftopp'd to liften to it, and being
very well pleas'd with the Voice, came up
to him and ask'd him his Name. The *Toledan* told him 'twas *Alvaro*; for when he
was fold to the Dey, he thought fit to
change his Name, purfuant to the Cuftom
of other Slaves, and hit upon that firft, by
reafon the Rape of *Theodora* by *Alvaro
Ponce* was continually in his Mind.

Mezzomorto, who underftood *Spanifh*
indifferently well, put feveral Queftions to
him concerning the Cuftoms of *Spain,* and
particularly concerning the Meafures the
Men

---

* Haram *is the Name given to all private Perfons* Seraglio's;
none but that of the Grand Seignior *being properly call'd the*
Seraglio.

Men took to render themſelves agreeable
to the Women: To all which *Don Juan*
return'd ſuch Anſwers as very well ſatisfy'd
the Dey

Alvaro, ſaid he to him, you ſeem not
to want Senſe, and indeed I don't take you
for a common Man; but whatever you are,
you have the good Fortune to pleaſe me,
and I will honour you ſo far as to make
you my Confident. *Don Juan* at theſe
Words proſtrated himſelf at the Dey's
Feet, and after having taken up the low-
eſt Border of his Robe, with it touch'd
his Eyes, Mouth and Head. To begin
with giving you ſome Marks of it, reply'd
Mezzomorto, I will tell you that I have
the fineſt Women in *Europe* in my *Seraglio*; amongſt them I have one which is
beyond all ſort of compariſon, and I don't
believe that the *Grand Viſier*, or the *Grand
Seignior* himſelf, is Poſſeſſor of a more perfect Beauty, tho' his Ships continually
bring him Women from all Parts of the
World. Her Face to me ſeems the Sun
reflected; her Eyes *Venus's* two Stars;
each of her Eye-brows may paſs for *Sagit-
tarius's* Bow, and her Shape is as exact as
that of the Roſe-tree in the Garden of
Eram: You may ſee that I am enchanted.
But this Miracle of Nature, tho' enrich'd
with ſuch rare Beauty, gives her ſelf wholly
up

up to a fatal Grief, which neither Time nor my Love can dissipate; and tho' Fortune has subjected her to my Desires, I have not yet satisfy'd them. I have constantly bridled them, and contrary to the common Custom of Men in my Circumstances, which aim no farther than sensual Pleasures, I have endeavour'd to gain her Heart by such a Complaisance and profound Respect as the meanest *Musulman* would be asham'd of ever owning to a Christian Slave ; yet all my Tenderness only encreases her Melancholy, and her Obstinacy begins at last to tire me. The Idea of Slavery is not graven in such deep Tracks in others, and even those were soon effac'd by my favourable Treatment of her. This tedious Grief fatigues my Patience; but before I yield to the violent Transports of Love, I must make one Effort more, in which I would use your Assistance; the Slave being a Christian and of your Nation, may make you her Confident, and you may persuade her better than any other. Advantageously represent to her my Quality and Riches ; tell her that I will distinguish her from all my Slaves; engage her to consider, if necessary, that she may one Day become the Wife of *Mezzomorto* ; and assure her that I shall have a greater Value for her than for

2

a *Sultana,* if her Highnefs fhould pleafe to tender me her felf.

Don Juan a fecond time proftrated himfelf at the Dey's Feet, and tho' not very well pleas'd with his Commiffion, affur'd him that he would do his beft to acquit himfelf in the Performance. 'Tis enough, reply'd *Mezzomorto;* leave your Work and follow me. I will order it that you fhall fpeak with this beautiful Slave alone; but have a care how you abufe that Truft, which if you do, your Rafhnefs fhall be punifh'd by Tortures unknown even to *Turks* themfelves: Endeavour to overcome your Melancholy, and know that your Liberty is annex'd to the End of my Sufferings. *Don Juan* left off working, and follow'd the Dey, who was gone before to difpofe the afflicted Captive to admit his Agent. She was with two old Slaves, who retir'd at his Approach. The charming Slave faluted him with profound Refpect; but could not help trembling, for fear of what might happen to her, every Vifit he made. He perceiv'd it, and to diffipate her Fears, Fair Captive, faid he, I come hither at prefent for no other reafon than to tell you that I have a *Spaniard* amongft my Slaves, which perhaps you may be glad to talk with; if you defire to fee
him,

him, I will give you leave to speak with him, and that also without any Witnesses.

The beautiful Slave having discover'd that she earnestly desir'd it ; I will immediately send him to you, reply'd *Mezzomorto*, if his Discourse can assuage your Griefs. These Words ended, he order'd the two old Slaves which serv'd her another way, and afterwards himself quitted her Apartment, and meeting the *Toledan*, he whisper'd to him, You may enter, and after you have talk'd with the fair Slave, come to my Apartment, and give me an Account of your Success.

Don Juan enter'd the Chamber, and saluted the Slave, without fixing his Eyes on her; and she receiv'd his Salutation, without looking very intently on him. But beginning to look on each other more earnestly, they burst out into Tears of Surprize and Joy. O God, said the *Toledan*, approaching her, am I not deluded by a Phantome? Is it really *Donna Theodora* which I see? Ah, *Don Juan*, cry'd the Fair Slave, is it you that speak to me? Yes, Madam, answer'd he, tenderly kissing one of her Hands, 'tis *Don Juan* himself. You may know me by the Tears which my Eyes, charm'd with the Happiness of seeing you again, cannot restrain : At the Transports of Joy which your Presence is only

capable

capable of exciting, I have done murmur-
ring at Fortune, fince fhe has reftor'd you
to my Wifhes——But whither does my
immoderate Joy hurry me? Alas! I forget
that you are in Chains! What ftrange Ca-
price of Fortune brought you hither? How
did you efcape *Don Alvaro's* rafh Paffion?
Ah, what difmal Alarms does that give me!
And how much am I afraid that Heav'n has
not fufficiently protected your Virtue!

Heav'n, faid *Donna Theodora,* has reveng'd me of *Alvaro Ponce.* If I had time
to tell you——you have enough, interrupted *Don Juan.* The Dey has permitted
me to be with you, and what may furprize
you, to talk with you alone. Let's make
the beft Ufe of thefe happy Moments, and
pray acquaint me with all that has happen'd
to you, from the time of your Seifure, to this
prefent. Ah, who told you that it was
Don Alvaro that feiz'd me? I know it but
too well, return'd *Don Juan.* Then he
fuccinctly related how he was inform'd of
it, and how *Mendoça* and he embark'd in
fearch of the Ravifher, and were taken by
Pyrates. After which *Donna Theodora* immediately began the Recital of her Adventures in thefe Words,

'Tis needlefs to tell you that I was extreamly furpriz'd to find my felf feiz'd by
a Troop of mask'd Men. I fwooned a-
way

way in the Arms of him that carry'd me
off, and when I got out of my Fit, which
doubtlefs was very long, I found my felf
alone with *Ines*, one of my Women, at
Sea in a Cabin of a Veffel under Sail:
Ines exhorted me to Patience, and by her
Difcourfe gave me room to conclude that
fhe had a Correfpondence with my Ravifher; who then prefum'd to fhew himfelf
to me, and throwing himfelf at my Feet:
Madam, faid he, pardon the way *Don Alvaro* has taken to poffefs you. You know
what tender Addreffes I made to you, and
with what Conftancy I difputed your Heart
with *Don Fadrique*, to the Time that you
gave him the Preference. If my Paffion
for you had only been a common one, I
had conquer'd it, and comforted my felf
under the Misfortune; but I am deftin'd
to adore your Charms; and, fcorn'd as I am,
I cannot free my felf from their Power.
But yet don't fear that my Love will offer
any Violence. I did not make this Attempt
on your Liberty, to affright your Virtue
by bafe Means; no, all I pretend to in the
Retirement whither I am conveying you,
is, that an eternal and facred Knot may
bind our Deftinies.

He faid feveral other things which I cannot well remember, they tend.d to hint
that he thought, in forcing me to marry

ry him, he did not tyrannife; and that I
ought rather to look upon him as a Paffionate Lover, than an Infolent Ravifher.
Whilft he fpake, I did nothing but weep
and defpair: Wherefore, without lofing time
in Endeavours to perfuade me, he left me.
But at his Retiring, made a Sign to *Ines,*
which I difcern'd was his Order to her to
reinforce with Addrefs thofe Arguments,
with which he defign'd to dazle my Reafon.

She acted her Part to the full: She fuggefted to me, that after the Noife of a
Rape, I muft of neceffity be forc'd to accept *Don Alvaro's* Offer, how great foever
my Averfion for him might be. That my
Reputation demanded this Sacrifice of my
Heart. The laying me under the Neceffity of fuch a hideous Marriage, not being
the Way to dry up my Tears, I remain'd
inconfolable. *Ines* did not know what to
fay to me farther, when on a fudden we
heard a great Noife on the Deck, which engag'd all our Attention.

This was occafion'd by the Surprize of
Don Alvaro's Men, at the fight of a large
Veffel making all poffible Sail towards us.
Our Ship not being fo good a Sailor as that,
'twas impoffible for us to avoid it. He
came up with us, and immediately we
heard a crying To Wind-ward, to Wind-
ward.

ward. But *Alvaro Ponce* and his Men, chusing rather to die than yield, ventur'd to dispute their Liberty with the Enemy. The Action was very sharp; I will not run into Particulars, but only acquaint you that *Don Alvaro* and all his Men were kill'd, after having fought with utmost Desperacy. As for us, we were conducted into the great Ship which belong'd to *Mezzomorto*, and was commanded by *Aby Aly Osman*, one of his Officers.

Aby Aly earnestly look'd at me with Surprize, and knowing by my Dress that I was a *Spanish* Woman, he said to me in the *Castilian* Tongue: Moderate your Grief for being fallen into Slavery, 'tis a Misfortune which was inevitable: But why do I call it a Misfortune! 'Tis an Advantage, for which you ought to applaud your happy Stars; you are too charming to be confin'd only to be obey'd by Christians: Heav'n never form'd you for those wretched Mortals : None but *Musulmen* are worthy to enjoy you. I will, adds he, return to *Algier*. Tho' I have taken no other Prize, I am persuaded that the Dey, my Master, will be pleas'd with this Expedition ; nor can I fear his blaming my Impatience, to put into his Hands, a Beauty which will afford him such delicious Pleasures, and be the whole Ornament of his *Seraglio*.

R   At

At thefe Words, which difcover'd what
I had to expeft, my Tears redoubled. *Aby
Aly*, who look'd on the Reafon of my
Fright with another Eye than mine, only
laugh'd, and made all the Sail he could towards *Algier*, whilft I afflifted my felf beyond all Bounds of Moderation; fometimes
I direfted my Sighs to Heav'n, and implor'd its Affiftance ; at others, I wifh'd
fome Chriftian Ships would attack us, or
that the Waves would fwallow us up; and
after that I wifh'd my Grief and Tears
might render me fo frightful, that the very Sight of me might ftrike a Horror into
the Dey. Vain Defires, alas, refulting
from my alarm'd Modefty! We arriv'd at
the Port, I was condufted to the Palace,
and fhewn to *Mezzomorto*. I don't know
what *Aby A'y* faid when he prefented me
to his Mafter, nor what he anfwer'd, becaufe they fpoke *Turkifh*; but I fancy'd
I could difcover, by the Geftures and Looks
of the Dey, that I had the Misfortune to
pleafe him : And what he afterwards faid
to me in *Spanifh* perfefted my Defpair,
by confirming me in that Opinion. I threw
my felf in vain at his Feet, and promis'd
whatever he pleas'd for my Ranfom: I
largely tempted his Avarice by the Offer of
all my Eftate : But he told me that he valu'd me above all the Riches in the World.
He

He caus'd this Apartment, the moſt magnificent in all his Palace, to be prepar'd for me; and has left no Means unattempted to diſpel that Grief which overwhelm'd me; he brought me all the Slaves of both Sexes, that could either ſing or play on any Inſtrument; he remov'd *Ines,* believing ſhe only fed my Melancholy, and I am waited on by old Slaves, who inceſſantly inculcate to me their Maſter's Love, and all the Pleaſures reſerv'd for me.

But all that has been done to divert me ſerves only to augment my Sorrows; nothing can comfort me. Captive as I am, in this deteſtable Palace, which every Day reſounds with the Cries of oppreſs'd Innocence, I ſuffer leſs by the Loſs of my Liberty, than the Terror with which the Dey's odious Paſſion inſpires me. For tho' I have hitherto found no other Treatment from him than that of a complaiſant Lover, I am not leſs affrighted, and very much fear, left abandoning that Reſpect which perhaps has hitherto reſtrain'd him, he ſhould at laſt abuſe his Power. I am continually afflicted by theſe dreadful Reflections, and every Moment of my Life is a freſh Torment.

Donna Theodora could not end theſe Words without Showers of Tears, which ſtabb'd *Don Juan* to the Heart: 'Tis not

R 2   with-

without Reafon, Madam, faid he, that you
form fuch a horrible Idea of what may happen to you: I am as much terrify'd at it
as you: The Dey's Refpect is nearer its
Declenfion than you imagine; this fubmif-
five Lover will foon throw off his feign'd
Complaifance: I know it but too well, and
know all the Danger you are in: But, continu'd he, changing his Tone, I will not
tamely fee it; Slave as I am, my Defpair
is to be fear'd. Before *Mezzomorto* fhall
force you, I will plunge into his Breaft —
Ah, *Don Juan*, interrupted *Donna Theodora*, what a dangerous Project are you ven-
turing at? Ah, be extreamly careful that
you never put it in Execution. What prodigious Cruelties, great God, will be the
Confequences of this Death! Will the
Turks leave it unreveng'd? Oh! the moft
dreadful Torments ——I cannot think of
them without trembling. Befides, is it not
to expofe your felf to an unnecessary Danger? Can you, by killing the Dey, reftore
my Liberty? Alas, perhaps I may be fold
to fome villainous Wretch, that may have
lefs Regard for me than *Mezzomorto* has.
O Heav'n! you ought to fhew your Juftice: You know the Dey's brutal Defires;
you forbid me the Ufe of Poifon and
Sword; it therefore belongs to you to prevent a Crime which offends you.

Yes,

Yes, Madam, reply'd *Don Juan*, Heaven will prevent it: I perceive that it inspires me; what at prefent occurs to my Mind, is doubtlefs fuggefted to me from thence. The Dey gave me leave to fee you, for no other Reafon than to encline you to yield to his Paffion: I am charg'd to give him an Account of our Converfation; but I muft deceive him: I will then tell him that you are not inconfolable; that his generous Conduct, with regard to you, begins to affwage your Griefs; and that, if he continues in the fame Meafures, he ought to hope for whatever he wifhes. Accordingly, when he comes to fee you again, I wifh he might find you lefs melancholy than ordinary, and feign your being in fome meafure pleas'd with his Difcourfe.

Oh horrid Conftraint! interrupted *Donna Theodora*; how can a frank and fincere Soul betray it felf to that degree? and what Advantage will refult from fuch a painful Diffimulation? The Dey, anfwer'd he, will pleafe himfelf with this Alteration, and refolve to gain you wholly by Complaifance. In the interim I will endeavour your Liberty: The Task, I own, is difficult; but I am acquainted with a Slave, whofe great Addrefs and Induftry may not be unferviceable to us. I leave you, continu'd he; the Affair requires Di-

ligence

ligence, and we shall see one another again.
I go now to the Dey, whose impetuous
Flame I will endeavour to amuse by false
Intelligence; and you, Madam, must prepare to receive him. Dissemble; force your
Nature: Tho' his Presence offend your
Eyes, yet disarm them of Severity and
Hatred. Prevail on your Mouth, which
only opens it self daily to bewail your Misfortunes, to learn a flattering Tone; and
don't fear shewing too much Favour. You
must promise every thing, in order to grant
nothing. 'Tis enough, reply'd *Donna The-*
odora; I will follow all your Directions,
since the fatal Evil which threatens me
imposes on me this cruel Necessity. Go,
Don Juan, imploy all your Cares in putting an End to my Slavery. 'Twill be a
great Addition to the Pleasure of Liberty,
to owe it to you.

The *Toledan,* pursuant to his Orders,
waited on *Mezzomorto,* who said with utmost Concern, Well, *Alvaro,* what News
do you bring me from the fair Slave? have
you dispos'd her to hearken to me? If you
tell me that I ought not to flatter my self
with the Hopes of ever subduing her cruel Grief, I swear by the Head of the *Grand*
Seigni r, my Master, that I will this Day
seize by Force what she has hitherto refu-
sed to yield to my Complaisance. Sir, an-
                                   swer'd

fwer'd *Don Juan,* that inviolable Oath is
needlefs; you will not be forc'd to make
ufe of Violence to fatisfie your Love, The
Slave is a young Lady who never yet lov'd;
fhe is fo proud that fhe has rejected the
Addreffes of the greateft Men in *Spain;*
fhe liv'd like a Sovereign Princefs in her
own Country, and is a Captive here. A
haughty Mind long refents the great Difference betwixt thefe Conditions; yet, Sir,
this proud *Spanifh* Lady will by degrees
grow familiar with Slavery, and I dare
venture to tell you that already her Chains
begin to be lighter. The great Deference
you have always fhew'd her, and the refpectful Cares which fhe did not expect
from you, have fomewhat abated her Sorrows, and do by little and little tame her
Pride. Sooth this favourable Difpofition,
and compleat the Conqueft of this fair
Slave by frefh Marks of Refpect, and you
will foon find her yield to your Defires,
and lofe the Love of Liberty in your Arms.

Your Words ravifh me, reply'd the Dey:
The Hopes which you have given me are
fufficient to engage me to do any thing.
Yes, I will reftrain my impatient Defires,
to fatisfie them the better. But don't deceive me; or art thou not thy felf deceiv'd?
I'll immediately go talk with her, and fee
whether I can difcover in her Eyes thofe

flatter-

flattering Appearances which you have obferv'd. Thefe Words ended, he went to
Donna Theodora; and *Don Juan* return'd
to the Garden, where he met the Gard'ner,
who was the dextrous Slave whofe Induftry he promis'd to ufe to fet the Widow
Cifuentes at Liberty.

The Gard'ner, whofe Name was *Francifco,* was of *Navarre.* He knew *Algier*
perfectly well, having ferv'd feveral Patrons before he liv'd with the Dey. Friend
Francifco, faid *Don Juan* approaching
him, I am extreamly afflicted at what I
have feen: There is in this Palace a young
Lady of the firft Quality in *Valencia,* fhe
has entreated *Mezzomorto* to fet his own
Price on her Ranfom; but he will not part
with her, becaufe he is in Love with her.
Alas, why does that trouble you fo much?
faid *Francifco.* Becaufe I am of the fame
City, reply'd the *Toledan;* her Relations
and mine are intimate Friends, and I am
no ways able to contribute to her Deliverance. Tho' 'tis no very eafie thing, reply'd *Francifco,* I dare engage to accomplifh it, if this Lady's Relations will be
pleafed to pay very well for this piece of
Service. Don't doubt it, in the leaft, return'd *Don Juan;* I will be refponfible
for their Acknowledgments, but more e-
fpecially for her own Gratitude. Her Name

is

is *Donna Theodora*; she is the Widow of
a Man which has left her a very great E-
state, and she is as Generous as Rich. I
am a *Spanish* Gentleman, and my Word
ought to satisfie you. Well, reply'd the
Gard'ner, I will depend on your Promises,
and go look for a Runagate *Catalan* of my
Acquaintance, and propose it to him——
What do you say? interrupted the *Toledan*, very much surpriz'd; Can you rely
on a Wretch, who has not been asham'd
to abandon his Religion for—— Tho' a
Runagate, interrupted *Francisco* in his
turn, he is yet an honest Man, who deserves rather to be pity'd than hated; and
if his Crime can admit of any Excuse, I
should indeed be willing to think him excusable : I'll tell you his Story in two
Words.

He is a Native of *Barcelona*, and a
Chyrurgion by Profession: Perceiving that
he did not succeed in his Practice, in his
Native Place, he resolv'd to settle at *Cartagena*, hoping that he might thrive
better by removing. He embark'd then
for *Cartagena* with his Mother, but they
met an *Algerine* Pirate, who took and
brought them hither. They were sold, his
Mother to a *Moor*, and he to a *Turk*, who
us'd him so very ill that he turn'd *Mahometan* to end his cruel Slavery, as also to
procure

procure the Liberty of his Mother, who was very rigorously treated by the *Moor*, her Patron. Then entering himself in the *Bafba*'s Pay, he made feveral Voyages, and got four hundred Patacoons, part of which he employ'd in the Ranfom of his Mother, and to improve it he intended to rob on the Sea for his own Account.

He became a Captain, and bought a fmall Veffel without a Deck, and with fome *Turkifh* Soldiers, who willingly join'd with him, he went to cruife between *Cartagena* and *Alicant*, and return'd laden with Booty. He went out again, and his Voyage fucceeded fo well, that at laft he fitted out a large Veffel, with which he took feveral confiderable Prizes; but his good Fortune failing him, he one Day attack'd an *Englifh* Frigot, who fo fhatter'd his Ship, that he could fcarce regain the Port of *Algier*; and as the People of this Country judge of the Merit of the Pirates, by the Succefs of their Enterprifes, this Runagate began to be defpis'd by the *Turks*; and growing very uneafie and melancholy, he fold his Ship and retir'd to a Houfe out of Town, where ever fince he has liv'd on the Eftate he has left, with his Mother and feveral Slaves. I frequently vifit him, for we liv'd together with the fame Patron, and are very great Friends.

He

He has difclos'd to me his moft fecret Thoughts, and within thefe three Days he told me, with Tears in his Eyes, that he could never be eafie, after he was fo unhappy as to deny his Faith; that to appeafe the Remorfe which inceffantly rack'd his Mind, he was fometimes inclin'd to quit the Turban, and hazard being burnt alive, to repair, by a publick Acknowledgment of his Repentance, the Scandal he had caft on the Chriftians.

This is the Runagate to which I defign to addrefs my felf, continu'd *Francifco*; fuch a Man as this you ought not to fufpect. Under Pretence of going to the * *Bagne*, I will go to his Houfe, and fuggeft to him, that inftead of confuming himfelf with Grief for withdrawing himfelf from the Bofom of the Church, he ought to think of means of returning to it: That to execute this Defign, he need only equip a Ship on pretence that weary of an idle Life, he would return to his old trade of Cruifing, and with this Ship we will gain the Coaft of *Valencia*, where *Donna Theodora* fhould give him enough to pafs the reft of his Days agreeably at *Barcelona.*

Yes,

---

* *That is, the Place where the Slaves meet.*

Yes, dear *Francisco*, cry'd *Don Juan*, transported with the Hopes which the *Navarre* Slave gave him, you may promise the Runagate every thing; you and he shall be sure to be rewarded. But do you believe this Project really practicable in the Manner you have form'd it ? It may meet with some Difficulties which I don't foresee, reply'd *Francisco*, but the Runagate and I will remove them. *Alvaro*, added he, as he was leaving him, I have a very good Opinion of our Enterprise, and hope at my Return to bring you good News.

'Twas not without Anxiety that *Don Juan* waited for *Francisco*, who return'd in three or four Hours. I have talk'd with the Runagate, said he, and propos'd our Design to him, and after mature Deliberation, we have agreed that he shall buy a small Ship ready fitted to go out, and it being allow'd to make use of Slaves for Sailors, he shall Man the Vessel with his own; that, to prevent Suspicion, he should engage twelve *Turkish* Soldiers, as tho' he really intended to go out to Cruise; but that two Days before that which he should assign for his Departure, he should embark in the Night with his Slaves, weigh Anchor without any Noise, and come to fetch us on Board with his Skiff, from a little Door of this Garden near the Sea. This is the

Plan

Plan of our Enterprife; you may inform the Captive Lady of this, and affure her, that within fifteen Days at fartheft, fhe fhall be freed from her Slavery.

How inexpreffible was *Don Juan's* Joy, to have fuch a comfortable Affurance to carry to off *Donna Theodora*! To obtain Permiffion to fee her, he the next Day fearch'd for *Mezzomorto*, and having found him : Pardon me, my Lord, faid he, if I prefume to ask you how you found the beautiful Slave. Are you better fatisfy'd——— I am charm'd, interrupted they Dey. Her Eyes did not turn away from my tendereft Addreffes; her Difcourfe, which always before confifted only of endlefs Reflections on her Condition, were not intermix'd with any Complaints; but fhe even feem'd to liften to mine with an obliging Attention. 'Tis to your Endeavours, *Alvaro,* that I owe this Change. I fee you know your own Country Women; I will have you talk with her again. Finifh what you have fo happily begun ; exhauft all your Wit and Addrefs to haften my Felicity, and I will then break your Chains; and I fwear by the Soul of our great Prophet, that I will fend you home to your own Country fo richly laden with Prefents, that the Chriftians when they fee thee fhall not believe thou return'ft from a Slavery.

The

The *Toledan* did not fail to flatter *Mezzo-morto*'s Error; he feign'd himself extreamly fenfible of his Promifes, and under pretence of haftening the Accomplifhment of the Dey's Joys, he haften'd to fee the Fair Slave, whom he found alone in her Apartment, the old Women which attended her being employ'd elfewhere.

He told her what the *Navarre* Slave and the Runagate had contriv'd, on the Credit of the Promifes which he made them. 'Twas no fmall Confolation for *Donna Theodora*, to hear that fuch proper Meafures were taken for her Deliverance. Is it poffible, faid fhe, in the Excefs of her Joy, that I may hope to fee *Valencia*, my dear Country, again? How tranfporting will the Blifs be, after fo many Fears and Dangers, to live at Eafe with you? Ah, *Don Juan*, how charming is that Thought! Will you fhare that Pleafure with me? Do you think, that in delivering me from the Dey, 'tis your Wife which you tear from him?

Alas, anfwer'd *Don Juan*, with a profound Sigh, thofe endearing Words would charm me, if the Remembrance of an unhappy Friend did not throw in a Bitternefs which fpoils all the Sweetnefs? Pardon me, Madam, that Nicety. and confefs alfo that *Mendoça* deferves your Pity; 'tis
for

for your fake that he went from *Valencia*,
and loft his Liberty. I can affure you that
at *Tunis*, where perhaps Slaves may be
worfe treated than here, he is lefs loaded
with the Weight of his Chains, than the
Defpair of ever revenging your Sufferings.
He doubtlefs deferves a better Fate, interrupted *Donna Theodora*; I take Heav'n to
witnefs that I am throughly fenfible of all
that he has done for me. I fhare with him
the Sufferings which I have caus'd; but by
the cruel Malignity of the Stars, my Heart
can never be the Price of his Services.

This Converfation was interrupted by
the Arrival of the two old Women who
waited on *Donna Theodora*, when *Don
Juan* turn'd the Difcourfe, and acting the
Dey's Confident: Yes, charming Slave,
faid he to the Widow *Cifuentes*, you have
depriv'd him of Liberty, who keeps you
in Chains. *Mezzomorto*, your Mafter and
mine, the moft engaging, and moft amiable
of all the *Turks*, is very well pleas'd with
you: Continue to treat him favourably, and
you will foon fee an End of your Griefs.
At the End of thefe laft Words he left
Donna Theodora, who did not comprehend their true Senfe.

Affairs remain'd during eight Days in
this Pofture at the Dey's Palace whilft the
Runagate *Catalan* bought a fmall Veffel
almoft

almoft wholly fitted for Sailing, and prepar'd for his Departure. But fix Days before he was ready to put to Sea, *Don Juan*
met with what very much alarm'd his
Fears.

Mezzomorto fent for him, and being enter'd his Clofet: *Alvaro*, faid he, you are
free: You may return to *Spain* whenever
you pleafe; and the Prefents which I promis'd you are ready. I faw the fair Slave
to Day, and oh, how vaftly different does
fhe appear from the fame Perfon whofe
Griefs have given me fo much Pain! The
fenfe of her Captivity every Day wears off.
I found her fo Charming, that I have this
Moment refolv'd to marry her. She fhall
be my Wife within the Space of two Days.

At thefe Words the *Toledan* chang'd Colour, and notwithftanding all the Reftraint
he laid on himfelf, could not hide his Difturbance and Surprize from the Dey, who
afk'd him the Caufe of that Diforder. My
Lord, anfwer'd *Don Juan*, all in Confufion, I am doubtlefs very much amaz'd,
to think that one of the greateft Lords of
the *Ottoman* Empire fhould fo debafe himfelf as to marry a Slave. I very well know
'tis not unprefidented amongft you; but
for the illuftrious *Mezzomorto*, who may
pretend to the Daughter of the principal
Officers of the Port,———I allow what
you

you fay, interrupted the Dey, I might at
the fame time afpire to the *Grand Vifier's*
Daughter, and flatter my felf with the
Hopes of fucceeding my Father-in-Law;
but I have an immenfe Eftate, and am not
very Ambitious. I prefer the Eafe and
Pleafures which I enjoy here in my *Vifier-
fhip,* to that dangerous Honour; to which
we are no fooner rais'd, than the Fear of
the *Sultans,* and the Jealoufie of thofe near
them, who envy us, precipitates us into
the loweft Abyfs of Mifery. Befides, I
love my Slave, and her Beauty qualifies her
to deferve the Dignity, to which my Affection invites her.

But, adds he, in order to deferve the
Honours I defign her, fhe muft change her
Religion. Do you believe that any ridiculous Prejudices will prevail on her to defpife my Offers? No, my Lord, return'd
the *Toledan;* I am perfuaded that fhe will
facrifice all to fuch a high Elevation. But
give me leave to tell you, that you ought
not to marry her fo haftily; do nothing
rafhly; 'tis not to be doubted, but that the
Thoughts of abandoning the Religion
fuck'd in with her Mother's Milk will ftar-
tle her at firft. Give her then time to confider of it; when fhe reprefents to her
felf, that inftead of difhonouring and con-
fining her under a Guard amongft the reft

S   of

of your Captives, you join her to your felf
by fuch a glorious Marriage, her Gratitude
and Vanity will by little and little remove
her Scruples. Defer therefore the Execution of your Defign for eight Days only.
I yield to your Reafon, interrupted the
Dey; tho' I am fo impatient to enjoy the
fair Slave, I will yet wait eight Days. Go
immediately to her, and difpofe her to accomplifh my Defires at the Expiration of
that time. I defire that the fame *Alvaro*,
which has fo faithfully difcharg'd himfelf
with regard to her, have the Honour to
offer her my matrimonial Faith.

Don Juan flew to the Apartment of
Donna Theodora, and inform'd her what
pafs'd betwixt *Mezzomorto* and him, that
fhe might regulate her felf by it. He alfo
told her, that the Runagate's Ship would
be ready in fix Days ; but fhe telling him
that fhe was in great Pain to know how
fhe fhould get out of her Apartment, fince
all the Doors of the Chambers, thro' which
fhe was oblig'd to pafs to reach the Stairs,
were clofe fhut; You ought not to give
your felf much Trouble on that account,
Madam, faid *Don Juan*; one of your Clofet Windows opens into the Garden, and
from thence you may defcend by a Ladder
which I will provide you. Accordingly,
the fix Days being expir'd, *Francifco* ad-
vertis'd

vertis'd the *Toledan,* that the Runagate was preparing to depart the next Night; which you very well think was expected with great Impatience. The time came at laft, and what render'd it yet more lucky was that it grew very dark. When the Moment deftin'd for the Execution of their Enterprize came, *Don Juan* rais'd the Ladder to *Donna Theodora*'s Clofet Window, who no fooner faw it, than fhe defcended on it with utmoft Concern and Hafte, and then lean'd on the falfe *Alvaro,* who conducted her to the little Garden-Door, which open'd on the Sea. They made all poffible Hafte, and before-hand feem'd to tafte the Pleafures of being freed from Slavery; but Fortune, between whom and Lovers there is not always a perfect Agreement, rais'd a more cruel Misfortune than all thofe which they had hitherto fuffer'd, and which they could not forefee.

They were gotten out of the Garden, and haftening to the Sea-fide to reach the Boat, which waited for them, when a Man, whom they took for one of their Crew, and which they did not in the leaft miftruft, came directly to *Don Juan* with a naked Sword, and running him into the Breaft: Perfidious *Alvaro Ponce,* cry'd he, 'tis thus that *Don Fadrique de Mendoça* is oblig'd to punifh a villainous Ravifher. You don't

de-

deserve that I should attack you like a Man
of Honour.

Don Juan could not resist the Force of
the Push, which threw him down; and at
the same time *Donna Theodora*, whom he
supported, seiz'd at once with Amazement,
Grief, and the Fright, swooned away on
the other side. Ah! *Mendoça*, said the
Toledan, what have you done? 'Tis *Don
Juan* that you have wounded! Juft
Heav'n, reply'd *Don Fadrique*, is it poſſible that I should assaſſinate my beſt Friend?
I forgive you my Death, return'd *Don
Juan*; Fate alone is to be blam'd, or rather
he deſign'd thus to put an End to my Mi-
ſeries. Yes, my dear *Mendoça*, I die contented, since I put into your Hands *Donna
Theodora*, who can aſſure you that my
Friendſhip for you has never been violated. Too generous Friend, said *Don Fadrique*, seiz'd with a violent Despair, you
shall not die alone ; the same Sword which
has been plung'd into your Breaſt shall puniſh your Murtherer. Tho' my Miſtake may
excuſe my Crime, it cannot comfort me.
At theſe Words he turn'd the Point of his
Sword to his Breaſt, run it up to the Hilt,
and fell upon *Don Juan*, who fainted away,
leſs enfeebled by his loſt Blood, than the
Surprize of his Friend's Diſtraction.

Fran-

Francisco and the Runagate, who were but ten Paces off, and who had their Reasons which detain'd them from running to the Assistance of the Slave *Alvaro,* were extreamly astonish'd to hear *Don Fadrique*'s Words, and to see his last Action. They then found their Mistake, and that the wounded Men were two Friends, and not mortal Enemies, as they thought. They then ran to their Assistance; but finding them senseless, as well as *Donna Theodora,* who yet remain'd in her Swoon, they were at a loss what Measures to take. *Francisco* was of Opinion that they should content themselves by carrying off the Lady, and leave the Gentlemen on the Shoar, where, according to all Appearances, they would immediately die, if they were not yet dead. But the Runagate was not of that Opinion: He concluded they ought not to be left; that their Wounds might perhaps not be mortal, and that he could dress them on Board, where he had all the Instruments of his former Trade, which he had not yet forgotten.

Francisco fell in with his Opinion, and very well knowing of what Importance it was to be expeditious, the Runagate and he, by the Assistance of some Slaves, carry'd into their Skiff the unhappy Widow

Cisu-

Cifuentes, and her two Lovers, yet more
unfortunate than fhe; and in a very few
Minutes reach'd their Ship. As foon as they
were all gotten on Board, fome of them
fpread their Sails, whilft others on their
Knees on the Deck implor'd the Affiftance
of Heav'n, by the moft fervent Petitions
which the Fear of being purfu'd by *Mezzomorto*'s Ships could infpire.

The Runagate, after having charg'd with
the Management of the Ship a *French*
Slave, who underftood it perfectly well,
apply'd himfelf firft to *Donna Theodora*,
whom he recover'd out of her Swoon, and
then took fuch fuccefsful Care of *Don Fadrique* and the *Toledan*, that they alfo recover'd their Sences. The Widow *Cifuentes*, who fainted away at the Sight of
Don Juan's being wounded, was very
much furpriz'd to find *Mendoça* there; and
tho' at the Sight of him fhe really believ'd
that he had fallen on his own Sword, for
Grief of having wounded his Friend, yet
fhe could not look on him otherwife than
the Murtherer of the Man fhe lov'd.

'Twas certainly the moft moving Scene
in the World, to fee thefe three Perfons
return'd to themfelves; and the Condition
out of which they had been recover'd, tho'
a Refemblance of Death, did not more deferve

ferve Pity. *Donna Theodora* earneftly look'd
on *Don Juan*, with Eyes in which were
painted, in lively Colours, all the Emotions of a Soul overwhelm'd with Grief and
Defpair. And the two Friends fix'd on
her their dying Eyes, feebly uttering the
moft profound Sighs.

After having for fome time kept a Silence equally tender and unhappy, *Don
Fadrique* thus broke it, by addreffing him to
the Widow *Cifuentes*: Madam, faid he,
before I die, I have yet the Satisfaction to
fee you deliver'd out of Slavery; would to
Heav'n that you were indebted for your
Liberty to me: But it has appointed that
you fhould owe that Obligation to the Man
which you love. I love that Rival too
well to murmur at it, and wifh that the
Wound which I have been fo unhappy as
to give him, may not prevent the full Enjoyment of your grateful Acknowledge-
ments. The Lady made no Anfwer to thefe
Words, but far from being then fenfible
of the melancholy Fate of *Don Fadrique*,
fhe was only influenced by the Averfion to
him, which the prefent Condition of the
Toledan had infpir'd.

In the mean time the Chirurgeon prepar'd to examine and probe the Wounds.
He began with that of *Don Juan*, and did

S 4   not

not find it dangerous, by reafon the Pafs had only glanc'd below the left Breaft, and had not touch'd any of the nobler Vital Parts. This Report of the Chirurgeon very much abated *Donna Theodora*'s Afflicti-on, and equally rejoyc'd *Don Fadrique*; who turning his Head towards that Lady, I am fatisfy'd, faid he; I leave this Life without Regret, fince my Friend is out of Danger : I fhall not then die laden with your Hate.

Thefe Words were utter'd with fuch a moving Air, that *Theodora* was touch'd by them; and as her Fear for *Don Juan* grew over, fhe ceas'd to hate *Don Fadrique*, and no longer look'd on him otherwife than on a Man which deferv'd her Pity : Ah, *Mendoça*, cry'd fhe, influenc'd by a generous Tranfport, let your Wound be drefs'd, 'tis not perhaps more dangerous than that of your Friend. Oh, yield to our Cure of your Life ; and if I cannot make you happy, at leaft I will not beftow that Felicity on another ; but out of Compaffion and Tendernefs for you, I will with-hold the Hand which I defign'd to give *Don Juan*, and offer to you the fame Sacrifice which he has made you : Content to reign in both your Hearts, I will live with you in fuch a Manner that he whom I don't
love

love fhall have no Reafon to complain of
the other.

Don Fadrique was going to reply, but
the Chirurgeon, afraid that Speaking might
prejudice him, oblig'd him to Silence, and
fearch'd his Wound, which he judg'd
mortal, by reafon the Sword had pierc'd
the upper Part of his Lungs, as he concluded from his exceffive Flux of Blood,
the Confequence of which was very much
to be fear'd. As foon as he had drefs'd
the Gentlemen he caus'd 'em to be carry'd to his own Cabin, to repofe them on
two Beds, one next the other, and conducted *Donna Theodora* thither, whofe
Prefence he thought would not be prejudicial to them.

Notwithftanding all this Care *Mendoça*
fell into a Feaver, and towards Night the
Flux of Blood augmented. The Chirurgeon then told him he was incurable, and
inform'd him that if he had any thing to
fay to his Friend, or *Donna Theodora*, he
had no Time to lofe. This News ftrangely afflicted the *Toledan*; but *Don Fadrique*
receiv'd it with Indifference. He fent for
the Widow *Cifuentes*, who came to him
in a Condition much eafier to be imagin'd
than defcrib'd.

Her

Her Face was cover'd with Tears which
ſhower'd down with ſo much Violence that
they diſturb'd *Mendoça*. Madam, ſaid he,
I am unworthy thoſe precious Tears that
you ſhed? Reſtrain them, I beg, for a Moment: I ask the ſame of you, dear *Don
Juan*, adds he, obſerving the inſupporta-
ble Grief which his Friend ſhew'd. I know
that this Separation muſt very ſenſibly afflict you, I am too well acquainted with
your Friendſhip to doubt it; but I beſeech
both of you to ſtay 'till my Death, and re-
ſerve theſe Tears to honour it with ſo many Marks of Tenderneſs and Pity; ſuſpend
your Grief 'till then, ſince that touches
me more than the Loſs of my Life. I muſt
acquaint you through what Meanders of
Fate I was conducted to this fatal Shore,
where I have tainted my ſelf with my
Friend's and my own Blood. You muſt
be in Pain to know how I could take *Don
Juan* for *Don Alvaro*, but I will immediately inform you, if the ſmall Remainder
of Life will allow me to make that melancholy Diſcovery.

Some Hours after the Ship in which I
was had quitted that where I left *Don Juan*, we met a *French* Privateer, which attack'd and took the *Tunis* Ship, and ſet us
on Shore at *Alicant*. I was no ſooner at
Liberty

Liberty than I thought of ranfoming *Don Juan*, to which end I went to *Valencia* and rais'd Mony; and on Advice that at *Barcelona* there were feveral Monks of the Order for Redemption of Slaves ready to fet out for *Algier*, I refolv'd not to lofe this Occafion. But before I left *Valencia*, I entreated *Don Francifco de Mendoça*, my Uncle, to ufe all his Intereft at the Court of *Spain* to obtain a Pardon for my Friend, becaufe my Defign was to bring him back with me, and re-eftablifh him in his Eftate, which was confifcated after the Death of the Duke of *Naxera*. I went then to *Barcelona*, where I ftaid not above eight Days before I embark'd with the Monks of the Redemption.

As foon as we were arriv'd at *Algier*, I went to the Places frequented by Slaves; but having run thro' all of them, I did not find what I fearch'd for. After this I in vain recollected the Faces of the Paffengers taken with *Don Juan*, and confronted the Lines of their Features which I could recall to mind, with thofe Faces that offer'd themfelves to my View; but I could not find any Perfon whom I remember'd to have feen. Not being contented with this, I ask'd all the *Spanifh* Slaves I met whether they could inform me of a
Cava-

Cavalier of their Nation which anfwer'd
the Defcription I gave them of you, and
taken at fuch a time. Some told me he
muft be fet at Work in a Country Houfe,
and others that perhaps he might be one of
the twelve Chriftian Slaves who were lately impal'd for beating the *Mahometans;*
and this was all the Fruit of my Enqui-
ries.

Yet òne Day I perceiv'd a young Man
looking very earneftly at me, whom I remember'd to be a Youth that formerly
ferv'd my Uncle. He concluded, at the
Sight of me, that I was not a Slave; wherefore approaching me he faid, My Lord,
may I prefume to ask whether you have
yet any Remainder of Concern for *Donna
Theodora?* When I anfwer'd him Yes:
Since 'tis fo, reply'd he, give your felf the
Trouble of accompanying me, and you
fhall foon hear of her. I went along with
him, and he brought me to his Patron,
who is the Runagate *Catalan* to whom this
Ship belongs. He talk'd long with him a-
lone; after which the Runagate came to
me, and inform'd me that his Slave had
juft told him my Name; and fince he af-
fures me, added he, that we may depend
on your Difcretion, I will difcover to you
where a Lady is whofe Fate you are concern'd

cern'd for. *Donna Theodora* is a Slave to the Dey, who will not take any Ranſom for her, becauſe he loves her.

The Grief which I ſhew'd at this News mov'd the Runagate: Comfort your ſelf, ſaid he, Signior *Mendoça*; I can aſſure you *Mezzomorto* has not yet offer'd any Violence to that Lady, and ſince you are in Love with her, I will make no difficulty of entruſting you with a Secret which 'tis your Intereſt to conceal. The Dey's Gard'ner is a Slave born at *Navarre*, of my Acquaintance; he has told me that in his Maſter's Palace is a Lady of *Valencia*, call'd *Donna Theodora*, who offers a very conſiderable Reward to any Perſon that ſhall free her from Slavery. I have undertaken this Deliverance, and am equipping a Veſſel which will be ready in few Days, and under Pretext of Cruizing I will make to the Coaſt of *Spain*, where I will reſtore this Lady to her Relations. But how, ſaid I, will you get her out of the *Seraglio*? Two of *Mezzomorto*'s Slaves, anſwer'd he, have undertaken this Task. He of *Navarre*, whom I have mention'd to you, and another of *Valencia*, as I am told; but I have not yet ſeen the laſt, tho' by the Charaɗer I have heard of him, he ſeems to be a Man of Quality.

I

I ask'd the Runagate, with some Concern, if he did not know the latter Slave's Name; 'Tis *Alvaro,* reply'd he, and that is all I know of him. And all that I desire to know, cry'd I, in a Transport; 'tis my Rival! And without asking any farther Questions concerning that Slave, or informing my self whether he was taken with *Donna Theodora,* I did not doubt but that this *Alvaro* was *Alvaro Ponce* himself.

I gave a horrible Character of him to the Runagate, whom I entreated to engage in my Resentment. Assist, said I, both my Hate and my Love. Help me to revenge my self on my Enemy, and put an End to *Donna Theodora's* Captivity; you shall not then have only what she promises, but I will superadd particular Marks of my Gratitude. The Runagate returning no Answer, but seeming thoughtful, I concluded that he was considering whether he should accomplish my Desires; wherefore, to determine him, I presented him with a very fine Diamant Ring which I had on my Finger; but he refus'd it, saying, My Lord, do you believe that I distrust your Promises, or that they are not sufficient to engage me to serve a Gentleman of your Family? If you saw me considering,

fidering, I was only thinking which Way
to fatisfie you; which will foon be: You
need only accompany me on the Night chofen for our Departure, when you may fee
your Enemy; and after you have reveng'd
your felf, you fhall, if you pleafe, take
his Place, and join with us in conducting
Donna Theodora to *Valencia.*

These Words too much flatter'd my angry Refentment not to ravifh me; I thank'd
the Runagate for his Zeal for my Service,
forc'd him to accept my Diamant Ring,
and left him very impatient to fee *Don Alvaro* fall by my Hands. Yet this Impatience
did not hinder my Search after *Don Juan;*
but defpairing to hear any News of him,
I left Mony for his Ranfom in the Hands
of an *Italian* Merchant, nam'd *Francifco
Capati,* who lives at *Algier,* and under-
took his Ranfom if he could ever find
him.

At laft the Night appointed for our Departure and my Revenge came, when I
went to the Runagate, who led me to that
Part of the Sea-fhore behind *Mezzomorto's*
Gardens. We ftopp'd at a little Door that
foon open'd, where came out a Man that
made directly to us, which was the *Navarre* Slave. He ask'd the Runagate in
what Pofture our Affairs were: My Veffel,

fel, anfwer'd he, has this Minute left the
Port, and I expect the Boat here. Accordingly he had no fooner fpoke than the
Skiff appear'd. I will then, faid the *Navarre* Slave, go tell *Alvaro* that he may
bring the Lady; at which Words he return'd into the Garden, and fome Minutes
after came up to us, and pointing with his
Finger to a Man and Woman which were
coming along: Thofe who follow me, faid
he, are *Alvaro* and *Donna Theodora.* At
this Sight, enrag'd to the laft degree, I drew
my Sword, run to the unfortunate *Alvaro,*
and perfuaded that it was my hateful Rival which I was approaching, I wounded
that faithful Friend, whofe uncertain De-
ftiny was the Caufe of all my Difturbance.
But Thanks to Heav'n, continu'd he, in
a fofter Tone, my Miftake will neither coft
him his Life, nor the eternal Tears of
Donna Theodora.

Ah, *Mendoça,* interrupted the Lady,
you injure my Affliction; I fhall never comfort my felf for the Lofs of you; for tho'
I fhould ev'n marry your Friend, 'twould
be only uniting our Griefs: Your Love,
your Friendfhip and your Misfortunes
would be the whole Subj ct of our Difcourfe. 'Tis too much, Madam, reply'd
Don Fadrique; I am not worthy your fo
long

long Mourning for me. Allow, I conjure you, *Don Juan* to marry you, after he shall have reveng'd you of *Alvaro Ponce. Don Alvaro* is no more, reply'd the Widow *Cifuentes*; the same Day that he seiz'd me, he was kill'd by the Pirate which took me.

Madam, said *Mendoça*, this News gives me Pleasure: My Friend will the sooner be happy; follow without restraint the Guidance of your mutual Passion. I see with Joy the Moment approaching, which will remove the Obstacle your Compassion and his Generosity hath rais'd, to prevent your mutual Happiness. May all your Days be spent in a Repose and Union, which the Jealousie of Fortune dare not disturb. Adieu, Madam, adieu, *Don Juan*; vouchsafe both of you sometimes to remember a Man, who never lov'd any Body so well as you.

The Lady and the *Toledan*, instead of answering, redoubling their Tears; *Don Fradique*, who perceiv'd it, and found himself very ill; thus continu'd : I grow too tender; Death has already surrounded me, and I forget to supplicate the Divine Goodness, to pardon my having shortned a Life, which it alone ought to have dispos'd of. At the End of these

T   Words

Words he lifted up his Eyes to Heav'n, with all the Signs of a sincere Repentance, and the Flux of Blood immediately occasion'd a Suffocation, which carry'd him off.

Then *Don Juan*, hurry'd by his Despair, tore off his Plaisters, and would have render'd his Wounds incurable ; but *Francisco* and the Runagate threw themselves on him, and oppos'd his Distraction; and *Donna Theodora*, terribly affrighted at this furious Transport, assisted them both in diverting *Don Juan* from his Design. She addres'd to him with such a moving Air, that returning to himself, he suffer'd his Wound to be again bound up; and at last the Interest of a Lover, by flow Degrees, abated the Rage of a Friend. But if he recover'd his Reason, it serv'd only to prevent the distracted Effects of his Grief, and not to diminish the Sense of it.

The Runagate, who amongst other things he had brought out of *Spain*, had some excellent *Arabian* Balsam, and precious Prefumes, embalm'd *Mendoça*'s Body at the Instance of the Lady and *Don Juan*, who assur'd him, that at *Valencia* they would perform all the Honours of his Sepulture. Both of them did not give

over

over Sighs and Tears during the whole
time of their being at Sea; but the reft
of thofe on Board were more chearful,
and the Wind being favourable, they
were not long before they difcover'd the
Coafts of *Spain.*

At that Sight all the Slaves yielded
themfelves up to Joy; and when the
Veffel was happily arriv'd at the Port of
Denia, every one had their Share of it.
The Widow *Cifuentes* and the *Toledan*
fent a Courier to *Valencia* with Letters
for the Governor, and *Donna Theodora's*
Family. The News of that Lady's Return was receiv'd with all poffible Expreffions of Joy, by all her Relations;
but *Don Francifco de Mendoça* was extreamly afflicted at the Lofs of his Nephew, which he difcover'd when he accompany'd the Widow *Cifuentes's* Relations to *Denia,* where he defir'd to fee the
Corps of the unfortunate *Don Fadrique.*
The good old Man then melted into
Tears, and utter'd fuch lamentable Complaints, as fenfibly touch'd all the Specta-
tors. He enquir'd by what Adventure
his Nephew fell : I will tell you, my
Lord, faid the *Toledan*; far from blotting
it out of my Memory, I take a melancholy Pleafure in continually calling him

T 2

to Mind, and feeding my Sorrows. He
then related to him the fad Accident; and
the Recital of his Story drawing frefh
Tears from him, redoubled thofe of *Don
Francifco.* As for *Donna Theodora,* her
Relations exprefs'd their great Joy to fee
her again, and felicitated her on the mi-
raculous Manner of her Delivery from the
Tyranny of *Mezzomorto.*

After a perfect Relation of all Particulars, *Don Fadrique*'s Corps was put into
a Coach, and carry'd to *Valencia,* but
not bury'd there; becaufe *Don Francifco
de Mendoça* being going to live at *Madrid,* refolv'd to have his Nephew's Body carry'd to that City. While all manner of Preparations were making for their
Journey, the Widow *Cifuentes* loaded
with Riches *Francifco* and the Runagate which follow'd them. *Francifco*
went to *Navarre,* and the Runagate immediately return'd to *Denia,* where he
had left his Mother, fold his Ship, and
went to *Barcelona,* where he return'd to
the Chriftian Religion, and lives there
very handfomly at this prefent time. In
the mean while alfo *Don Francifeo* receiv'd
a Packet from the Court, wherein was
Don Juan's Pardon; which the King, notwithftanding the great Value he had for
                                          the

the Houfe of *Naxera,* could not refufe the *Mendoça's,* who all join'd in follici-ting it. This News was the more agree-able to the *Toledan,* becaufe it procur'd him the Liberty of accompanying the Corps of his Friend, which he durft not have done without it.

At laft they all fet forwards, accompa-ny'd with a great Number of Perfons of Quality; and as foon as they arriv'd at *Madrid,* they bury'd the Corps of *Don Fadrique* in a Church, where *Don Juan* and *Donna Theodora* rais'd a noble Mo-nument over his Grave. They did not ftay there; but they kept themfelves in Mourning for their Friend for the Space of a whole Year, to eternize their Grief, and his Friendfhip; and after having given fuch fignal Marks of their Tendernefs for *Mendoça,* they marry'd; but by an in-conceivable Effect of the Power of Friend-fhip, *Don Juan* long retain'd his Me-lancholy for his Friend, which nothing was able to remove. *Don Fadrique,* his dear Friend, *Don Fadrique,* was always prefent in his Thoughts; he faw him every Night in his Dreams, at which he moft times utter'd the deepeft Sighs. But yet his Reafon began to difpel thefe me-lancholy Views; and *Donna Theodora's*

Charms,

Charms, with which he was captivated, triumph'd, by little and little, over the sad Remembrance of his Friend. To conclude; at last *Don Juan* liv'd happily, and very contentedly; but a few Days past he fell from his Horse, as he was Hunting, and hurt his Head; the Wound grew to an Impostume, so that the Physicians could not save him, and some Hours since he dy'd in the Arms of *Donna Theodora*, who is that Lady which the Women in vain endeavour to assist. She has a violent Feaver, is delirious, and is hasting after her Husband; so that both of them will soon be carry'd to *Mendoça's* Tomb, where with him they will expect the End of that World in which they have suffer'd so many Miseries.

C H A P.

CHAP. XVI.
Of DREAMS.

WHEN *Asmodeo* had ended his Story, *Don Cleofas* said to him, This is a very fine Image of Friendship, but 'tis rare to find two Men love one another like *Don Juan* and *Don Fadrique;* and I believe 'twill be more difficult to meet with two Ladies fo good Friends, as generoufly to make a reciprocal Sacrifice of their Lovers to each other. Without doubt, fays the Devil, 'tis what has not been yet, and never will be feen in this World: Women are not fo complaifant to one another. Suppofe two Ladies love each other in an ufual degree, their Friendship may be tender and fincere, and they may even forbear fpeaking ill of one another in Abfence; fuch good Friends may they be, and that, I affure you, is a great deal: Yet if you meet with them, and incline more to the one than the other, Rage prefently feizes the fair One that is flighted, not that fhe loves you, but fhe would be preferr'd. This is the Nature of all Women; they are too jealous one of another to be capable of Friendship.

As to *Donna Theodora,* fays the Scholar, I am charm'd with her Character: A Wife to die of Grief at the Death of her Husband! A Wonder's fallen out in our Days. 'Tis certainly wonderful, reply'd the Devil: There was a Lawyer bury'd two Months ago, whofe Widow was not at all like his we are fpeak-

ing of. The Man of the Robe being in the
Agonies of the Death, his Wife all in Tears
gave way to the Perfuafions of her Family,
and fuffer'd her felf to be carry'd out of the
Houfe to avoid fo fad a Spectacle: But before fhe went, the good Woman call'd her
Chamber-maid; *Beatrice,* faid fhe, as foon as
my dear Husband is dead go carry the ill
News to *Don Carlos,* and tell him I am fo
troubled at it that I will not fee him this two
Days.

The Story of *Donna Theodora,* fays *Don
Cleofas,* has taken up a little too much Time.
'Tis almoft broad Day; I begin to fee People
in the Streets; I am afraid they may fpy us out
on this Church. If the Rabble fhould once
have a view of your Lordfhip's Figure, they
will never have done fhouting. Fear nothing,
reply'd the Devil, I'll warrant they fhall not
fee us; I have the fame Power as the Poets
Gods, and as *Jupiter* hid himfelf in a Cloud
on Mount *Ida,* from the Eyes of the Univerfe,
that they might not fee him Carefs his dear
Confort *Juno,* fo I will raife a Mift that the
Sight of Man fhall not be able to penetrate;
however we will fee him, and all his Ways,
thro' it. No fooner faid but done; a thick
Vapour immediately encompafs'd them; yet
the Scholar faw thro' it as eafily as if it had
been a Sieve. Now, continu'd the *Demon,*
I will give you a Pleafure that you have not
met with before. You fee abundance of Perfons, Men and Women, afleep, and I'll tell
you what they dream of.　　　　　Stay,

Stay, if you pleafe, fays *Don Cleofas* interrupting him ; pray what's the meaning that
thofe Ladies in yonder little Tenament are up
fo foon; what makes 'em rife fo early? They
were never a-bed, reply'd the Devil, they
have been making merry all Night long. There
has been an Affembly; they have been finging
Caudalas, a moft admirable Confort. A Scholar of *Alcala* compos'd the Mufick, and the
Words were made by a Man of Quality, who
makes Verfes for his own Pleafure, and others
Pain. The Symphony confifted of a Bag-
pipe and a Spinet, and what is ftill more extraordinary, a young Girl fung the Bafe, and
an old Quirifter the Tenor. Very pleafant
indeed, cry'd *Don Cleofas*, ready to burft with
laughing; if I had been one of their Affembly,
I fhould not have help'd making a Jeft of
their ridiculous Confort. Sure thofe that
heard it did not think it fine. No certainly,
reply'd *Afmodeo*, there were fome among 'em
who every now and then threw in a malicious
Jeft, that put the Mufick very much out of
Countenance: But enough of this; let's come
to our Dreams, and we'll begin with that
great Houfe there on the right Hand. The
Mafter of it, whom you fee fleeping in thofe
rich Lodgings, is a liberal and debauch'd
Count; he's dreaming that he's at the Play,
that he hears a young Actrefs fing, and is
conquer'd by the Voice of this *Syren*. In the
next Apartment lies the Countefs, his Wife,
a great Reader of Romances. Her Head is
full

full of Knight Errantry, and Deeds of Che-
valry. She's in very pleafant Dreams; fhe
fancies her felf this Minute to be Emprefs of
Trebizond; that fhe is accus'd of Adultery,
and all the Knights who offer themfelves to
vindicate her Innocence, are overcome by her
Accufers.

In the next Houfe to this lives a Marquifs,
who is in Love with a famous Coquet: He
dreams that he has borrow'd a confiderable
Sum of Mony to make her a Prefent; and his
Steward, who lyes in that little Chamber there,
a Story higher, that he is growing Rich as
his Mafter grows Poor: You fee People do
not always dream extravagantly.

The Scholar interrupting him faid, I would
very feign know what Spark that is who is
afleep with his Muftacho's in Papers, like Ladies Favourites. 'Tis a Country Gentleman,
reply'd *Afmodeo*, a Vifcount of *Arragon*,
Proud and Vain; his Soul is this very Moment fwimming in Joy, for he dreams that
he's with a great Lord of the Court, who
gives him a Place. If I am not deceiv'd, faid
Don Cleofas, I fee a young Man in the fame
Houfe, who laughs in his Sleep. The Devil
reply'd, No, Sir, you are not deceiv'd, 'tis a
Batchelor who is alfo in a very agreeable
Dream; he fancies that an old Man of his
Acquaintance has marry'd a young and hand-
fome Wife. But juft by I fee three Men
who are in very mortifying Dreams; the firft
is a Chymift, who dreams that a Marquifs has.

a

a Guardian appointed him, and he has begun
to extract away his Patrimony. The two
others are Brothers, and Doctors; one dreams
that there is a Law made forbidding any one
to give a Phyſician a Fee unleſs the Patient
is cur'd: And his Brother, that there's an
Order publiſh'd requiring all Doctors to go
into Mourning for all the Patients that dye in
their Hands.   Would to God, quoth the
Scholar, this laſt Order was true, and every
Doctor was oblig'd to go to the Funeral of
his Patients, as the Lieutenant Criminal in
France is bound to be preſent at the Execution of the Malefactor he has condemn'd.
The Compariſon is juſt, reply'd the Devil, all
the Difference is, that the latter may be ſaid
to ſee his Sentence put in Execution, where-
as the other has already executed his.

Here *Don Cleofas* interrupted the *Dæmon*,
crying, See, ſee, who's that Gentleman there
that rubs his Eyes, and gets up haſtily? 'Tis
a Courtier, reply'd the Devil; a terrible Dream
has awak'd him: He dreamt the Firſt Mini-
ſter had look'd coldly on him. I ſee another
Courtier, who wakes in as great a Fright; he
dreamt that he was carry'd on a ſudden to the
Top of a high Mountain by two other Cour-
tiers, and that they flung him from the Top
to the Bottom.

Look upon that Houſe at the Corner of
that Street: There lives an Attorney; ſee,
he's a-bed with his Wife, in a Chamber hung
with old Tapeſtry-Hangings with antique Figures;

gures: He dreams that he's going to pay a
Visit to one of his Clients in the Alms-house,
and give him a Charity out of his own Pocket;
and his Wife, that her Husband has turn'd
a young Clerk, of whom he was jealous, out
of his House.

I hear some body snore, says the Scholar,
and believe 'tis that fat Fellow there in the
little Room on the left Hand of us. The very same, reply'd *Asmodeo;* 'tis a Prebend
dreaming he's saying his Prayers. Next to him
is a Mercer, who sells very dear Bargains to
People of Quality, but all upon Trust; he has
above 10000 Crowns owing him: He dreams
his Debtors are bringing him his Mony; and
his Creditors are dreaming that he's on the
point of breaking.

In the House next to the Mercer lives a famous Bookseller; he Printed a Book that went
off very well a little while ago. When he
bought 'it, he promis'd to give the Author
fifty Pistoles on a second Edition; and he
dreams now of Reprinting it without giving
him any Notice of it. Ah! does he so? says
Cleofas; I don't doubt but this Dream will
prove one of the truest that ever he had in
his Life. I am acquainted with those worthy
Gentlemen, the Booksellers; they make no
manner of Conscience of cheating their Authors. The *Dæmon* answer'd, Very true; but
you should speak what you know of those
worthy Gentlemen the Authors too. Upon
my Word, they have no more Conscience
than the Booksellers.   **In**

Books Printed for J. Tonſon.

Ovid's Epiſtles, tranſlated by ſeveral Hands. The Seventh Edition: Adorn'd with Cuts.

The Diſpenſary, a Poem, in Six Canto's. The Sixth Edition, with ſeveral Deſcriptions and Epiſodes never before Printed.

Remarks on ſeveral Parts of *Italy*, &c. in the Years 1701, 1702, 1703. *Roſamond*, an Opera, humbly Inſcrib'd to her Grace the Dutcheſs of *Marlborough*. The Campaign, a Poem, to his Grace the Duke of *Marlborough*. All three written by Mr. *Addiſon*.

The Hiſtory of *England*, from the firſt Entrance of *Julius Cæſar* and the *Romans*, to the End of the Reign of *King James* the Firſt; containing the Space of 1678 Years; with a compleat Index. By *Laurence Echard*, A. M. Prebendary of *Lincoln*, and Chaplain to the Right Reverend *William*, Lord Biſhop of that Dioceſe.

The *Grecian* Hiſtory, Volume the Firſt, containing the Space of about 1684 Years. By *Temple Stanyan*. Adorn'd with Cuts, and a Map of Ancient *Greece*.

The *Roman* Hiſtory in Five Volumes compleat, from the Building of the City to the Taking of *Conſtantinople* by the *Turks*. The two firſt Volumes by *Laurence Echard*, A. M. The three laſt reviſ'd and recommended by *Laurence Echard*.

The Life of *Pythagoras*, with his Symbols and Golden Verſes: Together with the Life of *Hierocles*, and his Commentaries upon the Verſes, collected out of the choiceſt Manuſcripts, and tranſlated into *French*, with Annotations, by *M. Dacier*. Now done into *Engliſh*. The Golden Verſes tranſlated from the *Greek* by *N. Rowe*, Eſq;.

Turkiſh Tales; conſiſting of ſeveral Extraordinary Adventures: With the Hiſtory of the Sultaneſs of *Perſia*, and the *Viſiers*. Written Originally in the *Turkiſh* Language, by *Chec Zada*, for the Uſe of *Amurath* II. And now done into *Engliſh*.

A General Eccleſiaſtical Hiſtory, from the Nativity of our Bleſſed Saviour, to the firſt Eſtabliſhment of Chriſtianity by Human Laws under the Emperor *Conſtantine* the Great, containing the Space of about 313 Years; with ſo much of the *Jewiſh* and *Roman* Hiſtory as is neceſſary and convenient to illuſtrate the Work. To which is added a large Chronological Table of all the *Roman* and Eccleſiaſtical Affairs included in the ſame Period of Time. By *Laurence Echard*, A. M. Prebendary of *Lincoln*, and Chaplain to the Right Reverend *James*, Lord Biſhop of that Dioceſe.

BOOKS *Printed for* J. Tonſon, *at* Grays-Inn *Gate.*

THE Works of the late Famous Mr. *John Dryden*, in four Volumes, in Folio; containing all his Comedies, Tragedies, and Opera's, with his Original Poems and Tranſlations.

The Satyrs of *Decimus Junius Juvenalis*, tranſlated into *Engliſh* Verſe, by Mr. *Dryden* and ſeveral other Eminent Hands: Together with the Satyrs of *Aulus Perſius Flaccus*, made *Engliſh* by Mr. *Dryden*; with Explanatory Notes at the End of each Satyr: To which is prefix'd a Diſcourſe concerning the Original and Progreſs of Satyr, Dedicated to the Right Honourable *Charles* Earl of *Dorſet*, &c. by Mr. *Dryden*.

Miſcellany Poems in Five Volumes. 8vo. Containing Variety of New Tranſlations of the Ancient Poets, together with ſeveral Original Poems, by the moſt Eminent Hands. Publiſh'd by Mr. *Dryden*.

The Works of Mr. *John Milton*, containing his Paradiſe Loſt and Paradiſe Regain'd; to which is added *Samſon Agoniſtes*, and Poems on ſeveral Occaſions compos'd at ſeveral Times. In 2 Vols. 8vo.

The Works of Mr. *Abraham Cowley*, in 2 Vols. 8vo. Conſiſting of thoſe which were formerly Printed; and others which he deſign'd for the Preſs, Publiſh'd out of the Author's Original Copies: With the *Cutter of Coleman-ſtreet*. The Tenth Edition, adorn'd with Cuts.

Poems, &c. written upon ſeveral Occaſions, and to ſeveral Perſons, by *Edmond Waller*, Eſq; The Seventh Edition, with ſeveral Additions never before Printed.

Poems and Tranſlations, with the *Sophy*. Written by the Honourable Sir *John Denham*, Knight of the *Bath*. The Fourth Edition. To which is added, *Cato-Major* of Old Age.

The Works of Sir *John Suckling*, containing all his Poems, Love-Verſes, Songs, Letters, and his Tragedies and Comedies. Never before Printed in one Volume.

Poems on ſeveral Occaſions; with *Valentinian*, a Tragedy. Written by the Right Honourable *John* late Earl of *Rochoſter*.

The Works of Sir *George Etherege*, containing his Plays and Poems.

The Royal Convert. A Tragedy. Written by N. *Rowe*, Eſq;

Ovid's

of Ignorance or Flattery: The other is a Gentleman of *Eſtramadura,* nam'd *Don Ballazar Fax Farrerirco,* who is come Poſt to Court, to demand a Reward for having kill'd a *Portugueſe* with a Blunderbuſs; he Dreams that they have given him a Viceroyſhip, and yet he is not ſatisfy'd.

Over-againſt this Inn lives a Notary; you ſee him and his Wife lying in two little Beds. In this very inſtant they are dreaming Things quite different; the Husband, that he's rubbing over an old muſty Deed; and, Madam, his Wife, that ſhe's at a Mercer's buying a new rich Gown, with ready Mony, at the ſame Price that a Dutcheſs refus'd it upon Tick.

Aſmodeo was about continuing his Oſſervations, but he was ſuddenly taken with a *Friſſon,* which hinder'd him; the Scholar ask'd why he ſhook ſo: Ah! reply'd the *Demon,* Signior *Don Cleofas,* I am undone. The Conjurer, who kept me in the Bottle, has found out that I am flown; he calls me, he threatens me, he conjures ſo forcibly that all Hell rings with it. I muſt obey him, I will carry you back to your Apartment, and then fly to the wretched Garret from whence you brought me. In ending theſe Words he embrac'd the Scholar, took him up, wafted him to his Chamber, and vaniſh'd.

F I N I S.

In another House continu'd he, I see a ti-
morous respectful Lover, who is just awake.
He is in Love with a brisk young Widow,
and dream'd that he had her in the Middle
of a Wood, where he said abundance of soft
Things to her, and she to him : As, *Ah !
there's no resisting you ; I should yield to
you, if I was not on my Guard against all
Mankind; they are so false, I dare not trust
them upon their Words, I am for Actions.
What Actions, Madam*, reply'd the Lover,
*do you require of me ? Must I undertake the
twelve Labours of* Hercules *to shew my Love?
No, no*, Don Nicasio, says the Lady, *I don't
demand any such thing of you, I only*——and
then he awake. Pray, says the Scholar, tell
me, why the Man, who is asleep in yonder
dark-colour'd Bed, talks to himself as if he
was possess'd. The Devil answer'd, Oh !
that's a notable Licentiate, who is in a Dream,
that puts him in a terrible Agitation ; 'tis no
less than that he's in a Dispute, and main-
taining the Immortality of the Soul against
an old Physician. Near the Licentiate lives
a Player, dreaming that he's talking Insolent-
ly to an Author, who is all the while Complimenting him. In yon Inn I observe two
Men, whose Dreams I must by no means o-
mit. One of them is an *Italian* of the Aca-
demy *de la Crusca* ; he Dreams that he's reading a bad Poem, he has written to some of
the Society, who mightily commend it out
of